MISTRESS BY BLACKMAIL
INTERNATIONAL BILLIONAIRES I: THE ITALIANS

CARO LAFEVER

A COLD-HEARTED BUSINESS TYCOON. A STRONG-WILLED STARVING ARTIST. A BATTLE FOR EACH OTHER'S HEART BOTH MUST WIN.

Determined to save her best friend from an arranged marriage, Darcy Moran marches into Marcus La Rocca's boardroom intent on forcing him to release his younger brother from the commitment. Except she's up against a formidable foe who's not only sure the marriage should happen, but takes one look at her—

And wants her far away from his brother.

Blackmailed into being his pretend mistress, Darcy finds herself transported into a world of luxury and high society, something a poor artist knows nothing about. Still, she's not a girl to be intimidated by anyone or anything, and she manages to reject all of Marc's lures even though lust for him threatens to overcome her will.

Marcus knows women and he knows what they like. But no matter how many gifts he showers on Darcy, she refuses them all. Frustrated with lust and entranced by her charms, he finds himself falling in love.

An emotion he promised himself he'd never feel again.

Sweet Echo, sweetest nymph that liv'st unseen
  Within thy airy shell
  By slow Meander's margent green,
  in the violet-imbroider'd vale.

— JOHN MILTON

CHAPTER 1

His brother was an idiot. Marcus La Rocca rocked back on his heels and stifled the urge to yell. The damn kid knew what was at stake, knew his assigned role. He'd agreed to the marriage months ago. *Dannazione*, he agreed enthusiastically. So why was he playing with fire at this late date? If his younger brother stood in front of him right now, he'd wring his sorry neck. But what good would it do? Matteo had been a thorn in his side from the moment he entered his life and would continue in the role for the foreseeable future.

Or until he succeeded in dragging the idiot to the altar.

"He doesn't know what he's doing." His mother, Serafina, sobbed into her lace handkerchief. She sat in one of several burgundy leather office chairs across from his steel-and-glass desk. The bright overhead light shined with a harsh glare on her dyed-black hair.

With wry amusement, he noted there was no smearing of her makeup and her eyes weren't red. His mother was a master at many things; she was pure genius at emotional manipulation. "He's twenty-five."

"A mere baby."

He snorted. Ten years ago, when he was twenty-five, he'd been running this company, making million-euro deals. Not running around and screwing around.

Her hands fisted and she threw him a glare. "You're never sympathetic."

"I ran out of sympathy a long time ago."

"You are always too hard on him." Her voice rose. "This is all your fault."

A phrase he'd heard so many times it could be tattooed on his brain. "Calm down."

"How can I calm down when my baby is in a whore's clutches?" She jumped from the chair and began pacing, her thin body trembling with anxiety.

Examining the photos his mother had provided, he silently questioned her conclusion. The woman seemed more like an innocent girl, not the seductive siren his mother seemed to fear. "She appears harmless."

"*Uffa!*" She threw her hands in the air and stopped, pinning him with another glare. "Those are the women you have to watch out for."

Assuming what she claimed held a kernel of truth, this was a problem. However, the last thing he needed was his fiery mother going off on a tangent. If he didn't rein her in, she'd likely screech to a tabloid, or worse, gossip with her gaggle of crows. The society crows would pass the information along faster than the tabloids could print their sheets. He had to tamp this down, buy some time so he could address this situation in his usual purposeful manner.

He shrugged his shoulders and gave her a blank stare.

"You don't believe me," she wailed.

"Momma," he replied. "Be reasonable. Matteo is engaged."

"*Sì, sì, sì,* and that is why—"

"For all my little brother's faults, he would not betray his commitment. Nor his family."

"He wouldn't mean to."

"Supposing what you say is true, he's only having a last fling. Irrelevant."

The handkerchief waved his words away. "She's moved in with him."

"What?" He stiffened.

"*Sì*," she proclaimed triumphantly. "One month before the wedding!"

Marcus paced to the wall of windows lining one side of the room. Looking down, he noted the London traffic coursing through the financial district where his office building stood.

Maledizione. He did not have time for this. He had to fly to Madrid tomorrow and then to New York a few days later. Why the hell couldn't his kid brother keep his pants zipped? Didn't he understand what this marriage meant to the business? This deal ensured Rocca Enterprises would be a big player in the emerging equity markets in Eastern Europe.

Hell, the kid liked the girl. Declared he was pleased. If Matteo had objected, Marcus would have let him off the hook and found another way to get the deal done. But he hadn't, and this deal and marriage had been on the books for months. If the marriage fell through now, there'd be no way to salvage the contract. Not with the Casartelli bride's pride and honor at risk.

"You're sure of this information?"

"*Sì*."

He glanced over his shoulder. "You've been keeping an eye on him."

"It's a mother's prerogative." She met his amused look with a defiant one of her own.

He turned and leaned on the window. The cold November wind blowing outside cooled the glass. And his irritation. Slightly. "I want all the information you've collected."

A gleam of victory lit in her dark eyes. "Now you are listening."

"If what you say is true—"

"It is."

"Then this is a problem that needs to be nipped in the bud before the Casartellis find out."

"*Sì! Sì!*" His mother's arms waved in the air, her eyes flashing.

"Momma."

His cool tone stopped her agitated movements and her gaze met his.

"I'll take care of this."

The magic words she'd been waiting to hear. He knew it and she knew it.

A smile beamed through her happy tears. "Marcus—"

"I need to get back to work." He ran his hands through his hair, trying to stifle his irritation.

Rushing over, she threw her arms around him. "Your father would be so proud."

"Momma—"

"Matteo's father would be so thankful."

Unlikely in both cases. But what did it matter? Both men had been dead for years and the responsibility for everything had been on his shoulders for what seemed like forever. It was his job to keep this financial empire intact and it was clearly his job to deliver his stupid brother to the wedding. The wedding that would ensure Rocca Enterprises' continuing prosperity.

Assuming his mother didn't babble and his brother didn't renege.

"No talking to your friends, Momma."

"Well, I don't think—"

"Momma."

She eyed him, gauged his temper as only a mother could do, and made the right decision. "I will leave all this in your capable hands, Marcus."

"*Grazie.*"

With a flurry of lace and purse and flounce and drama, his mother left the room. Leaving him with the mess.

As usual.

∽

Darcy Moran was a fighter.

At first she'd had to be and now, it was second nature. This situation, obviously, called for a fighter. It made no difference that her knees were doing some serious knocking below the edge of her one good dress. And it made no difference that the office building standing before her was a bit more grand and glorious than she'd imagined.

She had a fight to win.

It was the least she could do for her best friend.

He'd come through for her many times—the latest being when her ugly old landlord had objected to another overdue rent payment. If not for Matt, she'd have ended up on the streets. She figured she'd take a couple of weeks to get her feet back under her and then she'd start searching for another flat. Until then, she'd bunk on Matt's sofa.

Last night, though, she found out she could have his whole place in a month.

All to herself.

"Married?" She hadn't believed him at first. "Forced to marry?"

"I'm afraid it's true." Matteo Costa's big brown eyes shone with despair. She knew he used them all the time for effect, but still. Still.

"How could you let him do this?"

"He's the head of the family."

Her hands fisted in her jeans pockets. "He's not your lord and master."

"The next best thing." Her friend's expression grew more mournful.

"You must confront him," she instructed. "You need to tell him to go to hell."

"You don't know my brother."

"Thank God."

He sighed. "It's about the families. The connection. This seals the deal. In many ways, the marriage makes sense."

"You're barmy." Darcy frowned. "No one gets married to seal a business deal."

"No one but me."

"Don't give in," she cried. "Don't you ever give in."

"That's your rally cry, not mine." He leaned his head back on the flat's kitchen wall and closed his eyes. "At least Viola is pretty."

"You have got to be kidding." As if the pretty factor of his potential wife would have any impact on whether or not the marriage would work. Without love, it wouldn't. "You need to stop this right now."

"No," he said, one eye opening to squint at her rigid figure. "She is pretty. And stop shouting."

"You've got to tell your brother you made a mistake."

"He'd kill me."

"Better a quick death than a long protracted death by marriage."

"Cynic." Matt's stare turned shrewd.

"Realist." He'd asked and questioned, but she had no desire to confide about her past. He didn't know how she'd grown up and no amount of talking would ever give him a sense of what it had been like. What it had been like to see her parents fight and split and fight and split. What it had been like to land in foster care at the age of twelve. What it had been like to know she was all alone. Out of long practice, she'd shut the conversation down before the questioning went any further. She had more than enough information anyway.

By midnight last night, she made a decision.

The only decision she could make.

Matt had saved her many times. Now was the time she'd pay him back. She didn't know exactly how she was going to convince his big brother to stop the marriage, still she'd figure something out. Once she met the guy, she'd find some way to wrap him around her finger or bring him to his senses by finding his weaknesses and exploiting them. She'd become good at both a long time ago. Sure, he was a billionaire, but that didn't mean he had super powers.

He was just a man.

Darcy lifted her chin and stared with fierce intent at the massive building in front of her.

Time to make this happen.

She marched across the busy London street, ignoring the well-heeled crowd swirling past her. Marshaling her arguments, she lined up her words. She'd first have to get through the walls of security and secretaries before she reached her goal, still, she had charm. A quick tongue. Other talents.

ROCCA ENTERPRISES

The sign swept over the entrance, silver and elegant. Impressive. Intimidating.

She found it hard to picture her best friend coming from this environment. When she met him, she'd assumed he was like her: poor. The news that his brother was a billionaire, who ruled an entire empire of various businesses, had been a huge shock. The Great Man, Matt called him. With annoyance, yet sometimes she noted a hint of affection underlining his words.

There was nothing affectionate about this situation, however.

Her friend didn't have the courage to confront his brother. But she did.

Pushing through the doors, she entered the foyer. Sculptures of silver glass speared toward the cathedral ceiling. A wide wall of glimmering elevators lined the end of the foyer, swishing open and closed, filling and emptying with a dizzying number of women dressed to the nines and men dressed to impress. All rather overwhelming. For a moment.

Keep your focus.

She peered past the girth of an elderly woman walking by her and spotted the first hurdle.

Security.

Planted behind a wide desk, four uniformed guards scanned the crowd with sharp attention. She was short, but not short enough to sneak past sight unseen. Plus, her dress didn't come close to competing with the high-fashion women surrounding her. If she didn't act fast, she'd be spotted and stopped.

"Not on your life," she muttered.

She'd managed to pry a few critical pieces of information from Matt, without letting him know what she planned for his benefit. For example, everyone who worked for Rocca got a blue ID card, which they had to wear to get past security. All she needed to flit past this hurdle was one of those cards. Too bad her friend didn't have one. His brother wouldn't even allow him on the premises without prior approval.

Another strike against the Great Man. What an egotistical tyrant he must be.

Focus. Focus.

Scanning the crowd, she found a promising target. A behemoth of a man ambled toward the elevators, his jacket slung across his arm, his blue card flopping on the polished wool.

Well, actually, it was her blue card.

She slipped beside him, her keen gaze focused on what she needed to know. "Hi, John."

The man halted and looked down and down into her smiling face.

He blinked.

"How lovely to see you." She beamed at him and angled herself so his large body stood between her and the security desk.

Blinking again, he smiled back. "I don't think I know you."

"John, John." She batted her eyes as her hand deftly did its work. "How could you forget what we had together?"

"We…we…" The man sputtered to a stop and blinked once more.

"Well, I guess I'll have to let you go, then." She turned and walked away, swinging her hips as her mum had shown her long ago.

"Wait!" His voice didn't stop her.

Darcy smiled and snapped the lovely blue tag on her lapel. Nothing ever stopped her.

The Great Man had no idea what was about to hit him.

∾

"Boss." Blake Reston, head of his security, stepped into his office. "She's no longer at your brother's flat. We've located her."

Marcus had taken two days to calculate what needed to be done. After reviewing the information his mother had collected, within hours his security team had filled in the rest of the details on one Ms. Darcy Moran. In his methodical, careful way, he'd mulled over the situation when he'd been in Madrid and made a decision. Now it was only a matter of tracking down the prey and springing the trap. He glanced away from his computer screen. "Well?"

A gruff laugh escaped the blond man. "She's here."

"What?"

"She's been able to glide through the security on the ground floor and is currently on her way to…" Blake focused on his phone, scanning his messages. "It appears she's here to see you, big guy."

"Interesting." Standing, he slipped on his suit coat. "I can't remember the last time a person I was hunting came right to my door."

"I wonder what she's up to."

"Whatever she's up to, she's playing right into my hands."

The head of security stared at him with a knowing gaze. "You've figured out a plan."

"*Certamente.*"

"Willing to share?"

Marcus gave him a wry grimace before sitting down once more. "Don't I always share my plans with you?"

"Since I am usually a part of the plan, it's smart of you to do so."

"In this case, I don't believe I'll need your help." Flipping open the lone file on his desk, he once again examined the report about his target. It never hurt to be thorough, although he'd committed all of the data to memory. "The information we've collected about Ms. Moran shows she's got not a quid to her name."

"That is a fact."

"This would explain why she attached herself to Matt when they both were attending art school several years ago."

"Your cynicism is showing. Maybe they became friends because they liked each other."

"My cynicism is hard won and holds me in good stead." He scanned the documents one more time. "She's been playing her cards carefully, building rapport. However, the upcoming marriage has pushed her to act."

"Snag Matteo while she can."

"Correct."

"And now we come to your plan."

"My plan is to offer Ms. Moran a bigger prize."

The blond man eyed him, then laughed. "You."

"I plan to sweep her off her feet."

"Which you have quite a lot of experience doing with women."

"True." His smile faded. "Once Matt is safely married and our business deal is done with the Casartellis, Ms. Moran will be given a nice piece of jewelry and told to take a hike."

Blake walked to the window and looked down. "There is a chance she'll refuse."

"Not likely. But if she's stubborn enough to say no, I'll use the other key bit of information you found out about her."

The man stilled. "Her father."

"*Sì.*"

"You are one ruthless bastard." Blake said the words as he shook his head, yet the undertone of respect told Marcus what he needed to know. The head of his security thought his plan was solid.

"Do I detect judgment in your tone?"

His friend waved the question away. They'd gone through too many tense situations not to know what the other really thought.

He leaned back in his chair and contemplated what he had to do in the next few weeks. His voice hardened with resolve. "I do what I have to do to protect my family and my business."

"There is a chance she's actually in love with him."

His sardonic chuckle filled the office. "Please."

Blake surveyed him with amusement. "At some point this cynicism of yours is going to trip you up."

"I doubt it."

The desk phone buzzed. "Mr. La Rocca?"

"Yes, Angie."

"There's a woman here to see you." His PA's voice held

annoyance. "She's not on your schedule, sir. Yet, she's very insistent."

Marcus threw a mocking grin at the other man. "I love insistent women."

"Sir?" Angie's voice blurred into confusion.

"Show her in."

"Yes, sir." The phone went dead.

"Want me to stay?" Blake gave him an ironic smile.

"I don't believe I need your supervision to seduce a woman."

The head of his security snorted. "Then I'm out of here. I wish you luck."

"I don't need luck. I merely need to follow through with my plan."

Shaking his head again, the blond man slid through the private side door leading into the conference room. At the same time, the main office door opened with a crash.

To his PA looking irritated and flustered. Which was unusual.

And behind her stood…

A fairy sprite.

A dainty *ninfa*.

A sublime elfin creature.

She would barely reach his shoulder. Even in high heels. Certainly not in the clunky, plodding shoes she had on. The dress she wore did nothing for her—brown, ugly. Yet, it could not hide the body beneath. All lithe and elegant. Fine boned, but still with a delicious womanly curve to the hip and bust. The photos his mother brought him had not done her justice. Did not show the reality of her true beauty.

Every inch of his skin tightened and a particular part of his anatomy hardened. A flashing thought crossed his mind: He was glad he was sitting.

"Sir." Angie regained some of her moxie and stepped forward. "This is—"

"Darcy Moran." The delicate *ninfa* stomped into his office, her dark, feathered brows furrowed in a deep frown. "I have something to say to you."

Struggling to regain his control, Marcus eyed his prey. "I can see that."

"Mr. La Rocca—"

"You may go, Angie." His gaze never left the tiny woman who'd stopped stomping and now stood inside the room in rigid anger.

The door shut with a soft thump.

Her face was a lovely oval, her chin slightly pointed. Her black hair was cut short and curled around her petite ears. Her mouth was pure perfection. Plump, pink, and lush. Her eyes flashed with fire. He couldn't quite pick out the color across the length of the room, but they were light. Filled with the light of battle at the moment.

Remarkable. The air between them sizzled. He would not have been surprised if electric shocks sprang from both of their bodies.

Dio. He could almost forgive Matteo for moving this piece of art into his flat.

The woman crossed her arms in front of her. "You have a lot to answer for."

"I usually do." His tongue felt thick. His mouth dry.

"You can't force Matt to marry this Viola woman."

"Mmm." He clamped down on his libido and focused on the task at hand. The task at hand that had become remarkably more desirable in the last few minutes. This was no longer a chore; it would be a pleasure to take this woman to bed. In fact, having sex with her was now his primary aim. How lucky for him this coincided with his ultimate goal of detaching her from his brother.

"That's all you have to say for yourself?"

"Matteo has been whining? In his usual way?"

"He isn't whining. He's upset." Her graceful hands lifted and sliced the air with curt, angry movements. "He's in despair. Because of you."

"I'm sorry to hear it." He watched, fascinated as her whole body vibrated with energy.

"No, you're not. Or you'd do something about the situation." She began to pace. "Whatever I have to do, I'll stop you from doing this to him."

The passion in her voice when she talked about his brother sliced fury right through his lust. The sudden picture of Matteo and this *ninfa* in bed together pulsed through his brain, sending him into a full-throttled rage. Which astonished him. He rarely lost his formidable temper. Yet, it was definitely temper knotting in his throat. He couldn't help the biting words spitting from his mouth. "You are close to Matt."

Her eyes widened at the tone of his voice. "Definitely."

"My brother is a lucky man."

Something, a spark of shrewdness or cunning, flashed across her face. "Yes," she said slowly. "He is lucky to have me."

"So you have come to plead for your love."

Her body tensed. A pause of breathless silence passed between them. Then she finally nodded. "That's right. That's exactly right."

The knot in his throat grew, still he couldn't help tightening it further. "You love Matteo."

"Yes." She walked to the edge of his desk, staring at him across the shiny surface. "And for the sake of this love, I'm asking you to call off the marriage."

Her eyes were blue. The deep, vibrant blue of a Tuscany night sky. They were filled with emotion. *Love.* Something he long ago stopped believing in.

"No." He stared right into her eyes. "Never."

"Please," she whispered. "This would make me very happy."

"I will make you happy." He stood with an abrupt jerk. "But in an entirely different way."

CHAPTER 2

The Great Man was…well…great.

Darcy took in a deep breath and tried to suppress every quivering cell in her body. Every female cell. Yet this was impossibly hard to do. The man before her was the epitome of male perfection. She'd expected an older version of Matt. Rather lanky, rather messy, and definitely non-threatening in the sexual department.

Instead, she confronted every woman's dream.

Well, certainly hers.

A revelation in and of itself. She had blissfully assumed she was immune to desiring or dreaming. Never, in her entire life, had she gone gaga over a guy. Not once in her entire existence had she thought she'd die if a man didn't want her. When other women went on and on about some bloke, she wondered what the big deal was about *any* of the male species.

Clearly her mum had left her another important gift.

The gift of not losing her head over a guy.

She'd kissed guys, naturally she had. She'd had sex. She figured she should find out what all the fuss was about. Prove she wasn't scared, she wasn't scarred. So she'd done it. Once. She'd been proud of herself. Proud she muddled through the incident without gagging or losing her control. The experience had been rather untidy, but not anything she couldn't handle. And she'd been ultra-proud of herself for not suddenly thinking she'd fallen in love with the man.

Except standing before her right now stood the contradiction to her smug conclusions about her immunity to lusting after a man.

Her whole body hummed and sparked and buzzed and tingled.

He was tall, several inches over six feet.

Who would have known she yearned for tall?

He was broad. His shoulders pressed against the blue Italian-silk suit, filling it with muscles galore. The man must work out every day. Or maybe he got his exercise by pummeling his competitors and cracking the whip on his subordinates.

Why did all of those hard-earned muscles turn her on?

His dark-brown hair was clipped short, yet a hint of a curl made it wave around his classically handsome face and ears.

She had this horrible compulsion to reach out and wrap one of those curls around her finger. Reach up and nibble on one of those perfect male ears.

Then there was his face. Proud jut of a prominent nose. Strong edge of a jaw ending in a square, determined chin. Cheekbones carved by a master. Wide forehead and dark slashes of eyebrows that lifted at the end, giving him a faintly satirical look, even when he frowned.

As he was doing now.

Even the ominous frown could not deflect her fascination with him. She tried to pull her attention back to what she'd come for, but it was no use. His features wove into complete and utter male flawlessness.

She was dazzled.

Hopefully, she wasn't drooling.

When she first walked in here, she hadn't stopped, hadn't allowed herself to notice anything other than her goal. Tell the man off and get his promise to make things right for Matt. It wasn't until she approached his desk and he stood that she realized what she dealt with. All purposes and plots were wiped from her head by the hazy, heated glow welling inside her. A glow of sexual lust she'd only read about in books or seen on TV. A glow she never thought to feel. A glow which threatened everything she'd decided about herself.

No. No. *Not true.*

No one ever beat her. This man wouldn't either.

Forcing herself, she stopped focusing on his bountiful physical gifts and made herself meet his inspection with a determined glare of her own. When she met his gaze, though, shock zipped through her body and along her spine, blasting her rising determination to bits. She'd expected another version of Matt's soulful, brown, puppy eyes.

Instead, she confronted two silver-grey flashes. Like swords of old.

The eyes were glaring at her.

"M-m-make me happy?" Instant shame twisted inside. She never stuttered anymore.

The shame only fed the astonishing lust. Against her will, she still ogled the Roman god before her, trying to make sense of his words amongst all the rest of her rioting reactions. Marcus La Rocca stated he wanted to make her happy and yet he frowned at her as if she'd committed a cardinal sin? Confusion mingled with her shocking lust and embarrassment.

A man can be deadly. Her mother's years-old warning whispered along her nerve endings.

All at once, the man shielded the stunning eyes with his thick lashes. When he glanced back at her, all the anger had disappeared. In its stead was steel determination. "Correct. The past is the past and we must move beyond it. I must remember what is important in this situation."

"Making me happy is im-m-mportant?" Stuttering again. This had to stop. Darcy fumbled for her brain without success. The Great Man had scrambled her mind into a frenzied froth of desire and disorientation. Not a good combination given she was here to take a strong, principled stand against him.

"*Certamente*. This will be my primary purpose for the foreseeable future." His mouth firmed as if he were making some grand commitment.

"But," she blurted, "I don't understand. Why would you care if I'm happy?"

"Matteo will no longer have time to cater to your needs."

"My needs?"

"He will be too busy with the wedding preparations."

His confident words about the wedding-that-wasn't-going-to-happen immediately drained the sexual swamp and wiped away the old shame about her stuttering. Ice-cold reality slapped her awake.

No more lust. No more stuttering.

No more distractions.

She needed to remember why she'd come here and not get caught in this male's erotic allure. She needed to stop acting like a scared, cowed kid. She needed to remember she was here to bend this man to her will.

Why spend innumerable moments trying to understand what this man meant by talking about making her happy? This had nothing to do with her happiness and everything to do with Matt's. That's what she needed to keep her focus on.

Leaning across the desk, she tried to ignore the buzz in her blood as she got closer to him. "There isn't going to be any wedding. I'm here to make you stop it."

"Make me?" His tone iced with immediate disdain. "*You?*"

His blunt dismissal of her capabilities fired her blood in an entirely different way than lusting after him had. A swift surge of relief swept through her as her fighting spirit reappeared. Slamming her fists on her hips, she pierced him with another worthy glare. "I'll do anything for Matt."

"The best thing you could do for Matteo is leave him alone."

"Never."

"Then it will be I who *makes you* do it."

This wasn't going exactly how she expected. When she marched into this office, her hackles were already crackling at the scorn she'd received from this man's PA. She'd lost any ability to play it sweet because she was so consumed with indignation.

Wheedling would have been better or pleading. Especially with this man.

The abrupt fury continued to grow, though, fed by her shock at the physical reaction he caused in her and the arrogant words he kept uttering.

The heat of battle flushed her skin. "Try. You'll regret it."

He leaned across his desk and she involuntarily stepped back. The mocking twist of his mouth should have stoked her anger. Instead, it made her heart flutter. When he planted his hands on the desk, his wide shoulders bunched beneath the silk and her heart went from fluttering to pounding. "Do not issue challenges, Ms. Moran. Not to me."

The glare he gave her was fierce. Rather frightening, if she were a frightening type of girl. Which she was not. "It wasn't a challenge. It was a warning."

The air grew still, yet hummed with energy. She held her breath, waiting for the next clash of swords, the next swift strike she'd be ready to parry.

Abruptly, he turned away to stare out the floor-to-ceiling windows behind the desk. She felt as if an invisible string between them had broken. Her breath chopped through her in a mini-gasp.

"*Santo cielo*," he growled, as his hand ran through his hair.

Her gaze slipped along the long line of his back and down his powerful legs. Her mind flipped away from the righteous fight she waged for her friend and landed again in the swamp of sexual heat pulsing deep within her. The heat inside burned and blistered her determination to win. She sucked in cool air, praying it would bring back her pride.

"This is counterproductive." His words were low, husky. "It does us no good to fight."

"I agree." An olive branch. She grabbed the peace offering eagerly. She didn't want to fight with this man at all. She wanted to do something entirely opposite. The realization shot a lance of fearful anticipation down her spine.

Turning back to her, he gave her a wry grin. And two dimples popped on the sides of his mouth. Two disarming, distracting dimples.

The impact this man had on her. It was enough to make an un-frightened girl terribly frightened.

"We will begin again," he stated.

"Um." Her mouth went dry. "Sure."

Slipping his hands in his pockets, he rocked back on his heels. "We will agree not to speak of my brother anymore."

Uh-oh. So much for olive branches. "I can't agree to that."

"You must." Storm clouds immediately threatened in his eyes. "Matteo is now irrelevant."

"Matt is the reason I'm here. He certainly isn't irrelevant."

"You will have nothing more to do with him." His tone turned deadly with—jealousy? Nah, not that. Maybe the Great Man didn't think she was worthy of being with his brother? That seemed more likely.

Her hackles vibrated once more. But her brain had finally kicked into gear.

Okay, time to change course. She'd picked up on the fact he thought her and Matt were an item. She figured this would be a card to play. Except now the tactic was backfiring on her. It was earning her hostility from this man rather than cooperation.

Sugar rather than vinegar, lovey. Her mother's words echoed in her memories. *Men always respond better to sugar.*

First, she'd set him straight on the nature of her relationship with his brother. Then she'd start to apply the sugar. In large quantities. "Listen. About me and Matt—"

"We will not speak of him anymore."

He issued commands like a seasoned potentate. Yet she hadn't grown up rough without realizing how to stand her ground with the best of them. "I came here to specifically speak of Matt. I'm afraid you're out of luck."

"I do not operate with luck." His dark brows furrowed in distaste. "I make a plan and proceed to carry it out."

"Well, bloody good for you," she muttered. "Listen, you need to know Matt and I—"

"You will soon find that all my plans are successful. As my plan for you will be."

Her hackles burned under her skin. All thoughts of sweetness and light snapped out of her in a crackle of outrage.

The man might ooze sex and testosterone that called to the very core of her female body. However, he was insufferably, utterly too arrogant for belief. They'd just met. He knew nothing about her. Still, he instantly made a plan which involved her and assumed she'd merrily dance to his tune? He needed to be cut off at the knees by somebody.

Who better than Ms. Darcy Moran? Fighter extraordinaire?

"How lucky for you." She gave him her best, absolute best, fake smile. "I'm breathless with anticipation to find out what your plan is for little old me."

She watched with satisfaction as his entire body tensed. Yes, yes. She was good at knocking people down a notch when it was needed. Sugar might be her best weapon, but it wasn't her only one.

His mouth tightened in a grim line. No dimples in sight. "I don't appreciate your sarcasm."

"Sorry." She pouted, taking wicked delight at his frustration. "Can't help myself."

With three swift steps, he rounded his desk and stood right before her. She braced, forcing herself not to step back. The move would be a signal of weakness in this battle of wills. And she wasn't going to give in. Not for Matt. Not for herself.

"You play with fire, Ms. Moran," he ground out the words, a threat winding through them.

He stood so close. Too close. An overwhelming desire to touch swept through her. To spread her hands across those broad shoulders. To lean into his strength. To breathe in the scent of his skin. She struggled to remember his arrogance and ignore her lust. "I'm not playing at all, Mr. La Rocca. There is nothing playful about you forcing your brother to marry."

His low snarl made her jerk her head up from her contemplation of his broad chest. Her gaze met his. Stormy grey eyes threatened certain disaster. "Matteo is no concern of yours any longer. You will never see him again."

Darcy's mouth dropped open. Not have Matt as a friend anymore? Not have his warm encouragement, his endless support, his unswerving belief in her talent, in her? Her mouth slammed shut.

"No way." She gritted her teeth. "I'm n-n-not going to lose him."

Silver fire flashed down on her like cracks of lightning. "From now on you will be too busy with me to have any time for my brother."

"With you? What are you talking about?"

He pointed a long finger at her, then back at himself. "You. Me."

She gave him a blank stare.

"Us. Together."

Darcy was positive her eyes popped out of her sockets. "Are you crazy?"

His gaze narrowed. "No."

"There is no us. You. M-m-me. Together." Shame at her inability to control her tongue made the words rushed and touched with the beginning of hysteria. "There's no way—"

"I have decided," he cut her off. "You are with me now. Not Matteo."

"What planet are you from?" Her heart rate soared. With outrage. Definitely outrage. "You can't command people."

He gave her a solemn look through his thick lashes. "Actually, I can. I do."

"Not me."

A whiff of his cologne wrapped around her, a spicy mix of pure temptation overlaying the smell of the man himself. Innately virile, potent. His scent mocked her statement, mocked her resolution to win the battle with this man.

The corner of his mouth lifted as if he could sense the struggle inside her. "There are different ways to command a person, Darcy."

Her name on his lips was soft and lilting. Enchanting her against her will. The tone tugged and mocked, exactly as his scent had.

Fight. Straightening her spine, she stared him down. "I didn't give you permission to use my first name."

"Then what should I call you?" he murmured. *"Mia regina di fata?"*

"What?" Unwillingly, she was mesmerized by the way the words slipped off his tongue.

"Or perhaps *il mio piccolo uno.*"

The movement of his mouth captivated her, the lips wrapping around each word, the roll of the accent, the slight slur as if he were under a spell also. "It's rude to speak in Italian when I can't understand what you're saying," she objected, trying to pull out of the web he was weaving.

"My apologies." He gave her a slight bow. "I will translate."

"Don't bother if you're calling me something nasty."

"They are compliments, I assure you."

Darcy wasn't sure compliments from this man would be better than slurs. His impact on her body and brain was beginning to scare her. It was a bit too much. He was a bit too much. She inched away, putting some distance between them. "It doesn't matter what you think of me or call me—"

"Not true." He took one step and came as close as before.

"I came here for a specific reason and I refuse to be distracted."

"I am distracting you?" The slow, devastating smile came once more. Along with the disturbing dimples. His teeth were amazingly white and even. "I must admit this delights me. It will be fun to *distract* each other, *sì?*"

Dragging her attention from his smile, she tried to concentrate on her mission. "I'm here for Matt."

"No. You are here for me." He trailed one long finger across her cheek. "You are as delicate as a flower petal."

The electricity of his touch sent a frisson of raw power through her entire body. He took her breath away. He took her words away. He took her ability to move away.

"I believe I promised I would translate. My fairy queen." His voice twisted around her, inside her. Warm and melting like butter. He caressed the words with his faint Italian drawl. "Or my little one. Which do you prefer?"

"Yours?" Her heart thumped into a gallop at the thought of being his. But her brain jerked to life at a faster clip.

You're mine.

One male had claimed she was his a long time ago and she'd barely escaped. The man before her might be potent stuff, but her teenage memories superseded even the Great Man. She stepped back, away from him. "I'm not *yours*. I never will be."

The silver gaze never left her face. "I'm afraid I must disagree."

"And I disagree totally with what you're doing to your brother, Mr. La Rocca." He'd been able to derail her like no other man ever had. She wasn't going to be distracted anymore, though. Not by his words nor his potent appeal. "I'm here to point—"

"Why you came here initially is immaterial." He continued to smile his distracting smile. "What is important is how we handle things going forward."

"There is nothing immaterial about forcing Matt—"

"What you must see is I am much more capable of making you happy than Matteo."

"I don't need you to make me happy. I'm perfectly happy right now."

"You will be happier with me." His big body loomed over hers, encircling her with his presence. "I promise you, I have much more to offer than my brother."

"You have nothing to offer that I want."

Really? her body questioned.

"Really?" He leaned down, his face mere inches from hers. His breath whispered across her mouth, mint and man. "I think I have many things you want. I will take pleasure in giving you every single one."

She stared over his shoulder and tried to think. Tried to pull her brain back to normal. But once again, her mind filled with a cloudy haze of pure desire. The man was seduction personified. She couldn't quite believe he was serious, yet it didn't seem to matter to her blurring brain or her burning body. "You can't be serious about all this."

His finger smoothed across her jaw and pushed her chin so her eyes met his. His shone, glowed a hot pewter. Somehow, he'd moved closer. "I am always serious. You will come to know this."

"You…you…"

"I have decided on what I will call you. *Tesorina* suits you the best." Both of his hands lifted, slipping across her cheeks and through her hair, melting her where she stood. Sending tingles of sensation across her skin, into her soul. "Little treasure."

The words became muffled as his mouth moved softly, slowly over hers.

～

SHE SMELLED LIKE SUNSHINE.

She tasted like a tart cherry.

She felt like warm silk.

All of it mixed with sweetness and spice. And nothing very nice.

Grazie a Dio.

He liked her spunk, liked her feisty spirit. Her fiery temperament would add zest to their bedroom adventures. He relished the thought of taming her. His body hardened as he pulled her toward him. *Dio*, he was really looking forward to it.

Slipping his tongue across her mouth, he tasted her, sipped her. "Open your mouth, *Tesorina*," he whispered on her lips. "Let me in."

Her lashes lifted. Her night-blue eyes met his, glazed with the passion he'd created inside her. The sight filled him with a fierce delight. This next month would be no chore at all and she would derive as much pleasure during this time as he. He would drive every memory of his brother out of her head and her body. The thought of her with Matteo burned in him. He relished the thought of claiming his prize and vowed she would never think of any other man except for him for at least this next month.

"Open for me," he commanded, his words harsher than he'd meant them to be. Yet, he suddenly had a driving need for her to acknowledge his claim.

Her eyes cleared and sharpened. Two small hands slapped his chest. "Let me go."

Startled at the sudden change, he stared at her mulish face. His hands tightened on her waist. "You were with me all the way."

"You grabbed me." She pushed him, and the feel of her hands on his chest drove his blood into a frenzy.

"You kissed me." His temper, his well-controlled temper, roared to life once more.

"No." Blue lasers of rejection met his gaze. "*You* kissed *me*."

"*Maledizione*." He gripped her tighter.

"You can bellow in Italian at me all you like, Mr. La Rocca." Her chin thrust out with her words. "But you will release me or I'll scream."

The determination in her voice finally speared through his throbbing need to pin her to the floor and teach her what she honestly wanted. It also cut right through his temper—the temper he never allowed himself to lose.

Irritated surprise flashed through him.

He stepped away from her, lifting his hands up in a sign of compliance. "*Perdono*."

"If that means you're apologizing, apology *not* accepted." Tugging on the edge of her ugly brown suit jacket, she pretended to ignore him.

His temper bubbled behind the steel wall he always contained it with. This woman had a knack for cracking through his control, which he didn't appreciate. "Then I will retract the word. It was not needed anyway. I did nothing to you that you did not want."

"That's not true—"

"Nothing you weren't a full participant in."

Her gasp of outrage fed his growing ire. He itched to grab her, shake her into acquiescence. Rather than making that strategic mistake, he stalked to the window and scowled down at the seething traffic. "Let us get to the bottom line," he snarled. "I don't have any more time to waste on you."

"Fine. Give me what I came for—your commitment to release Matt from this marriage—and I'll be gone from here in a flash."

Turning, he glared at her. Her hair was mussed by his hands. Her eyes were huge and blue in her delicate face. Her lips were plump and puffed from his brief kiss. His burning anger mixed with an aching lust. She forced him to use his last cruel card. So be it. Why was there some primal part of him taking delight in breaking her to his will? "You leave me no choice."

Her dainty eyebrows frowned. "What do you mean?"

"I am done trying to reason with you."

"This is your idea of reasoning with me?" She huffed. "Issuing commands I'm supposed to follow? Stealing a kiss when I don't want anything to do with you?"

"I am afraid I will have to disappoint you on your wish to have nothing to do with me." He stepped behind his desk and lifted the folder. Slapping it down, he pinned her with an icy stare. "For the near future you will be with me all the time."

"I will not." Her pointed chin jutted.

A harsh laugh escaped him. "From this point on, Ms. Moran, you will do exactly as I say."

"Ha!"

"I will take great pleasure in seeing this happen." He shoved the folder towards her. "Some light reading for you."

She eyed it with distrust. "What is it?"

"You wish me to translate once more?" He sat down in his leather chair, his gaze never leaving her. "The report is about your father."

Her lithe body froze. "How do you know my father?"

"I don't know him. I know of him."

She gave him a nonchalant wave of her petite hand. But he was not deceived. She vibrated with unease and she no longer met his gaze. "So?"

"Sooo," he drawled out the word. "He is in trouble."

"Oh, no." Her head jerked up from her contemplation of his carpet.

"This is not the first time, is it, Ms. Moran?"

She stared at him as if he were a rattlesnake ready to strike.

He obliged her. "My security team has determined your father is neck deep in a heroin ring."

"Bloody hell. I told him I would give him money—"

He snorted in disgust. "You are naïve if you think the tiny amount of money a starving artist can give is going to be enough to feed a heroin addiction. Your father is dealing to feed his habit."

"I thought he'd finally made a decision—"

"Don't be a fool." His tone was overly harsh yet he couldn't seem to help himself. Frustration and anger still simmered in his blood. He craved her submission, her defeat, with a ferocity that surprised and stunned him. But the craving compelled him forward. "Your father has two destinations. The one he takes will be determined by you."

"Me?" she squeaked.

"*Sì.*" Lust and fury roared in his head, in his heart, in his body. The passionate mix drove him to conquer. "My security team will either turn your father over to the police—"

"Don't—"

"Or deliver him to a recovery facility."

Dead silence answered his words.

"A very expensive, successful recovery facility."

She stood rigid—her face white, blue eyes stark in contrast to her skin. He had a sudden desire to pace to her, sweep her in his arms, tell her he would protect her.

However, this was not his goal or his duty. His goal was to bring this woman in line. His duty was to his business, his family, his brother. She was merely an object of his fleeting desire.

And his adversary.

"Well, Ms. Moran? Which will it be?"

CHAPTER 3

Being treated like unwanted baggage was nothing new.

As a kid, she'd always been treated this way.

Still. It rankled.

Darcy glanced across the long length of the limo seat. The Great Man ignored her. As he'd ignored her in the limo that drove them to Heathrow. As he'd ignored her on the long flight to New York. As he ignored her now. He'd been far more interested in his phone, which he was currently talking into, or his laptop, which he'd had in front of him the entire eight hours on the plane.

She shouldn't care. She should be thankful his attention wasn't on her. It was pretty damn scary to think this man and his goons had rifled through her life enough to find out about dear old dad. What else did he know about her?

Not that she had anything much to hide.

Except herself.

Her hands trembled and she stuck them between her legs to warm them. The chill running through her body couldn't be warmed by the heat seeping from the vents. Trying to recover her composure after coming through the whirlwind of dictates, plans, and commands issued by this man was a decided chore. Within seconds of her capitulation, he'd barked orders into his phone.

His brother was to be sent to Italy, to spend the next month cozying up to his fiancée. Her meager belongings were to be immediately packed and delivered to his penthouse. Her mobile phone and passport were handed over at his bidding. And she, the unwanted baggage, was going to New York with him.

As his blackmailed mistress.

In name only.

She'd been able to get a couple of words in. One demand.

No sex.

He'd looked at her, quirked an eyebrow and then laughed. His demeanor had changed from impatient dictator to wicked tempter. *Tesorina,* he'd caressed the word as he murmured it. His silver eyes gleamed with humor. *I will allow you to make the first move.*

He'd stated the words with absolute arrogance and complete confidence.

He would *allow* her.

Darcy threw a glare across the length of the seat, but he was staring out the window as he talked into his phone in rapid Italian. Her glare bounced right off him and back onto her.

For several hours she had been overwhelmed, so what?

It was understandable. Also, forgivable.

Now, though, it was time to find her courage and reinstate it. Time to resurrect her fighting spirit. Admittedly, he'd gained the upper hand and forced her into this situation. Yet she'd learned well over the years—every situation held a silver lining. The silver in this situation was not his eyes, but the fact she had a month where apparently she was going to be spending a lot of time following him around. A month to charm, cajole, and change his mind about Matt and the bloody wedding-that-wasn't-going-to-happen.

There was every reason to hope she could do what she'd originally set out to do.

Feeling a bit more cheerful, she looked through the window and watched as the city lights glistened and glowed through the icy sleet dripping down the pane.

There was another silver lining.

She could enjoy her first trip to New York.

Her first trip anywhere outside of England.

The Great Man hadn't thought it worth telling her how long they'd be in the city, still it would be at least a day or two, wouldn't it? He'd be busy with his all-important business meetings, so odds were she'd have a chance to see some of the sights. She'd read about the art galleries in this city. If a girl focused on this situation in the right frame of mind, this was brilliant.

A man she despised would foot the bill for something she adored doing.

My, my, how she loved irony.

Actually, she was downright cheerful. Giving her window reflection a jaunty grin, she promised herself she'd find a way to make this new situation work to her benefit and Matt's.

"What is so funny?"

His dark growl rolled across the seat and straight up her spine. It reminded her there was a big bad wolf in her plot line and she was going to have to use every one her skills to charm him if she wanted to succeed in bending him to her will. She hadn't handled it well in his office, true. For the last few hours, she'd sunk into a numb zombie state, also true. Maybe he thought this was how she usually acted—either screeching like a banshee or stumbling behind him like a dumb animal.

Well, he was about to get a dose of the real Darcy Moran.

She gave him her best smile. The one that always got her

anything she wanted from anybody she dealt with. "I'm excited to be here."

"Is that so?" His only reaction was a slight lift of one satanic brow. "I was under the impression you wanted nothing to do with me. I'm glad to hear you're excited to be with me."

Darcy stared at him with shock. The man hadn't even blinked when she'd used one of her best weapons on him. What if her lures didn't work? What was she going to do then? Swinging her head away from his penetrating stare, she looked out the window again.

Come on. You've conquered a lot worse than this man.

She pushed past her worries. She was capable of winning this contest of wills. More than capable. After all, she had many more weapons to use. She had a wily, sharp brain. She'd survived the worst as a child by cunning and fast talking. She'd escaped danger many times using myriad tricks to protect herself. Somehow, she would dazzle and manipulate this man into submission.

Brushing a wisp of hair from her forehead, she tried to ignore the shaking of her hands. A little voice in her head screeched a warning she couldn't ignore, though. How would she lure and enchant him without falling under *his* spell?

Impossible, another voice inside her tutted. The man had blackmailed her. There was no way she'd ever feel attracted again to him.

No, she was completely safe. But he wasn't.

She peeked at him, through her long lashes, which she knew she used to excellent effect. His eyes narrowed and his big body stiffened.

Ha!

She would win this battle. She would prove her mettle. He might have won the first clash. The war was only beginning, however.

"I'm excited to be in New York for the first time."

Purposefully, she lowered her voice, layering a touch of husk into her tone.

"With me," he added. He observed her as if he were about to pounce, yet he wouldn't. The man had too much pride. Maybe even as much as she had.

Easy-peasy, another voice chimed in her head. She was safe. Very, very safe. She could tease and play and provoke all she wanted. Because of his pride, he'd wait until she made the first move simply to prove a point.

He'd be waiting forever.

She threw her best smile at him once more. This time, she noticed the slight tensing of his jaw. Anticipation ran around inside. The man was going to be eating out of her hand in short order. "The city is what excites me. All the places and happenings will provide me many hours of enjoyment, I'm sure."

"And I am sure I'll provide you many more hours of enjoyment than any city could." He lounged on the leather seat, a male filled with supreme confidence. "After you admit I excite you."

"My, that ego of yours is quite impressive," she drawled.

"I have other impressive qualities." His deep voice curled around her, his gaze promising sultry sin.

She succeeded in stopping the quiver threatening to run through her blood. But for the life of her, she couldn't think of what to say in response.

Where was her quick tongue? Her quick wit?

The beep of his phone caused him to looked away, releasing her from his scrutiny. Releasing her from any need to rebut him. His expression turned from wicked teasing to grim determination. The Italian words rolled out of his mouth, staccato with tension and rapid force.

Exactly as Matt had indicated, his older brother lived for his work, lived and breathed his company. Although he had made himself her enemy, she struggled with a faint welling of compassion for the guy. He didn't have a clue what was important in life. Friends. Family, if you were lucky enough to have one. Finding something you did with your heart, like her painting. Instead, it appeared from the hours she'd spent with him, he buried himself in work every time it called. Yet, this didn't make him happy. The look on his face, whenever he worked, made it clear. He wasn't doing this for the love of the work.

Why did he work so hard if not for the love of it? He had enough money amassed in his bank coffers to live the rest of his life in ultimate ease. What drove this man to work non-stop?

He clicked off his phone and glanced her way.

"The only thing you do is work, isn't it?" she said, giving him a pitying look.

"No." His eyes went hot. "I make time for other pursuits."

"Really?" She countered his suggestive gaze with one of disbelief. "I can't imagine it."

"Pleasure." He drew the word out, slurred it with his accent. "I pursue pleasure on occasion."

The limo's temperature seemed to instantly spike thirty degrees. Her cold hands went slick with sweat. She pulled them from between her legs and ran them across the smooth surface of the seat. The warm leather made her brain think treacherously of another kind of warm skin.

The man knew how to turn on the heat. A hot stare and a couple of words, and he had her thinking of stuff she never, ever thought of. Bodies and skin and sexual stuff. Still, he'd run into a worthy adversary. He could turn the heat to boiling and she wasn't going to get burned.

She'd play the game, though. She definitely knew how to play the game.

"What gives you pleasure?" She gave him a faint smile as if

she were only mildly interested in the answer. "Sports? The theatre?"

"No," he volleyed back. "Sex."

His blunt word slammed the ball right onto her side of the court. She was ready for him. "I'm amazed you would take time away from making your next billion for such a simple pleasure."

"Simple?" His mouth quirked in sardonic humor. "There is nothing simple about having sex with me. As you will soon find out."

"Dream on."

He chuckled and the damn, distracting dimples showed themselves in all their fine glory. "I will have many dreams of you, *Tesorina*. Eventually, I will make them come true for both of us. Of that you can be sure."

Before she could respond, the limo slowed, then stopped.

"Finally." He slipped his mobile phone into his pocket. "We are here."

She peered out the window to see five flags whipping in the wind and an impressive marble entryway. "Where's here?"

"The Plaza." His door was eased open by the doorman and he stepped into the biting cold of a November winter.

Slipping across the length of the seat, she was instantly conscious of how rumpled she appeared. She still wore her one good suit, though it had long ago given up any semblance of freshness, and was wrinkled and creased. Much like her hair and probably her face.

The doorman, dressed in a smart, navy suit with gold braiding, gave her a surprised appraisal. Darcy lifted her chin. What did it matter what she looked like? She wasn't going to be intimidated by anyone.

La Rocca glanced over his shoulder at her. His gaze narrowed.

Her chin thrust out another notch. She certainly wasn't going to let *him* intimidate her.

"It's a good thing I made arrangements," he murmured under his breath, condescending satisfaction oozing through each word. He gave her one last scan before turning away.

Bristling, she watched him as he started climbing the red-carpeted stairs. What gall. What arrogance. What the hell did he mean by *made arrangements*?

She gritted her teeth and controlled the urge to snarl.

Okay, he held more power than her for now, but she wouldn't allow him to dictate anything more than where she stayed for the next month. That was the limit of her cooperation.

"*Vene,*" he barked at her, gesturing with impatience.

What did that mean? Except she knew what it meant. Follow him. Do what he told her to do. Be an obedient—

"Darcy." He turned to stare at her, his satanic brows frowning. "Do I need to remind you of your father's predicament?" Not waiting for her reply, he swung around and climbed the last of the stairs, the doorman rushing to open the door before him.

Grumbling under her breath, she followed him up the staircase and through the gold-embossed doors.

Straight into heaven.

Pale marble floors gleamed like satin. Inlaid tile swirled in patterns that made her want to kneel and run her hands across them. Huge chandeliers, glistening with fractured glowing glass, splattered warm light on the lobby. A marble embossed circular table stood in the middle of the room laden with a stunning display of gardenias and greenery arching to the ceiling.

Every drop of artist's blood in her rose in acknowledgement of pure beauty. "Blimey."

The Great Man turned to stare at her. "You like this?"

"Yes." Immediately, she chastised herself for letting her true reaction to this extravagance show. After all, she'd been able to keep her composure throughout these last luxury-filled hours.

While she'd been transported to the airport in a sleek limo. When she'd been ushered into a lavish private plane. As she'd been offered expensive champagne as they lifted off. Pride had saved her. She would not let anything this man did or said or owned intimidate her or impress her. Or at least let him know it did.

Except now, now she'd shown him…

"You see?" He strode to her side and leaned down to whisper the rest of his words in her ear. "I promised you I would provide many things for you. Many things that will pleasure you."

His breath slipped around her, rich and warm. The heat of his body encircled her, mixed with the musk of his scent, earthy and exotic. In one single moment, he wiped the beauty of the lobby away, leaving in its place *his* beauty. He was a pleasure to smell, she thought in a daze. He'd be a pleasure to taste.

The lobby blurred as his presence enveloped her.

"Mr. La Rocca." A man dressed in a tuxedo approached. "How nice of you to visit us once more. If you would follow me, I will show you to your room."

The Great Man stepped back.

A shudder of something she didn't want to admit feeling rippled through her, but she was a realist. The blackmail had not doused the lust for him. "Bloody hell," she muttered.

"*Vene.*" He barked the word over his shoulder again as he strode towards the elevators.

His arrogance doused the last remaining spark of lust in a flash. All right, she knew the danger now. So she would tease from a distance. She would cajole from several feet away. She would make sure she never got close enough to be tempted.

And she would win. She would come out of this situation with the win.

"Darcy." His voice now vibrated with irritation. He turned to glare at her from the elevator doors. The concierge gave her a look of astonishment. The apparent fact she was accompanying the Great Man had managed to crack his smooth facade.

Never let it be said that Darcy Moran wasn't worthy of being anywhere she wanted to be. Thrusting up her chin, she swept towards them as if she were Queen of England.

La Rocca smirked.

The other man's eyes widened.

She reached them just as the doors of the elevator hummed open and she stepped in. The men followed. She positioned herself on the other side of the concierge near the wall. Looking at the man, she gave him her best smile. He stiffened and then smiled in a stunned sort of way.

Typical.

It was always this way when she used her finest weapons. Let the Great Man put that in his hat and stew on it. She glanced over to see his reaction.

La Rocca met her gaze from the other side of the man, and drat him, chuckled.

Fine, let him continue to underestimate her. She swung her focus to the front and watched the lights flash as they climbed the floors.

He'd be sorry, very sorry when she won.

Within minutes, they were being ushered into a room filled with Louis XV furniture, Persian rugs, and antique paintings. Her frustration and irritation seeped away when she stepped into the beautiful place. As the two men talked, she circled the living room, slipping her hand across the plush upholstery, admiring the downy carpet with its splashes of vibrant red mixed with muted green and gold. She walked to the fireplace and scanned the oil painting of a Renaissance lady dressed in a vivid purple, her serene visage ruling all she surveyed. Pulling her gaze from what was clearly a masterpiece worth thousands, she noticed the staircase arching to another floor.

This was a hotel? Her mind boggled. The only kind of hotel

she ever experienced was when her pop and mum got thrown out of their flat and they'd been forced to stay in a hotel room with only one bed. She'd slept on the floor that night, breathing in the smell of cigarette smoke.

"The bedroom is upstairs."

The words jerked her attention from the surroundings and put it solidly on him. The concierge had left.

They were alone.

He lounged on the doorframe, looking impossibly handsome and polished. His suit showed not one tiny wrinkle. His hair swept back from his face in perfect formation. His eyes were clear and alert, even though they'd left London late in the night and it was now close to midnight here. She had slept on the plane, yet as far as she'd seen, he'd never stopped working.

She felt like a wet rag in front of a crisp linen handkerchief.

"You're tired."

"A little." She stepped behind an antique velvet sofa feeling a need for some protection from his perfection.

"Why don't you go upstairs and sleep." He took a quick glance at his watch. "I have some work to do."

"Work. Again." She stared at him. "At this hour?"

"I can put work aside, *Tesorina*, if you wish to indulge in my other pursuit." His lazy grin teased her. "Pleasure."

"No."

"Much to my regret. However, I'm a patient man." He waved to the stairs. "Go on. I'll be here in the study."

A sudden thought flashed in her brain. She'd been so caught up in the whirlwind which was Marcus La Rocca she hadn't thought, hadn't remembered. She glared at him with resentment. "I don't have any clothes."

"I took care of it." He turned and paced toward the study.

"What?"

Glancing over his shoulder, he pointed skyward. "Go and see."

What overconfidence. The man went ahead and got her some clothes without consulting her? She marched to the elegant stairs, vowing to hate every article of clothing and throw them right in his face.

The upper floor was dominated by the bedroom and bath. Her gaze went to the armoire. Throwing open the doors, she gasped. The closet was stuffed full of scarlet satin flounces and frothy cream creations. She couldn't help herself, her artist hands slid over the gorgeous fabrics. There were dresses and suits, even a long gown in ruby red which fluttered through her hands. She opened the drawers and found cashmere jumpers in a riot of colors along with elegantly cut slacks in fine wool. Another drawer provided a lacy bounty of panties and bras.

A heated blush rose up her throat at the thought of him ordering these for her.

Then, she lost her temper.

She stomped down the stairs and zeroed in on the computer light emanating from the study.

"You can't possibly be serious," she snarled at the man whose back was to her.

He turned and gave her an annoyed glare. "I believe I have informed you of my seriousness in all things."

Holding up a bra, she nailed him with a glare of her own. "I can pick my own underwear."

"But it is not necessary. I have already done so."

"Without my consent."

He shrugged. "I didn't think you would mind a whole new wardrobe."

"I do mind."

"Tough." He stood and sauntered toward her. "No woman of mine is going to appear as a bag lady."

No woman of mine.

The words shot through her like an arrow, leaving a trail of unwanted enchantment behind.

Bag lady.

That stung and infuriated her.

"I'm not your woman. I'll dress any bloody way I want to."

"You agreed to be my woman for the next month." His silver eyes flashed. "You'll dress in a manner fitting to your new role."

"I'm here with you only because you forced me—"

"I gave you a choice." His accent became more pronounced. "You chose me."

"I chose the lesser of two evils, but that doesn't mean I have to bow down to all your commandments."

"Actually, it does." Leaning in, his every word brushed her skin. "It means exactly that. With one exception."

At the mention of their bargain about sex, a blush stained her cheeks. Embarrassment fired her temper higher. "I'm not going to tart myself up for you."

"Tart?" His satanic eyebrows rose. "I was quite clear about what I wanted in your wardrobe. I don't believe Bergdorf Goodman does tart."

Her mouth dropped at the mention of the high-class store. She was poor, still she'd read, dreamed, heard how the rich lived. She'd simply never thought of herself experiencing the lifestyle. She should be enjoying this. Why was her temper getting in the way of taking what was offered?

Because she had principles. She wasn't like her mum. *She wasn't.*

"I finally have you speechless. How delightful."

"You must have spent a fortune."

"I had a feeling the silence wouldn't last long." His hand slapped onto the doorframe, effectively pinning her to the wall. "What I spent is no concern of yours. Go upstairs, put on one of the dozen nightgowns I bought you, and enjoy. Like any other woman would."

"I don't—"

"Remember your father, Darcy?" he whispered in her ear.

"Remember your poor father who is even now getting treatment for his addiction?"

She sucked in a hot breath and met his threatening frown. "I hate you."

Pushing himself off the doorframe, he strode to the desk and his ubiquitous computer. "It is a surprise when a woman is given a brand-new wardrobe and says she hates the man who gave the clothes to her. Nevertheless, I will survive the shock. And your stated feelings for me."

She should say something. Something witty and sharp and nasty. Something that would make *him* lose his temper to the point he couldn't put one cognitive thought together.

Sitting, he stared at the screen and began to type. "Go to bed."

She cursed him under her breath. Yet, what could she do? She couldn't wear this same droopy dress for days on end. Plus, she couldn't go to bed nude…

Wait a minute.

She ran to the stairs and up the steps to gape at the bed.

The one bed.

Turning around, she opened every door. The door to the bathroom, with its gold fixtures and swirling leaf pattern on the floor. The door to the outside terrace, with the cold wind whipping and the lights of Manhattan spread out before her.

There was only one bedroom.

She flew down the stairs and into the study.

"*Dio,*" he said, his gaze never leaving the laptop's screen. "What now?"

"Where are you sleeping tonight?" she gasped.

"In the bed upstairs." Leaning back in his chair, he eyed her quivering figure.

"No, you're not." Pure panic flared. She'd never slept with anyone before. Never since the horrible night when she'd forced the male away. And been forced to run away.

He sighed. "I don't enjoy all this drama."

"I'll get another room."

"Do you know how expensive this place is? I doubt you have the funds."

"I'll find another hotel."

"Don't be ridiculous." He swiveled, his focus again on his computer screen as if everything which could be said had been said. "We will sleep in the bed together like adults."

"I'm not having sex with you."

"I do not appreciate screaming women," he observed with exasperation. "In fact, I don't allow them in my presence if I can help it. Also, no one said anything about sex."

"I'm not getting into that bed with you." A well of nausea slid into her throat.

"Let's get something clear." The silver sword of the glare he gave her sliced into her words, her emotions. "For the next several weeks, you have agreed to be my willing mistress."

"In public only."

"No." He cut her another icy look. "The only thing I agreed to was not making the first move as far as our sexual relationship goes."

"We have no sexual relationship and we never will."

"You can say whatever you like, but we both know what's going to eventually happen between us." He lifted his hand to silence her next words. "My goal is to make sure everyone knows you are my woman."

"For God's sake—"

"This means you will be on my arm in public, smiling at me, allowing me to touch you—"

"I never agreed—"

"There will be numerous parties we will attend. All of them will have paparazzi who will take pictures. Those photos will land in the tabloids."

Another bolt of horror shot through her. She didn't want her name in the papers. This could draw attention. Unwanted attention. Sure, it was unlikely *he'd* be reading the New York tabloids. Still, she didn't want to take the chance. "I didn't think of that."

"You can think about it now." He turned back to his work. "I usually avoid tabloid coverage, yet in this case it is necessary."

"Why?"

"My mother loves the tabloids. She will see the pictures of us and will most certainly share them with my brother."

This whole situation was insane. She'd played her hand wrong from the very start and now look where she was. Dealing with threats she couldn't ward off. Quarreling with a man who tied her in knots. Facing a situation she couldn't face. All because of a misunderstanding she'd first thought would help her and Matt.

She had to stop this now. She had to make this man understand. "You n-n-need to know Matt and I are not together."

"I do know this. I'm the one who made sure of it."

"N-no. You don't understand." She tried to keep her tone level, except her breathing kept hitching in her throat. The stuttering only made her agitation worse. "We've n-n-never been together. Ever."

He swung around to frown at her, a curl of disgust on his lips. "Don't take me for a fool."

"It's true." Her voice wobbled as she forced the words out and she cursed at herself internally. It was imperative she made him believe her. "It's n-never been like that with your brother and me."

A snort of disbelief came from the man sitting before her. "What happened to the grand passion you confessed to me only yesterday? The great love of your life which you tried to use to manipulate me into releasing Matteo from his obligations?"

"Well." She stumbled through her head for the correct words. "I d-d-do love Matt. Just not in that way."

"Right." The word dripped with contempt, as he returned to his all-consuming work. "It is of no consequence to me what your feelings are about my brother."

"You have to see this makes all the difference in the world." Her hands flew in the air, panic making them flap in a furious dance. "You can let me go home to London."

"Not a chance." His words landed between them like stone pellets.

"Matt won't believe we're together if he sees a dozen, a thousand photos of us."

Glancing over his shoulder, he gave her a grim smile. "Sì, he will believe we are together. I'll make sure of it."

"This is so unnecessary—"

"You will also make sure to leave the impression to everyone we meet that we are lovers."

A shiver of tremulous fear mixed with excitement slipped through her. "I can't—"

"Listen." He pinned her with another of his steely glares. "The bottom line is I don't believe anything you say. I only believe in one thing."

"What's that?" She stamped down on the unexpected pain his words caused her.

"My plan," he replied. "The plan you agreed to in order to get care for your father."

"I don't think if M-matt sees us together—"

"This is the purpose of our current relationship. I want to let Matteo know you are now with me."

She stared into his narrowed gaze and realized her protestations were hopeless. He was never going to believe she and his younger brother hadn't been a couple. He was never going to let her out of the deal she'd agreed to.

"Have I made myself clear?" He continued down his relentless path.

"I'll play your game," she acknowledged. "Still, sharing a bed is going too far."

He tapped his finger on the desk in exasperation. "Maids talk. My new lover will be of interest. Do you think I'd take a chance of word getting out we had separate bedrooms? This would defeat the entire purpose of you being with me."

"I'll sleep on the sofa."

He gave her figure a long perusal from head to toe. A panicked thrill shivered over her skin. "You are small, but not that small. You'll be very uncomfortable."

"I don't care." She forced the frantic tears back. No matter what, she would not cry in front of this man. Ever.

"I do, *Tesorina*. I promised you pleasure. Not a painful night on a sofa."

"I can't do this," she cried. "I can't."

"You will. Or your father will be in quite a bit of trouble."

She stood there, breathing in, breathing out. The jumble of emotions and thoughts brewing inside threatened to overwhelm her. The only other time she'd felt this sense of shock and fear surging in her was when she was seventeen. Seventeen and so, so scared. The memories swirled through her, sweeping over the current emotions in a maelstrom.

"The woman's complaints have stopped." Cynicism and scorn oozed from his every word. "I'm relieved."

She wouldn't allow herself to walk away from this latest confrontation a loser once more. She had to get at least a piece of his hide, poke him enough to draw pain. Or she'd never forgive herself. "You don't like women do you?"

"I like them just fine." He swung around to his computer and began typing. "In certain areas of my life."

"I'll rephrase. You don't respect them."

His gaze landed on her. His eyes were cool, cloaked. "No. In my experience, there is nothing much to respect about a woman."

Her hands fisted at her sides. The urge to smack him on the side of his head was hard to control. She'd teach him a lesson about respect. If it was the last thing she did, she'd teach him. "What woman did this to you?"

His laugh was harsh. "I'm not talking to you about my past, Ms. Moran. It has nothing to do with you."

"It certainly—"

"Let's get this straight." His silver eyes turned to ice. "You are here for one purpose. To keep you away from my brother until he is safely married. We are not in a relationship. I do not have to care what you think of anything I do. You will do what I tell you to do for the next month, and then you can go and do any damn thing you want."

"What I want is to see Matt. A man who's ten times the man you are." She hoped this barb would bite. Bite hard.

"No." The ice turned to storm clouds, threatening her with certain calamity. "You will never be with Matteo anymore. I'll make sure of it."

The bite had clearly bitten him, but he'd struck back with deadly intent. His words cut the heart out of her. Nausea and tears welled in her throat. "Y-y-you can't stop me."

The childish lament mixed with the awful stutter only made her feel worse. Feel powerless. Feel like she was a kid all over again.

"I can and I will." He stated the claim with utter confidence. Turning, he effectively dismissed her. "I will always have your father's criminal activities to keep you in line. Even after we have long parted company."

The maelstrom inside her roared. She wrapped her shaking arms around her.

"Go to bed, Ms. Moran." The ice now resided in his voice.

"Tomorrow you will start your new role and you better be prepared to please."

CHAPTER 4

She slept like a child. Marcus watched as she slipped one hand under her cheek and whimpered. She was curled on her side, the covers gracing her shoulders, the pink of her silk nightgown highlighting the cream of her neck. Her inky-black hair was a startling contrast to the milk-white of her petal-soft skin in the shadows of the bedroom.

He wanted to touch. He desperately wanted to touch.

Touch once more. Hold her like he had only moments ago, as he lifted her off the floor where he'd found her, and slipped her under the feathery duvet.

The woman's stubborn determination astounded him and annoyed him.

Yet he'd given one promise to her. And he never broke a promise.

Not even to a woman.

Putting his hands beneath his head to keep them from straying, he stared at the ceiling and willed his erection to subside. He'd had the thought when he booked this room that sleeping with her would surely be a promising push towards addressing the sexual heat between them. He hadn't believed her silly declaration in his office.

No sex.

He'd chuckled under his breath as he instructed his PA to make the reservations.

He wasn't laughing now.

The woman had pluck and pride. She wasn't going to go down without a fight. Much to his displeasure. Eventually, she'd give in to this desire running between them. The current, the electric pull, the demanding, drugging need…there was no way she wouldn't capitulate. Meanwhile, though, it appeared he was in for some long nights and some cold showers.

Why the hell was he putting up with this behavior?

Rolling over, he surveyed her once more. He could have done this another way. He could have paid her a sum which would ensure she stayed far from his brother. He could have used her father as a threat before trotting her off to be taken care of by his security team for the next month. Instead, he'd ensured she was in his presence, by his side, in his sights for the foreseeable future.

Why?

There was the sexual draw. Yet, he'd been drawn to many women sexually. Sex was the only draw women ever had for him. None of the women he'd taken were such a pain in the ass. Why the hell was he putting up with her screeching, her stomping? Why didn't he shove her on the plane back to London and lock her away until after the wedding?

She murmured in her sleep, her plump lips parting to breathe. The driving desire for her lashed at his control and concentration. Without intending to, he lifted his hand, ran a finger down her cheek, then slid it across her mouth. She felt as soft as a kitten, as downy and plush as the ripest peach. He remembered with stark clarity the taste of her. The sweet mixed with zing and zest.

The woman moved restlessly, arching into his touch.

Her hair flowed through his hands, silken strands warmed by her skin. It curled around his fingers, tugging him closer. He leaned in, watching as her long, black lashes fluttered on her creamy cheeks and then, lay still. Her pointed chin, the one she seemed to be continually jutting into the air when she was yelling at him, the chin begged for a kiss. A touch of his mouth brought another sigh from hers. She moved, moved into his arms, snuggling into the curve of his shoulder. The smell of her wrapped around him, honey mixed with cinnamon and sunshine. Appropriate for a sprite who was sugary sweet one moment and all sexy spice the next.

His arm rested on her curving back, his hand on her slight hip.

Che diavolo. There was no way he was going to let this woman out of his sight until he'd touched every part of her, kissed every inch of her, been deep inside her. Then this unwilling fascination for her would disappear. She would become like all the other women he'd had in the years since Juliana.

Nothing special.

Nothing memorable.

Nothing he would allow into his heart.

∼

She was safe.

Swimming between sleep and wakening, Darcy hung on tight to the unfamiliar feeling. One she hadn't experienced in so long... Well, she couldn't remember when she'd ever felt this way.

What did it matter? Living in the moment was one of her best skills.

She snuggled into the cozy covers. Unlike the sheets and bedding she was used to that scratched and snagged, these were silky on her skin, velvety and light. A firm warmth permeated from underneath her pillow. It smelled delicious, musky with a touch of something she couldn't describe. Something oddly familiar.

The comfort of the covers and pillow was intensified by the heat along her back. Had she gone to bed with a heating pad? She didn't even own one.

Again, what did it matter? Her brain musty with sleep, she burrowed deeper into the covers, arching her whole body into the heat.

Safe. I'm safe.

Sunshine filtered across her face. She'd have to get going soon. She had things to do. Matt wouldn't put her up forever. Getting her own place was a priority. Still, just a few more minutes of this bliss. Just a few more minutes.

She purred in contentment.

"*Tesorina*," a deep, humor-filled voice rumbled in her ear. "If you make noises like a kitten and arch into me like one, I must assume you wish to be petted."

Her eyes popped open. An antique painting of some Renaissance king glowered at her from the opposite wall in arrogant disdain. Sudden memory slapped away her feelings of being safe.

The panic rushed in right behind.

Yanking herself out of his arms, she jumped from the bed like the proverbial scalded cat.

La Rocca chuckled behind her.

How could she have fallen asleep last night? She'd been sure when she marched up the stairs—tight with the familiar fear and intense anger at his arrogance—she'd been positive there'd be no sleep for her. Not until he rose from the bed and left for one of his inevitable business meetings. She'd pulled off one of the covers from the massive bed and lay on the floor, promising herself she'd be far too uncomfortable to miss his appearance in the room.

She hadn't even heard him come in.

She hadn't even felt him pick her up.

She hadn't even noticed his arms encircling her.

How could this have happened? She never let anyone touch her. Never for long. Certainly never for a whole night.

"You have an amazing figure." The husk was deeper, richer in his voice. "The sunshine through your nightgown makes for an astonishing display."

Gasping, she twisted to face him, wrapping her arms around herself in a vain attempt to conceal.

"As I'm sure you know." Irony laced his words.

He was naked. At least, his chest was naked. The sight of his male gloriousness froze her in her tracks. Rather than running for the bathroom and a good set of clothes, she turned into a twit who could only gaze at perfection and lose all sensibility.

His shoulders were broad and thick with muscle. In his business suits, he exuded a sleek, lithe grace. Naked, though, he showed his true colors. A warrior body, ready for battle. Ready to conquer. Ready for action.

Action you aren't willing to give him, her brain yelled.

Why not? her body hummed.

His skin was dark olive, a rich, satin covering for those fabulous muscles. It glistened in the sunlight as if he were sweating slightly. The hint of moisture only increased the urge she had to reach out and touch. Glide the tips of her fingers over the warm flesh and feel his life flow pumping through his body.

A swirl of dark hair graced his pectoral muscles and the center of his chest, then thinned into an arrow pointing down,

down, down. For a desperate, depraved moment, she was quite angry at the sheets for hiding where that arrow ended.

"Do you like what you see?" He smiled, the dimples appearing. "I do."

Taking her lust by the throat, she turned and hurried into the adjoining bathroom. She slammed the door on his chuckle and muttered a very dirty word.

What the hell was wrong with her?

She'd lost her cool and lost another battle last night. Instead of telling the Great Man to take a hike, instead of demanding he get her another room, or instead of insisting she would sleep on the couch downstairs—

"Daft cow." Darcy glared at the mirror.

She'd fallen asleep, let down her guard, and found herself in a bed with him. Then to top it off, rather than telling him off for moving her, touching her, taking her in his arms as she slept, she'd stood like a git and drooled.

And he knew it. Damn it.

Safe? She must have taken some kind of crazy pill. Safe with this man? Wherever that feeling had come from, she needed to send it right back. Because the last word she would use for Marcus La Rocca was safe.

She yanked the borrowed nightgown off her and stomped into the shower, and punishing herself with cold water. Standing under the pounding spray, she lectured herself.

Keep your focus on winning.

Seduce this man with your charm.

Play your game. You know the game.

She stepped from the shower feeling more assured. Staring into the mirror again, she stuck out her chin and watched with satisfaction when the light of battle flickered in her eyes.

There she was. The girl she knew. The survivor. The fighter.

She'd lost the first few skirmishes between them. So what?

The war would still be won.

The Great Man was simply another person in a long line of people who had stepped into her life and thought, for whatever reason, she was a pushover. Maybe it was being short. Or skinny. Or maybe it was because she met everyone with a cheery grin. She was used to being underestimated. Hell, it often worked in her favor.

Being underestimated would work this time, too.

She slipped on a bulky bathrobe she found hanging behind the door. Much to her relief, it covered her from the top of her chin to the tips of her toes. The arms slid down to cover her hands.

She was ready to meet her adversary's dimples and distractions.

The bathroom door swung open with a bang.

He was gone.

The sunshine drifted along his pillow and the cream sheets that had covered his body. The light seemed to make the bed glow and shimmer, as if it waited for the Roman god to once more grace it with his presence.

Darcy snorted at herself. What muck.

She was glad he wasn't here. It left her in peace to dress and gird herself for their next skirmish.

For a moment, she thought about making a statement by dressing in her droopy old suit, but when she opened the wardrobe, the only items she found were the plush and pleasing pile of new clothes. The few items of clothing she owned had disappeared.

Her temper fired. How dare he sneak in here and take it away?

But she wasn't willing to march downstairs in only this bathrobe, however much it covered. It would make her feel nervous and exposed, knowing she was naked underneath it. Knowing he knew she was naked under it.

What was a girl to do?

Do the practical thing. And what did it matter if she enjoyed the feel of the silver lace bra as she put it on? What did it matter if she ran her hand down the emerald green cashmere jumper before she slipped it over her head? He'd never know she turned and twisted in front of the mirror, admiring the way the grey linen slacks hugged her hips and butt making her feel like the classiest woman on earth.

Sucking in her breath, she stared at herself.

Charm, Darcy. Charm.

Play the game, lovey, her mum chimed in. *Always play the game.*

His gaze met hers as soon as she started down the stairs. Then it traveled over her body in lazy perusal, touching on the roundness of her breasts highlighted by the soft cashmere, making them tingle. It eased along her waist and hips, causing heat to rise under her borrowed clothes. It slipped to her legs and to the tips of her boots. She could swear even her pinky toes quivered under his inspection.

"It's a good beginning."

The quivering stopped short as her temper bubbled. Any thoughts of charm blasted out of her head. "I am not some doll you can dress."

"I don't wish to start the day as I ended the last." Turning his back on her, he walked to a table laden with breakfast dishes. "Arguing with you."

Her hands fisted at her sides at his dismissal of her words. "Too bloody bad. Where is my suit? I want it returned. It's my best dress."

"That thing?" He gave her an amazed look over his shoulder. "I've done you a favor and disposed of it."

"You had no right."

"If that is the best you have, it is a good thing I came into your life."

"The worst day of my life was when you came into it." No

truer words could she have spoken and she hoped like hell they cut his hide.

To her irritation, amusement crossed his face. His eyes twinkled as he sat down and waved her to the other chair. "Let's at least eat before you continue to harangue me."

One hairy leg appeared as the duplicate of her bathrobe slid off a part of his body. Her gaze unwillingly gravitated to the strong, flexing muscles, ending at his feet. The man had gorgeous feet. They were long, the arch graceful, the toes elegant.

Elegant toes?

Had she lost her mind?

His chuckle yanked her attention to his face. The silver eyes sparkled at her. The sunshine shone on his dark hair, turning the strands into a mix of gold and mahogany. "You appear hungry for something besides food."

"Not at all." She met his gaze with a fierce glare.

"Then come." He waved her toward the table. "Have something to eat and you'll have the energy to snarl at me once more."

Her tummy rumbled. It had been more than twenty-four hours since she ate on the plane. And she'd been too tense with him by her side to do much more than nibble. The smell of bacon and coffee swirled around her.

A woman had to have sustenance if she was going to win with this man.

Eggs Benedict with hollandaise sauce to die for. Chunks of potatoes with dill and pepper. Freshly squeezed orange juice. She appreciated good food when she had it. Which wasn't that often. When she had a few extra coins, though, she enjoyed going to farmer's markets. She bought the best she could afford and then experimented in the kitchen until she created a new and exciting dish to try with friends.

"You eat well." His attention never left her as he wolfed down his own portion. "I like that in a woman."

She cut into the last part of her Benedict. His arrogance stirred the temper she'd managed to squelch as she ate. "I don't care what you like in a woman."

His lazy grin was the only response.

Laying her utensils on her plate, she fired the next shot in their ongoing war. "What? Not working? Why it must be nearly eight o'clock in the morning."

"I have a meeting in an hour and then several after that." He leaned back in his chair. "Don't worry, *Tesorina*. I'll make plenty of money on this trip to keep you in style."

"Gosh." Her tone was all sweetness and light. "That will mean you'll be busy throughout the day, won't it? Keeping me in style will cost you a pretty penny. Keeping me happy will cost you more than you can give."

The dimples flashed. "I believe I am *up* to the task in both areas."

Fighting her blush down at his double entendre, she plowed on. "I guess that means I have quite a bit of time by myself. I have several sights I'd like to see."

A frown replaced the dimples. "I'm afraid your day is already planned and it does not involve walking around New York City alone."

His phone buzzed. He flicked it on. A line of tension made his forehead furrow as he read the text. If only the man had a clue about what was important in life.

Still, she wasn't here to enlighten him, even if he paid her any attention. Which was doubtful. No, she couldn't allow herself to soften towards him and give him some much-needed advice. She had a war to win. "I can plan my own day."

"You'll be spending the day at the hotel salon." His words were distracted, his gaze centered on his phone. "The clothes are good, yet only the first step."

"The first step to what?"

Her tone must have alerted him. There were problems. His focus swung back to her and his gaze grew icy. "I thought we had resolved this last night. I don't appreciate this attitude you exhibit with me."

"I don't want to spend my day being slathered with lotions and potions," she spat at him. "I would much rather explore New York City."

"I'm sorry to disappoint you." His tone told her the exact opposite. "I'm afraid you need further assistance before appearing as my woman this evening."

"I look fine without a ton of makeup plastered on my face."

"You have a very odd idea of what will be done to you. I have told them what I want and I believe you will be pleased."

"I won't be."

"Is that so." He cocked his head with an air of disdain and disbelief. "Except that is not the point. The point is for me to be pleased and I have every assurance I will be."

Before she could punch him in the nose, he stood. His presence, the potent power of his body, silenced her for exactly long enough for him to get a list of his commandments announced before she could respond to his last salvo. "I'll return at seven. Wear the red gown. We'll be attending a formal event."

She finally found her tongue. "I don't want—"

"Your wants are immaterial." He prowled to the stairs, his mobile in hand, his attention already distracted once more. "It is mine that are paramount."

"You are the most arrogant—"

"Again, I must remind you." He stared at her, his gaze stormy with irritation. "Your father, Darcy. Your father."

He turned and ascended the last steps, disappearing into the bedroom. The man used his weapon against her well. Another win added to his column.

She could run up the stairs and fight with him some more.

That would mean risking seeing him naked, though. Which would only exacerbate this unfamiliar lust she wrestled with.

There was the crux of the problem. Why he kept winning this battle of wills. She'd come down here and promptly fallen into that pesky swamp of lust by ogling his feet for God's sake. She'd let herself get distracted and boom. Any thoughts of charming him disappeared when he did his usual arrogant routine. Rather than letting his arrogance roll off her, she'd let her agitated lust turn into pugnacious demands.

Which only irritated him.

A new approach was what was needed to win the day. It was up to her to master this new and frightening response to this bloke. She merely needed to figure out how to quash the lust once and for all.

"He's just a man," she whispered to herself. "Like every other man on the planet."

This was how she had to view him. Simply another guy. And apparently, she had the entire day to drill this into her skull. So, she'd sit and get slathered and plastered and use the time wisely.

Focus. Focus.

There would be no more swampy lust no matter how many dimples or feet he flashed. There would be no more attitude from her no matter how egotistical he was. As a substitute, she would deploy her own weapons.

Memories of her mum washed through her.

The long red nails. The blue sparkly eye makeup and bubblegum-pink lipstick. The high laughter, the inevitable glass of wine as she readied herself, the glazed eyes.

A little girl picked up a lot if she only watched and listened.

She usually shied away from it all. Used other skills. Yet some memories didn't fade.

He wanted her glamorized like a pretty doll? She could do that in spades. He wanted her dressed in a fancy new gown, ready and waiting for her lord and master? She could do that. And much to his surprise, bring him to his knees before her.

Today, she would climb out of this swamp of lust.

Tonight she'd push him into it. He would be the one distracted and disturbed.

She'd win this battle and then the war with the Great Man using the ploys she'd learned so well from her mum. Ploys that had driven Lucy Moran to her death would be used well by her daughter. Darcy Moran would be a winner, not a loser.

Thanks, Mum. Really. Thanks.

CHAPTER 5

Marcus slipped his phone into the pocket of his suit coat and eased back on the limo seat. Darkness had descended on the city, but the lights of Times Square blazed as if it were day.

The day that had seemed as long as a month.

Raking his hands through his hair, he cursed under his breath.

He'd wondered. All day.

Dannazione. Worried.

The sprite had appeared horrified at the thought of spending an entire day being pampered. What kind of woman was she? Any other woman of his acquaintance would have purred a thank you. *Dio,* maybe even given him a kiss.

Not Ms. Darcy Moran.

No, just as with her brand new wardrobe, she'd thrown it right back in his face. He'd had to put his foot down so many times in the last twenty-four hours, she should be nothing more than a squashed bug.

A chuckle escaped him.

He was always good at sizing up the competition. Or in this

case, the enemy. So he figured he shouldn't hold his breath about finding a submissive doormat waiting for him at the Plaza.

Instead, he'd likely be dealing with a hellcat ready to fight.

She'd been gone by the time he showered and dressed this morning. Apparently the concierge followed instructions and arrived to lead her to the salon. Yet, the sizzle of her anger hung in the air above their breakfast dishes. He'd called to make sure she obeyed instructions. Once he'd made sure she was where he wanted her to be, he put her out of his mind.

Or tried to.

It was merely to ensure she was following orders that he made the calls to the salon through the course of the day. He was only checking to make sure she hadn't taken flight. This was the only reason he quizzed his security team regarding her whereabouts a few times.

Okay, several times.

What mattered was she'd stayed put and did what he told her.

But he could predict what would happen when he got to his suite. The little sprite would stomp and screech. She had her pride so she would make her point by hurting his ears and irritating him. He'd end up putting his foot down once more. Perhaps he would even have to stuff her into a gown and shoes before carrying her through the door.

His body burned in excitement as images of his opponent in lacy panties and bra slid through his brain. Fighting him as he slipped a dress over her head. Tiny fists waving in his face. Eyes blazing defiance. Plump pink lips pouting, while that damn pointed chin of hers jutted out in bold rebellion.

He tugged at his tie, loosening the stranglehold around his neck.

Why was the thought of another row with her making him excited?

His phone buzzed against his chest. Sliding it open, he scanned the message. Good. The deal was done. The one he'd negotiated during the day with half his brain tied around all things Darcy.

Satisfaction coursed through him. As well as annoyance.

No woman distracted him from business. Not since he'd been twenty-one. He learned a hard lesson then, one he'd mastered well. No woman was worth taking his attention from what was truly important. Making the next deal. Amassing more power. Ensuring there would always be plenty of money.

Yet Darcy had.

He tapped the phone on his knee. It would not do and this would not happen again. He would make sure of it. All he had to do was remind himself of the fool he'd been with Juliana.

Sì. Juliana.

The ugly memory washed through him and settled like a hard mass in the center of his chest. It felt right in some way, familiar. It was good he remembered. Remembered everything and how it had changed him for the better.

He was now no longer trusting. Instead, he was thorough. A man who didn't assume something was done to his satisfaction until he checked on it himself. A man who didn't take someone, man or woman, at their word. He listened to what someone promised or proposed and then tied them to it using his power and money. It was one of many reasons why he was so successful. He never left anything to chance or luck. He was always prepared for whatever an adversary tried to use to oppose him. He'd seen and experienced every trick in the book and knew how to overcome each one.

The *ninfa* clearly knew quite a few tricks.

The peeks from beneath her long lashes. The husk in her voice. The drama of last night's screeching demands to get his attention one way. The curling into his arms in bed to gain his attention in another. The pretend horror when he'd called her on the sunshine pose.

The woman was trying to play him.

He chuckled.

He had to give her some credit. She was good. Not good enough to win against him, but hell, he was a hardened warrior in the game-playing arena.

Now that he thought about it, the fact she went to the salon and stayed was no surprise. Without a doubt, she had no real intention of denying herself the luxury. Why should she? She'd hit the jackpot. No, the entire confrontation this morning was a sham. A way to jerk his chain and keep his attention. She was playing a game, saying one thing, wanting another. For all her flat denials, she slipped on the clothes he'd given her. For all her pretend shock, she'd slept by his side, snuggling into him. For all her fake outrage, she spent the day right where she wanted to be.

Sì, the woman was playing her game.

He answered a few texts and emails. Called his manager in London and then placed another call to his Rome office. He finally snapped the phone off. Glancing out the window, he caught a glimpse of a billboard, high above the street. A model pouted and posed in a slinky pink nightgown.

The memory of her, this morning, filled his mind.

The sunshine had shot right through the filmy cloth gracing her body. The firm roundness of her bottom, the surprising length of her legs, the slender back and dainty shoulders. Then she'd turned to face him, her arms trying to pretend to hide her delights from his perusal. He'd seen enough, though. The lush thrust of her delectable breasts, the tiny waist, the petite hips.

Sei bella.

His erection pressed along the zipper of his pants, pulsing and pounding. Exactly as his blood did.

Sì, so beautiful.

With grim determination, he stared at his phone. He would not allow her this control over his thoughts. The strength of his response to her mere memory was not acceptable. He clamped down on both the irritation and his libido.

The only problem with the woman who waited for him at the Plaza was he needed to bed her. This was the only small hold she had on him, the only fascination he carried for her. That was all. This was easily taken care of. She would capitulate soon. He'd seen it in her eyes this morning. She wanted him. It would have been so easy to sweep her off her feet, into the bed. However, he had his pride.

He could wait.

Wait for her first touch. Prove his point and win once more.

The limo eased to a stop at the hotel stairs.

As he strode through the lobby and into the elevator, he prepared himself. Set his shoulders straight, slipped his tie into place, buttoned his suit coat. Arranged his expression into one of forbidding resolve.

He opened the door expecting an immediate battle cry.

No one met his entrance with words or missiles. He shut the door behind him with a thump. Glancing around, waiting for an attack, he found himself standing in the middle of the living room.

She was upstairs. He could hear her humming.

Humming?

Pacing to the crystal decanter of brandy he'd ordered last night, he poured himself a shot. He swirled the liquor in the glass, watching as it sloshed against the side.

She was happy? She wasn't meeting him at the door with more accusations and insults?

The husky, low voice above continued to hum. The sound slid across his skin and soaked into his soul. He threw his head back and swallowed the shot in one gulp.

This was only another version of her game. He could play along.

"You're here." She was using the husk in her voice again for good effect.

Turning, he looked to the stairs.

Despite the determined conclusions he made in the limo, his breath caught in his throat. His blood turned to heated oil. His cock hardened into a hot thrust of lust.

The ruby-red dress wrapped around her body like a caress, highlighting her pocket Venus figure to perfection. A tight sash emphasized her tiny waist, the round curve of her hips. Her breasts were pushed high, displaying a surprisingly impressive cleavage to his ravenous inspection.

"You fancy?" Her eyes danced as she spread her arms wide, showing herself off.

The makeup had been expertly applied. He'd known it would be well done. What he hadn't realized, hadn't been prepared for, was how it deepened her eyes into mysterious pools of deep-night blue. How the bright-red color on her lips highlighted the plump appeal.

She smiled.

It hit him. A womanly weapon that nearly brought him to his knees. The smile lit her face with vivacity, filled her eyes with excitement.

A giggle escaped her. "I think you like it."

A cold wash of alarm jerked him from her power. He turned his back on her, poured another shot of brandy and drank it down. "You'll do."

A tense silence fell between them.

"That's good," she finally said, her tone cool. "I would hate to think the money you've spent would leave you disappointed."

He heard the click of her heels as she descended. He continued to stare at his empty glass.

"Are you changing before we go?" There wasn't any

inflection in her voice to tell him what she was thinking and feeling.

"*Sì.*" Without looking her way, he paced to the stairs.

"I hope you'll take some care with your clothes."

He stopped at her words.

"I wouldn't want to be disappointed either."

Allowing himself to glance at her, he ignored the desire lacing through his body. "*Tesorina*, since I have never given you any expectations, how could you possibly be disappointed?"

The blast of her fuming scowl heated his neck as he ascended the steps. The resumption of their battle felt good, felt safe. What did it matter if he also felt irritated once again?

And also deprived.

~

WHO WAS THAT WOMAN?

Darcy peered around one of several tuxedoed men surrounding her. The men she'd charmed and corralled as soon as she arrived at the charity ball.

To be left to her own devices.

For all the talk about being seen together, Marcus La Rocca promptly dropped her like a stone when they entered the lavish ballroom. He'd disappeared into the large crowd, leaving her standing alone. A million miles away from anyone she knew. A thousand miles away from anything familiar. In the middle of a seething mass of elegantly dressed, rich people.

The type of people she knew nothing about.

Driving to the ball, she'd worried and fretted over the paparazzi they were sure to encounter entering. Profound relief swept through her when the limo dropped them off in the underground parking lot.

But the relief had disappeared along with La Rocca. A different kind of fear attacked, trickling down the back of her throat, making it hard to breathe. How could she cope in this strange environment, with these polished, fashionable people?

Then, like always, the fighter in her appeared to save the day.

Grabbing a glass of champagne, she stuck out her chin and jumped right into the crowd. Within minutes, she flirted and charmed and laughed and teased with everyone surrounding her. She'd become the life of the party. It was inevitable. Did her blackmailer think she'd turn into some kind of wallflower, pitifully waiting for him to come to her side? He was in for a shock if that was the case.

She watched as the woman slid a hand down his arm. The Great Man looked at the hand and then, straight into the woman's eyes.

Something clutched at Darcy's gut. Jerking her attention away from the interplay, she focused on the men before her. Who all smiled back when she smiled and flirted with her when she flirted. Who appreciated how beautiful she was. Much to her satisfaction, they were all charmed and with infinite ease she wrapped them right around her pinky finger within minutes.

Unlike La Rocca.

You'll do.

The words stung and burned, even hours later.

Darn it. The words hurt.

Which made her mad at herself. Why the bloody hell should she care what he thought? Clearly, her new façade was a brilliant hit with every other man she'd encountered at this charity ball. The makeup, the haircut, the lotions and potions had done their job. She'd rather enjoyed it if she had to confess. Surprise, surprise. The gown—the beautiful dress she'd fallen in love with as soon as she slipped it on—well, it was also perfect by the amount of attention she was receiving. She fit right into this crowd of the rich and famous.

Like a duck to water.

Who cared if one man didn't think much of her?

She couldn't help herself. She glanced across the room once more. The woman kept pawing him. He was letting her. Darcy eyed the woman, noting the lush figure, the long, blond hair, the height. A high-fashion model, maybe. Or a past lover? Or perhaps both.

Something ugly twisted inside her.

She scanned his face. No dimples. No grins. He looked the same as when he was stressed about some business email or text. Except she would lay odds on the fact this wasn't a business deal being negotiated between the couple.

Yet, there was something important happening. Of that she was sure.

Darcy Moran knew her body language. It had been a matter of survival when she was a kid. One peek at her mum's face and she'd known when to hide. One peek at her pop's and she'd known when to run. Being an artist only sharpened those skills.

There was something going on over there.

Something odd.

It was almost as though she could feel the tension in his body.

Glancing back at her gaggle of men, she threw them a tease and laugh, got them chuckling, and then swung her focus back to the couple across the room.

She knew. Knew the tension streaming through him. It had only been forty-eight hours since they met and yet she sensed the taut tension radiating from his body. The woman touched him again, and he finally smiled. But it wasn't the smile she'd seen this morning when he'd been in bed showing off his gloriousness. She'd swear his eyes weren't sparkling.

The smile was cold and icy.

The woman dropped her hand and with a flip of her hair, walked away.

Silver flashed as he glanced over and met Darcy's gaze. His frozen smile slipped from his face, replaced by a dark frown.

Whipping her head around, she laughed at one of the men's jokes. She made sure her eyes glowed, made sure her grin encompassed everyone surrounding her. If she couldn't manage to bring Marcus La Rocca to his knees before her, she would darn well get every other man at this party to do the deed. At least this would be something to crow about with the Great Man. There was no way she'd give him the idea she cared one iota about what he was doing or who he allowed to touch him.

"Excuse me, gentlemen." His words silenced the chatter. "I'm afraid I must take away your entertainment."

Her temper simmered. She wasn't mere entertainment. She was the life of the party. "I'm enjoying myself."

"I can see that." His voice was mild, though his eyes crackled with sharp lightning. "However, something has come up and we must go."

She gave him a chilly smile. "You go. I'll stay."

"Impossible." He returned her smile with an icy one of his own. Was it her imagination or did every one of her ardent admirers take a step back? "I couldn't leave you here alone."

"Really?" She arched a brow in disbelief. "Yet this is exactly what you did when we got here, Marcus."

His big body stiffened. She realized it was the first time she'd ever said his first name. Was this the reason for the sudden electricity sparking between them? But no. One glimpse into his eyes and she knew it was something else entirely. Why the hell would she think he'd be sentimental about something so little as his name tripping off her tongue?

Instead, it was clear; he was incensed at her rebellion.

She was baiting quite a formidable foe. Still, he deserved it. He'd belittled her and deserted her. Now he thought he could claim her like some baggage yet again? Unwanted for a time, but now claimed as his?

"Darcy," he murmured, his tone dripping with displeasure. "You are a constant challenge."

Her faithful fans faded from her side like smoke.

"Mmm." He surveyed the area. "It appears your party is over."

She found her arm held in an inflexible grip. "Hands off, bloke."

"Not for the next month."

His long legs started moving and it was all she could do to keep up with his pace. The crowd parted—eyes watching, tongues wagging, fingers pointing. She was literally being frog-marched out of the ball. "This is complete bollocks."

"True." He tugged her arm beneath his. "I can't remember the last time I dragged a woman from a room."

"We just got here." Embarrassment warred with irritation. "They haven't even served dinner."

"Never fear." He glanced at her and abruptly, astonishingly, the dimples emerged. "I'll make sure you are fed."

"That isn't the point." She would *not* let this surly man off the hook because of some dimples. *She would not.* As he pulled her across the foyer towards the front doors, a doorman hurriedly produced their coats. "I thought the point was to be seen together."

"Correct." He slid his arms into his black Armani jacket. "We will take care of that right now."

Through the door they went. Right into a sea of flashing lights and a chorus of yells.

The fear clutched in her throat and fisted shut any remaining words she had. The flashbulbs bloomed in her face, and she had a sudden image of her picture being carefully cut from a tabloid. Taped to a wall. Gloated over and obsessed over. Ugly, slimy memories rose like haunting wraiths swirling around her, grasping and gouging and gripping her in their talons.

"No!" The cry came from her heart; a spiked scream of fear. Marcus jerked his head around to stare at her. What he saw caused his satanic brows to tighten into a fierce frown. With a sharp tug, he wrapped her in one hard arm and picked up his pace. Striding through the crowd, he ignored the catcalls, the questions. Even though she now lay sheltered in his grasp, she was unable to push the ghosts of her past away.

He would see the pictures.
He would find her.
He would kidnap her.

It seemed like hours to her, yet it must have been only seconds before they were safely ensconced inside the limo. The car pulled away from the curb and the press and the photographs, leaving her limp with exhaustion.

"What's wrong?" He inspected her with sharp eyes. "You have gone completely white."

"Nothing."

His dark brows rose. "You appear as if you're about to faint and I am supposed to believe it is nothing? Don't take me for a fool, *Tesorina*."

"I don't like my picture being taken. That's all." She slumped into the warm leather seat, pulling at the lapels of her new faux fur coat to conceal her face from his scrutiny.

"That's the whole point of this outing." Apparently taking her at her word, he slid the omnipresent mobile phone from his pocket and then slipped his finger across its screen. "To be seen together."

"I d-don't see why there have to be so many pictures."

"The more pictures, the more chance my brother will see one and get the message."

"Your brother isn't going to care about us being together." Frustration at his stubbornness chipped a bit of her fear away. "Other than knowing both of us and being rather curious as to how we got together."

He jerked his head up and pinned her with his glare. "The love of your life not care?" he mocked. "You have such little hold on him?"

"He is not the love of my life," she gritted.

"But you confessed a towering love for him when we first met." He continued to glare at her, silver swords flashing. Did the memory bother him? Is this why she glimpsed fierce anger in his gaze? "You begged me to release him into your arms."

"I did not beg."

"Close enough." He returned his attention to his emails.

"You misunderstood what I was saying."

"I misunderstood nothing." His fingers moved over his phone. "Don't try and convince me I can let you go and you will behave with Matteo. It is an exercise in futility."

Silence descended. Darcy curled her hand on the fake fur, taking slight comfort in the rich feel of the coat. The comfort wasn't enough to banish the old fear chugging through her veins, though. The realization hit her; the longer she hung out with the Great La Rocca, the more and more exposure she was going to get in the press. More press exposure = more chance she'd be found.

Bloody hell. For a smart girl, she'd behaved rather stupidly, hadn't she?

It was imperative to get away. Now. What could she say to penetrate this man's thick, arrogant hide? Which words could she use to convince him this was a stupid waste of his time and hers?

"Stop trying to figure a way around me," he grumbled from across the seat. "I can see your scheming and conniving from ten meters away."

Some woman had really, really done a job on this man. And she was unjustly reaping the rewards.

"You might be able to dazzle those men back at the ball into falling at your feet," he continued. "However, I am a different kind of man."

A thrill spiked in her. He'd noticed the attention her charm elicited. The realization gave a small stroke to her ego.

Then, his last words penetrated her brain.

The thrill tightened her fear into outright panic. Not only did she have to get away from him because of the press, but he had just slapped another realization right in front of her.

He *was* a different kind of man. This close proximity to him —to his muscled body, his bold stare, his potent masculinity— was casting a lure around her. His allure drained her of her spunk, garbled her thinking. If she was always with him for this coming month, she was very afraid she might do the unthinkable: let go of her pride and fall into his arms.

He would win the war between them. Then, when he walked away, she would be left alone to fight her demon once more.

Safe?

A hysterical laugh burbled in her throat.

Being with this man wasn't safe. Being with him was the most unsafe she'd ever been since she was seventeen.

A deep sigh came from him. "It is such a waste of time, *Tesorina.*"

She peered at him. His attention was back on her. A quirk of a smile graced his mouth. The silver now glowed in his eyes. His big body leaned back in casual elegance on the fine leather.

"It is a waste of time," she agreed, hoping he'd finally listen. "You're holding me against my will for no reason whatsoever."

"Against your will? For no reason?" A disparaging sound slid across the seat. "You made a choice to be here. And you and I both know there's a very good reason."

Turning from his cynical stare, she stared at the back of the driver's head. What was the use of arguing with him anymore? The stubborn arrogance he exuded shielded him from any doubts or second thoughts.

A deep dread settled inside.

"Let us agree it would be best if you stopped your endless womanly machinations and instead took the only reasonable avenue before you."

"Womanly machinations?" His accusation stung, and frustration and fear turned to outright fury. What was the difference between his bullying and her attempt to stand her ground? She was merely protecting herself by using the skills she'd acquired the hard way. Her temper spiked through the last of the lingering nightmare of being photographed. "Reasonable avenue?"

"It would be reasonable for you to enjoy the situation you are in to the fullest rather than arguing with me at every turn."

"Do I have a choice?"

"No." His voice turned harsh. "It would be extremely smart of you to stop trying to manipulate me."

"I use my charm and personality to get my way. So?" She shot a fuming glare across the seat. "You use your power and money to get yours. What's the difference?"

His steel gaze shimmered with the light of battle. "The difference is I'm honest about what my plans are. You, a typical woman, are not."

The man had a chip on his shoulder the size of Wembley Stadium. His attitude about women reeked of cynical distrust. Which was something she could kindly point out to him. "What woman did this to you? Made you so suspicious of anything they do or say?"

He moved back along the leather. "I have no idea what you are talking about. I allow women to do many things to me. When I want them to."

She ignored the sexual gleam in his eye. She knew it was a ploy to take her off track. "I think you may want to contemplate a bit of counseling."

"Counseling?" His satanic brows rose in disbelief.

Giving him a pitying look from underneath her eyelashes, she smiled with satisfaction when his body stiffened. She had turned the tables quite neatly. If she was being burned by their association, why shouldn't he be? Why not throw more wood on the fire? "My bet is there are some old experiences you might want to discuss."

"I have no need for psychobabble." The sexual gleam had turned to ice in his eyes. "And as I don't indulge in bets, you will be disappointed."

He glanced at his mobile, dismissing her once more. Or was it a form of hiding from her scrutiny? Her questions? Her digging?

"No, you don't." She grabbed the phone from his hand and slid it under her coat.

"Don't be childish," he growled. "Give it back."

"No can do." Her grip tightened on the prize. Then another weapon appeared in her brain. "Who was that woman tonight?"

An irritated finger tapped on his leg. "I talked to many women tonight."

"Tall. Blond. Beautiful." The words came from her mouth, a staccato accusation in spite of herself. "Hard to forget."

The finger froze. "No one of importance."

She'd been right. The rigid line of his jaw, the blank tone in his voice, it all told a story. A story she wanted to know with a desperation that surprised her. "My guess is she's very important. What's her name?"

"Jealous? How fascinating."

He was quick at recovery, she'd give him that. "Don't try to change the subject."

"I find your jealousy much more fascinating to discuss, though."

"I'm not jealous."

"I think you are," he murmured, his accent thickening. "Don't worry. You are currently the only one I want in my bed."

His words sizzled through her, lighting a disturbing fire deep inside, banishing any thoughts of inquiring about his past with another woman. A flush of sexual excitement burned through her, leaving only pure need behind.

"Such a waste of time, this sparring and arguing." He leaned over and a long finger touched her brow, then whispered along her cheek and across her lips. "Why not stop this fighting and spend our time doing something far more pleasurable?"

The sizzle exploded deep within. It shocked her. His touch didn't bring forth her usual reaction—the need to pull away, the instinctive desire to keep her distance. Instead, she wanted him to come closer, touch more of her.

Why him? Why this man? After all these years, after she'd been sure she'd never feel the sexual pleasure other women talked about—

He inched closer and did what she so desperately wanted. She felt his breath on her cheek. His hand slipped along her jaw, moving her mouth closer to his. His distinct scent enveloped her, rich and redolent of musk, man. Sex. She breathed him in, wanting him.

No, she shouldn't. She couldn't.

Could she?

In the midst of her turmoil, one of his phrases finally caught her attention and saved her from herself.

You are currently the only one I want in my bed.

Currently?

"No." She pushed the word from her mouth, her lips almost brushing his with the word.

The heat of his gaze brought a blush to her skin. She forced herself to meet his glittering eyes. "No," she whispered again.

Before she could do or say anything more, his hand slipped beneath her coat, moving along her waist. Making every cell in her body jump to life. Making her gasp. "I said—"

"I believe this is mine." His hand slid out of her coat, his phone held tightly in his grip. He gave her a grin as he swung it in front of her.

What a fool she was. Thinking he was making a move. When what he was really after was his lifeline, his real passion. A streak of hurt zipped through her brain and settled into her heart. Which only made her more of a fool.

She scowled at him.

Chuckling, he moved away from her, back to his side of the limo seat. "I like your spirit. It will be infinitely enjoyable when you bring it to my bed."

Breathing in a shaky breath, she tried to pull herself together. Tried to put on a brave face. "You'll b-be waiting a long time."

"But eventually the wait will be over," he returned the volley without missing a beat.

She turned her head away from him.

Yet there was no escaping him, was there? No escaping the press who followed his every move. No escaping her lust for him. No escape for the next month.

Fear wrapped around the lust, making her sick.

Icy rain began to fall. Darcy watched as the rivulets of water slid down the window.

CHAPTER 6

The lavender velvet brushed on her palm. It shimmered in the sunlight shining through the limo windows. For November, the day was surprisingly warm. She hadn't even worn a coat. Instead, she'd opted for the most beautiful garment in her expanded wardrobe. A purple velvet jacket paired with a matching short skirt. Tall black heels and fancy black silk stockings with matching garters finished the attire with flair.

Darcy felt like a movie star or a member of the royalty.

Or the mistress of a very rich man.

His voice spoke Italian beside her. Into the phone, of course. They were on their way to another of his interminable business meetings. This must be…she thought for a moment…at least the tenth meeting she'd attended during the last two days. He hadn't allowed her to disappear from his sight. She'd been dragged to luncheons with old men. Board meetings with alarmingly smart men and women. There'd been the charity brunch where the Great Man gave the keynote speech in front of a group of swooning ladies. Plus, the trips to the theatre and opera in the evening.

She hadn't had a moment to herself. Not a moment to see some of the sights she'd promised herself.

She was having a fabulous time.

Amazing. She never saw herself as a wine-and-dine kind of gal. She never pictured herself enjoying the company of some of the richest people in the planet. She certainly never imagined herself understanding most of what was discussed around a long, impressive table in a corporate boardroom at a public meeting.

She'd loved every minute of it. Charming the old men into telling her stories of their grandchildren. Smiling at everyone in the boardroom until she saw the tension ease, replaced with cordial talk and occasional laughter. The gaggle of women, who had first scrutinized her as if she weren't worthy of the La Rocca; well, even they had succumbed to the Darcy Moran magic. One of them even hugged her as they left the brunch, pleading with her to return next year.

Now that had finally gotten a reaction from him. He'd lifted his dark brows.

At least, it was a reaction.

Because all the while she cut a swath through New York society, Marcus La Rocca stood by her side and gave no real acknowledgment of her accomplishment. Rather than giving her her due, he'd demanded and dictated. He announced where they were going next. Told her what to do.

Her hand fluttered across to grip the door handle.

Remembered irritation simmered inside her. He hadn't complimented her after the old men at first said *no* to his proposal, but then, after a lunch with her, said *yes*. He hadn't noticed when she eased the way for him in the stuffy boardroom. He certainly hadn't uttered a word about how she could charm women as well as men.

Nope. She'd only gotten a raised eyebrow for all her efforts on his behalf.

Why the hell was she doing it? Why was she exerting herself to smooth his path before him? Why did he keep dragging her with him if he barely paid her any attention?

Darcy flattened her fingers on the plush velvet of her skirt. She'd asked. Questioned him on why she had to trot behind him. Stated her desire to take off on her own. To no avail. He waved her words and desires away, intent on getting his way. Which was typical. Still, what could she do?

Your father, Darcy. Your father.

He'd said it so many times during the last few days she heard it in her sleep.

Smoothing her hand on her skirt, she sighed.

"Stop doing that."

Her hand froze. "What?"

"You are driving me crazy." His eyes blazed. With anger?

She was simply sitting here minding her own business. On her way to another of his meetings where she'd probably have to, once again, save the day. But was the man appreciative? Obviously not. Why should she expect anything different than his usual chilly manner towards her?

"What are you talking about?" she said. "I'm sitting here because you demand it. I am going to another meeting because you wanted it. I am dressed the way you—"

"Touching." The silver of his gaze burned like hot metal. "You keep touching."

"Huh?" She stared at him in shock.

"You are always doing it." His hand raked through his hair, leaving it ruffled and oddly appealing. "Running your hands over furniture, over car seats, *per l'amor di dio*. Over your damn body."

"I do?" She glanced at her offending hands.

"*Sì*." The word shot out like a bullet. "It drives me crazy."

What was she supposed to say?

I'm sorry I like to touch things? Because I dream of touching you instead.

A wash of color flooded her cheeks as she remembered this morning. After starting every night on the floor, inevitably, she found herself in the bed when she awoke. For once, today, she was the first one to wake up. The past two mornings she opened her eyes to no one and counted herself lucky. Yet, when she meandered down the stairs, there he always was.

At his laptop, on his phone. Working, working.

This morning, though, he'd been beside her asleep.

The early sunlight slid along his naked shoulder, burnishing the olive skin until it glowed. Again, she noticed how long his dark lashes were. Usually, the stunning silver of his eyes garnered all her attention. The lashes graced his cheeks, making him appear younger and sweeter.

Before she knew it, she'd succumbed to his appeal.

The rasp of his beard felt wonderful along the palm of her hand. The softness of his lips on the tips of her fingers gave a startling contrast. His hair curled warmly through her fingers as she slipped her hand through the dark strands.

He'd murmured, moved.

Like a dart, her hand snapped back to her side just in time.

He'd opened his eyes and looked at her flushed face. Then, he chuckled.

"Did I miss something?" he whispered.

"Nothing," she mumbled before scampering from the bed and into the sanctuary of the bathroom.

His phone buzzed, pulling her out of her memories. With an impatient jerk, he turned away from her. Italian words intermixed with English immediately rolled from his mouth, only a slight edge to his tone giving any hint he'd been scolding her moments ago. She had to admit, she'd grown fond of listening to him talk. He had a rich, deep voice, and whether he was speaking in his lightly accented English or in his native tongue, the words wrapped around her, making her feel hot and bothered.

But lust was not the only thing she struggled with now.

Darcy stared at the crowds of people swarming on the sidewalk and wished with a sudden, harsh desperation that she could join them, fade into them, walk away from him.

Walk away from the lust for him and his distrust of her.

The man thought he welded one almighty weapon against her. He thought she only wanted his body, wanted his sex. Yet, during the last few days, she'd come to feel more for him.

She'd seen and sensed what she'd already known. What Matt had already told her. The man had no time for friends, much less family. The man was all about business. No one they met slapped him on the shoulder or asked him about his day. Every one of them, from the smart board members to the society ladies to the business types, every one of them saw Marcus La Rocca as a money machine.

Her heart ached for him.

Silly her. The man wasn't asking for her compassion. He would laugh in her face if she succeeded in articulating what was in her heart; a tumbling mass of reluctant passion and unwilling affection. Nevertheless, it was clear why she'd been using every ounce of her charm to make his day easier, his deals smoother.

She cared. She really, really cared about him. Somewhere along the way, the swamp of lust churning inside her had turned into a deepening pool of—

Darcy clutched the door handle and stared down at her white knuckles.

Run lovey, her mum whispered. *Run before you turn out like me.*

THE SPRITE WAS SITTING OVER THERE LOOKING as if she were about to jump from the car. Marcus watched her from the corner of his eye, trying to understand what the hell was going on inside her head. It was an impossible task. Every other woman of his acquaintance was an easy read for his cynical perusal.

Darcy Moran was not.

Juliana Calvi was. Now.

He stared through the limo window, remembering the moment she'd walked across to him at the ball two nights ago. Her lovely dark hair now dyed a harsh blond. Her gleaming brown eyes, the eyes he thought the most beautiful in the world years ago, now filled with lust. Not for him. But for his money and power.

Her husband had died, she hummed.

She was free, she purred.

He'd felt nothing except distaste and a violent urge to run, not walk, away from her.

Juliana was not a fool. She left before she was told to.

Release, a strong sense of release had rushed through him. Then he glanced over and seen his supposed mistress surrounded by her adoring crowd. And another, entirely unexpected emotion burned through his blood.

The same emotion welled in him now.

Not jealousy, *per amor di Dio*.

Merely irritation.

An irritation he felt every time he saw Darcy. Irritation at her continued stubborn holdout in the bedroom. Irritation at how easily she caused every man in any room she entered to fall all over themselves to get to her side. *Dio*, even the women she met fell right under the *ninfa's* spell.

Which had worked in his favor several times in the past few days, he had to admit.

Why the hell had he decided to drag her around New York

with him? It had been impulse the first day. She'd come down the stairs dressed in a smart pantsuit, lovely and lush. He was about to leave for a series of meetings, about to walk out the door and get on with what was important in his life. Long, black lashes batted across her wide eyes when he announced he was leaving. Pink bow mouth pouted at the news she was to stay put.

Somehow, she ended up in the limo with him.

His phone buzzed. He took the call, watching her as she peered through the window at the city. He'd been surprised at how easily she landed on her feet in every situation. Surprised at how quickly she had people eating from her hand. For all her humble circumstances, Darcy Moran could hold her own with the richest and most powerful.

Which only made her more dangerous.

The woman was a master at her game. He'd underestimated her power. For two days now, he watched the charming Darcy operate her magic during the day and dealt with the cuddly Darcy at night.

Why the hell was he letting this woman become a part of his business? Why had he taken her to all these functions, clearly giving the impression she was important to him? He never allowed any woman in his personal life to attend any business function. His sex life was entirely separate from his business.

What sex life? His libido rumbled.

Within minutes of entering the bedroom every night, he held an armful of sleeping, sexy woman. A stubborn sprite who still started her night on the floor. A woman who never reached for him while she was awake. And his damn pride wouldn't allow him to be the first to make a move. Make a move, and then, have her crow at his defeat. Which was not acceptable.

The situation was driving him insane.

Which was exactly her aim, wasn't it?

She wouldn't touch him outside of the bed, yet she touched

everything else surrounding her. She patted an old man's cheek. She hugged the women at the brunch. She slid her hand along the limo seat every time they got in. Worse, far worse, she constantly touched herself. Twirling a curl around her finger. Brushing her mouth with her hand. Smoothing her palms across her legs.

He snapped at the manager on the phone. Ended the call. Seethed inside.

"Blimey."

The yearning lilt in her voice tugged at something inside him. Glancing across the seat, he noticed her face was alight, her hands waving in the air rather than lying on her lap.

"What?" he growled, still aggravated that this tiny woman was leading him on a merry dance.

"This is one of the places I wanted to see."

He glanced out of the window. Cobblestone streets competed for attention with tall, cast-iron buildings. Staircases and railings ran up and down every building creating a sense of movement and action. The sidewalk teamed with vendors selling purses, jewelry, and art.

"It's merely another New York street," he dismissed.

"No, it's not. It's SoHo." She said the words as if she were speaking to a demented moron.

He'd heard of the place. Artsy, new age, that kind of thing. He'd never had the time or inclination to visit this part of the city. Glancing through the window once more, he noted the sizable crowds bustling in and out of the line of bistros and art galleries. Storefronts blazed the names of high-end fashion.

He finally got it.

"You want to shop." This he could understand. This was predictable.

"Not at all." She gave him another one of her endless pitying looks. "It's the art I'm interested in."

Art. He'd forgotten. It was supposedly what she did for a

living. Moreover, according to his reports, she didn't do it very well. She hardly had a pence to her name at any given time. However, he supposed he could see the draw of this place for a wannabe.

She sighed and gazed through the window with a wistful gaze.

The thing inside him tugged once more. He didn't know what it was, but it twisted inside. Staring at his mobile phone, he noted the meetings on his calendar. Examined the agendas he'd outlined for each of them.

The sprite beside him sighed once more.

Placing a call, he barked instructions in Italian to his PA. He instructed the driver to stop. He opened the door and got out. Extended his hand. *"Vene."*

Her eyes, wide with surprise, stared at him. "What?"

"Do you want to see this or not?"

"Yes!" She gave him a smile that lit a spark deep inside him.

That thing, the thing he couldn't define inside him, untwisted.

~

London was dreary and cold.

The city fit her mood.

Darcy folded her arms around her as she glowered at the skyline. They'd left New York three days ago as abruptly as they arrived. Marcus announced they were leaving and within an hour they were on his private plane zipping through the air.

He'd ignored her on the entire flight.

Unwanted baggage once more.

Yet, unlike the flight to New York, this time her reaction was very different. She hadn't felt irritation. This time, to her horror, she'd been hurt.

With a snort of disgust, she turned away from the amazing

view and scanned the grand mausoleum she'd quickly grown to despise. The place reeked of wealth and class and modern design. Black and white leather furniture on icy white carpets. Monochrome photos of the city were placed with military precision on the walls. The only hint of color was provided by two large green plants that looked like they'd been shipped in from some African grassland. The long fronds continually hit her face when she walked by.

Not a hint of personality in the entire place. No family pictures on the walls. No special treasures gracing the pristine tabletops.

Not one hint of what kind of person lived here.

The kitchen was stocked full of every cooking device known to man. However, if anyone had cooked a meal there in the past ten years, she'd eat her last painting. The workout room with its mirrored walls resembled a colony of tall black skeletons with various juts of chrome and knobs of white. Marcus spent an hour every morning in the torture chamber.

She never went near the room. It gave her the creeps.

The four bedrooms, with en suite baths, were decorated in the same black-and-white scheme. All of them possessed as much character as a lump of coal. Come to think of it, a lump of coal would fit right into the entire décor. Black and dark and cold.

What she could do with this place, given half a chance.

The lighting was terrific. Which made sense since they were on the top of a tall high-rise. The penthouse must have cost a fortune since it took over the entire floor. The sunshine on the first day they arrived had dazzled her and hidden the basic coldness of the place. With some colored paint on the plain walls, big bold couches and chairs scattered on oriental rugs, her biggest, brightest paintings hung here and there—

"Good luck with that," she grumbled under her breath.

Face it, Darcy.

The place matched the man. The glimpse of humanity she thought she'd seen in New York City was a figment of her imagination.

SoHo.

Her heart ached at the memory. It had been a golden day.

"Seriously?" She'd stepped onto the busy sidewalk of Canal Street. "You're going to come with me?"

"*Sì.*" Sliding the offensive phone into his suit pocket, he arched a dark brow as he waved the limo away. "Is there a problem with that?"

"No. Not at all." Glancing around at the crowds, she pushed back the flustered feeling fluttering inside. After all, she'd spent quite a bit of time with this man during the last few days. Yet this was different, she knew it in her gut. They weren't going to be on show in Soho. They weren't going to be acting any kind of role. "Where do you want to start?"

"Lead the way." His rich, accented voice lifted at the end as if he were amused at letting her make the decisions for once.

No one could say that Darcy Moran didn't know how to trail blaze when given the opportunity. She strode through the crowds, passing the cries of the street vendors hawking their fake purses and junk jewelry until she arrived at the first art gallery she spotted. "Here."

"Here it is." His big presence loomed behind her, not only his body, but his personality and verve. Usually, she didn't enjoy large men who used their size to make her feel small and insignificant. In Marcus La Rocca's case, though, she didn't feel that way.

Safe.

That's what she felt.

The gallery was filled with a hodgepodge of modern art, everything from oil paintings to statues made of steel. Compared to the bustling street outside, the hall was quiet, almost hushed. Walking to the first row of paintings, she studied the way the artist had layered oil onto a series of silk plackets.

"No touching here." Tease edged his words.

Glancing at him, she chuckled when she met his dancing eyes even though her spirits sank. Marcus La Rocca was hard enough to ignore when he strutted through his day like a general ready to do battle. This La Rocca version was far worse for her sensibilities. This one, with the teasing voice and the dancing eyes, threatened to make her heart melt instead of just her body. "I wouldn't touch. I know better."

"I don't know." His focus switched to the painting in front of her. "You have a tendency to touch before thinking."

True. Especially true with him.

Trying to avoid the memories, she swished to the next painting. This one was stark—black slashes of paint sliding down into a blood red pool at the bottom.

A shiver of remembered fear went through her.

He threatened her, the last time he'd found her. He left a nasty note on the door of her flat telling her what he meant to do to her.

She'd left within the hour, leaving many of her belongings behind.

"What?" La Rocca stepped to her side, his gaze keen on her face. "What is it?"

"Nothing." Flashing him a jaunty grin, she moved away. "I just don't like that painting."

The buzz of his phone echoed in the cool, silent gallery.

Turning around, she gave him a look. "I knew it wouldn't last for long."

"You presume to know me so well." His hand twitched at his side as if he ached to reach into his pocket, but he didn't.

Instead, he gave her more trouble. Trouble like his dimples and his smile. Trouble like revealing a strong, olive-skinned neck when he tugged off his red power tie right then and stuffed it into his suit pocket. The same pocket that held the buzzing phone.

Buzz. Buzz. Buzz.

"Don't tell me you're not answering that." Pushing away his trouble, she layered thick sarcasm onto her words. "Color me completely surprised."

"I'm not answering. Maybe because I like to keep you surprised." His smile flashed to a grin, going from merely distracting to downright devastating.

Buzz. Buzz. Buzz.

She shouldn't do this. She shouldn't fall into the interplay going on between them. This male-female, sexual-friendly, exciting-disturbing play. She had learned the tricks, but something about this exchange made her gut clench.

His temptation was too great, however, and she loved having fun. She always had. "I'm thinking maybe I should make a painting of this event. You without a phone."

His eyes went bright. "I think a painting of me is an excellent idea."

A snort escaped her. "You are so arrogant."

"Worth painting, though, don't you think?" He took a step nearer. Just one simple step. Yet, he filled the air around her with his vitality. "Don't you, Darcy?"

Instead of doing what she should do—stop this, she pulled her courage around her, looked right into his eyes, and kept playing. "I don't think you'd like the painting."

"No?" he husked, his rich, sexy scent enveloping her.

Buzz. Buzz. Buzz.

"I'm afraid I'd have to paint what I usually see." She gave him a pout. "The phone nailed to your head, a frown on your face."

"Mmm." Leaning in closer, his breath brushed on her cheek. "Nails and frowns. Is that what you see right now?"

His eyelashes were incredibly dark and now that she was so close to him, she noticed the silver turned to a misty grey on the edges of his irises. He was right. She would love to paint him. And there wouldn't be any nails or frowns. There'd only be the beauty of this male, the beauty of his eyes and his skin and his mouth.

Not his heart, though.

His heart was not beautiful.

She took a step back. Then, another.

One satanic brow rose and his dimples disappeared.

Buzz. Buzz. Buzz.

They stared at each other as the phone clicked off, the message going to voicemail. Darcy was sure he was going to pull the plug on this adventure and dig that phone out of his pocket. But he surprised her again.

"Shall we continue?" he murmured before striding to the next painting.

He'd followed her for the rest of the day. Stopping when she tried on a silly feathered hat. Nodding when she waved them into another gallery. His smile had even come out a time or two again, though never the grin that made her heart tremble.

Throughout the day, her heart trembled quite a lot.

Maybe she'd grown weak because he took her to Sardi's for dinner that night. Maybe her brain skipped into la-la-land as she gazed across the white tablecloth at his masculine elegance. Or maybe her brain took a dip into pretend love later in the night, overcome by lust. As they entered the hotel room, the chemistry zipped and zagged between them. She felt the heat, the burn and mixed with it, the fear.

He'd known, she was sure. Still, he gave her a gentle smile, touched her cheek, and told her to go to bed. She'd shivered under the covers. Waiting, wanting, worrying. Somehow, she fell asleep, only to wake in the middle of the night with strong, warm arms around her.

Safe.

And so close to love.

That itsy-bitsy love sat dead like a lead weight in the bottom of her stomach now. Which was what she deserved. Because the very next day, the Great Man reverted to type—cold and contained, not a dimple in sight. He'd announced their departure with icy disdain. Ignored her on the plane. Ignored her when they arrived at the penthouse.

Ignored her existence for the past three days.

Darcy plodded down the hall to her bedroom. The one she slept in alone. His announcement of separate bedrooms had surprised her and hurt her. Darn it. Plus, double darn it, she missed him at night. Just as she missed him during the day.

She missed his hard warmth beside her. The sense of safety.

She missed his laugh and his dimples.

She missed the stimulation of his company. Not only the sexual hum between them, but the intelligence, the drive, the electricity of his presence.

Plopping down on her bed, she eyed the picture of the London Eye with distaste. The black-and-white photo sucked every ounce of joy from the edifice. Smoothing her hand across the grey silk coverlet, she gave it a moue of disgust. She would not moon over bedding thinking of his eyes. *No way.*

Thankful. That was the word.

She should be thankful he wasn't parading her in front of the London press as he had in New York. The odds were in her favor that those particular pictures would never land on a wall to be obsessed about.

More importantly, she should be very, very thankful that Marcus La Rocca showed his true colors these last few days. His behavior shocked her out of the fantasy she'd been weaving around him. He was nothing like that fantasy man. Not the smiling man who enjoyed her company. Not the simple man who ate Sardi's spaghetti with gusto. Certainly not the man who held her so tenderly at night.

In actuality, he was a tyrant of the first order.

"Stay put," he commanded every morning as he left for his office.

What had she done? She'd done what he told her to do. She'd spent her time mooning and yearning and moping over a man who didn't deserve any of it.

Time to stop this stupid behavior, pronto.

Time to face reality.

In three weeks' time, she'd be released from this gilded cage. Back into the real world where a girl needed to make a living. Unless a miracle occurred, she wouldn't have Matt to lean on while she got her feet on the ground.

Wait.

Matt. And the wedding-that-wasn't-going-to-happen.

She glared at the London Eye and berated herself. Somewhere in the midst of New York City glamour and La Rocca appeal, she'd lost the thread of her reasoning. Lost the whole point of being around the Great Man. She'd forgotten about her friend and his predicament.

"What a tosser you are," she muttered.

Time to change things. Rather than spending her time following the Great Man's orders while secretly pining away for his attention, she needed to get a grip and make things happen.

First things first. Tomorrow was Sunday.

Darcy smiled as a brilliant idea sprung into her brain.

CHAPTER 7

*I*t was a superb London day.

Sunny and exceptionally warm. The crowds were large for this time of year, a fact Darcy was grateful for.

Bayswater Road was her usual haunt on any given Sunday. She'd prop her oils along the hedges, set up her easel and chair, and usually do a brisk business drawing caricatures. Her oils moved a little slower. Still, all in all, she often walked away at the end of the day with a good stash of pounds.

Today was shaping up to be a banner day.

She'd already sold one oil in less than an hour. And she'd done three drawings in rapid succession. If the day proceeded like this, she'd have a nice beginning to a deposit on a new flat.

Surprisingly, she found it easy to slip away from the grand mausoleum. The Great Man held to his recent pattern and disappeared before she even awoke. His security team had spotted her leaving, but hadn't made any attempt to return her to the fancy prison. One lone man had followed her onto the Tube. He trailed her as she got to Bayswater Road and greeted an artist buddy who'd willingly stored her artwork when she was kicked out of her own flat. The security guy had faded into the woodwork as her buddy helped her display the art he'd carted over from his nearby home. She didn't mind the following and watching. It was part of the deal, she supposed.

In an odd way, it made her feel wanted, even safe.

There was that dang word again.

She snorted at herself.

"Darcy, my lass." Alvin, one the regulars sauntered by, several of his watercolor canvases under his arm. "Where've you been?"

"I only missed last week, Al." She gave him a jaunty smile. What was she going to say? *I was whisked away to New York by a billionaire.* That would get a good laugh.

"You never miss any week." Rubbing his hand across his bald head, he eyed her. "I was worried."

"You never have to worry about me." She twirled her brush pen in the air. "Survivor is my middle name."

Her older friend humphed as he placed his paintings along the hedge beside hers. "You're a dainty little thing. Not a big lug like me. So, I'll worry if I want to."

Waving his comments away, she smiled at a passing couple. They immediately stopped, chatted with her as they perused her paintings, and eventually agreed to her charming offer to do their portraits.

They were lovers, that was clear.

She outlined their faces on the big sheet of blank paper. Drew their eyes, concentrated on their mouths. Tried to ignore the tenderness in the gaze of the man when he looked at the woman.

An ache of longing bloomed inside her.

She threw a laughing smile at the couple. "Ah, to be in love."

They laughed with her.

The crowd swirled around them. Chinese words mixed with Irish lilts, Indian accents blended with Cockney. More artists and craftsmen arrived, adding their acrylics, sculptures, pastels, and collages to the display. The last of the autumn leaves rustled across the sidewalk. Sunshine warmed her back.

Darcy fought to push away the ache, replacing it with determination.

Pining for something that was never going to happen was a waste of time. She'd learned the lesson well as a child. Better to accept reality and play the cards dealt her. In this case, she'd hunker down until the La Rocca storm passed and then get on with her life. If she could find a way to help Matt, she would, but emotional survival right now was her main goal.

She'd be fine. Wouldn't she?

Yes, she would.

Drawing complete, she showed it to the couple, accepted their praise and their money. The man gave a kiss to his lover as they walked away holding hands, happy and complete. Fulfilled in each other.

The ache turned inside her.

She pasted her best grin on her face, glanced around for another likely customer, looked across the street—

To meet the gunmetal glare of an angry Italian.

∼

THE RELIEF MARCUS felt when he spotted her was way out of proportion to the importance the sprite held in his life.

Minimal.

Which was why the amount of relief surging through his veins was unacceptable in every way. He'd been successful these past three days at driving her from his mind completely.

Naturally. If he put his mind to anything, he accomplished it.

The stark reality, one he had a hard time accepting, was he could no longer handle the temptation of being with her for any length of time. He knew himself well enough to know he was very close to losing the bet between them. Very close to taking what he wanted and everything else be damned.

The degree of lust for her irritated him.

Yet, he couldn't deny its existence.

So he'd sat in his office and spent his time on what was important. He stayed away from the lure of her. It was necessary. He realized it as they'd walked down the streets of SoHo. Realized his interest in her was swiftly morphing into more than sex.

The shock he'd felt had been exactly the antidote to her draw that he'd needed.

When he entered his London office and given it some clear thought, he'd been revolted by his actions. Canceling important business meetings to address a woman's yearning sigh? Utterly, absolutely unacceptable.

The last three days cemented his determination.

Sex. That's all he wanted from Darcy Moran.

Sex.

Today, like any other day, he was at his office before six a.m. and worked his way through a hundred emails as he drank his morning coffee. But some sixth sense nagged at him. At first, he dismissed it as merely the lingering desire to be with her. A desire he'd successfully squashed during the last few days. Somehow, though, before he had fully come to grips with his instincts, he found himself pacing into his penthouse.

His empty penthouse.

The fear had flashed like a gigantic lightning bolt through him as he stared at her empty bedroom. His hand actually shook —*shook*—as he called his security. Anger had quickly followed after he heard their report. The fury washed any hankering to be with her right out of his system. In its place rose his recollection of what role the sprite really held in his life.

She was nothing but a pretend mistress. Nothing but a potential pitfall to an important business deal. His only duty was to keep her contained, not make her happy or gaze at her across a breakfast table or lust after her every minute he breathed.

She was nowhere near his brother.

This was what was important.

She hadn't been kidnapped or stolen. He'd been absurd to even entertain the thought.

His security team had done their job, albeit not in the way he expected. However, they had tracked her, knew where she was when he'd called from the empty penthouse, irate.

They assured him it wouldn't happen again.

Now the only thing he needed to do was lay down the law one more time to her. One more time for the thousandth time. Then continue to stay away from her for his own sanity until she gave up her silly notion that sex wasn't in their immediate future.

Marcus hoped his glare was boring into her thick head and making a clear statement without him having to say a word. But it appeared from her behavior when she saw him he was in for a disappointment.

She stilled for a moment, then shot him a cheeky grin. Twirling around, she spotted another in a long line of suckers, and within seconds, gained a new customer.

He marched across the street, stepped onto the sidewalk, and came to a stop.

Caricatures? She did caricatures? And she called herself an artist?

He smirked. How *cute*.

He'd attended enough gallery openings for business reasons to know true art when he saw it. He'd even made some judicious purchases for investment purposes. His brother's avid interest in sculpture and determination to make it his career had been a curious choice, yet at least it kept the kid out of trouble. He'd been perfectly happy to hand over the necessary funds to keep Matteo comfortable and content in London's finest art school. *Merda*, he even funded a scholarship for a needy student at his brother's urging.

In this instance, the money hadn't been the issue.

The important fact was he figured the young fool would be close at hand and easy to keep an eye on. Rather than roaming the streets of Rome, picking up girls, and getting into trouble, his brother was under his control. There was also the added benefit of not having to take his mother's calls on a daily basis. The endless screeching and wailing about the latest Matteo disaster had given him a never-ending headache.

For four years, the whole deal went well. Matteo had behaved. His mother spent her time shopping rather than screeching. And he'd been left alone to make more deals and more money.

"Aren't you darling," the sprite cooed at her young male customer, who promptly blushed at her words.

His smirk grew. Did she think he was going to go all jealous on her because of this young sprig she was drawing? Did she think if she kept ignoring his presence, he'd slink away?

Not a chance.

He could bide his time for now. Eventually, he'd have her complete attention.

After he got that, he'd have her complete obedience.

He eyed the long sidewalk filled with various artwork, some downright awful, some with potential. The crowd was relaxed and playful. Kids ran by hanging onto balloons. A group of young girls giggled and batted their eyes at him as they passed. A fishmonger's loud voice called out his list of delicacies including oysters and crab.

The sprite cooed another of her absurd compliments.

Marcus strolled across to a line of paintings propped behind her. In the background, he heard her soft, lilting voice become higher, louder. The sprig bantered back with teenage enthusiasm.

Ignoring both of them, he eyed the oil before him. A sturdy stone cottage nestled itself on a rolling hill. The glow of candlelight sprinkled gold on the waving leaves of an old oak tree. With a bit of a shock, he realized it was good. The technique was excellent, the color choices highlighting the sense of homeyness. He could almost feel the warmth of the light, the wisp of the wind.

Something twitched inside him.

He stepped to the next oil. Immediately he knew it was the same artist. Something about the use of color told him. The painting showed two children running down an alley. One of them, a tiny girl with a shock of long, black hair, was staring over her shoulder with fear.

Marcus stared at the night-blue eyes in the picture.

Eyes filled with fear.

The similarity was striking. The memory of another pair of eyes shining with fear struck him right in the chest, along with the immediate recognition of who the artist had to be.

He jerked around and stared at the *ninfa*.

The same night-blue eyes peered back at him from beneath her long, black eyelashes, wariness lacing this stare.

Why was she hiding her talent in this long row of wannabes? Why hadn't she damn well insisted his stupid brother include her in last year's big gallery showing? Rocca Enterprises had funded the entire event, with the proviso that some new artists would be included in the display. He'd let Matteo choose who would be included along with himself. His brother had been ecstatic.

Why the hell hadn't he included his talented lover's paintings?

The young male sprig left with one last longing gaze at Darcy. Marcus stared at his lanky figure as he strolled away, the prized caricature in hand. Her protection had disappeared at exactly the right moment.

Pacing to the chair opposite her, he sat. "Draw me."

The wariness in the blue depths started to sparkle. A fake frown appeared on her delicate brow. "I don't think you'll like the results."

"Try me."

She waggled her pen at him before whisking it across the broad paper. Silence descended between them, the only noise coming from the crowd of people surrounding them. Marcus watched her face as she drew. Watched her focus narrow. Watched her front teeth worry her lower lip as she concentrated.

His blood thickened.

He'd missed her these last few days. It wasn't something he wanted to admit, but a man needed to be honest with himself, if no one else. He'd missed her high spirits, her teasing. The dancing eyes when she glanced at him and threw him a joke. The way she scrunched her brow when she questioned his sanity. The pointed chin she gave him as she lashed at his ego.

The soft smile when she dressed up for his pleasure.

The soft skin against his when he held her sleeping body.

The soft laugh when she won the business deal for him in New York.

He scowled.

Darcy arched her brows. "Is that the look you want me to draw?"

"What?"

"If so," she responded. "I don't need you to pose. I know that particular look by heart."

"What are you talking about?" Exasperation crackled in his voice.

"The dark frown." She mimicked her words, her brows lowering.

He glared at her, lust and frustration and confusion churning inside him.

"The forbidding frown that's supposed to freeze me in my tracks," she continued.

"Clearly I have not yet been successful in the freezing process." Irony wove through his words as he forced himself to stay irritated in the face of her teasing. "If I had, you'd be safely frozen in the place you are supposed to be."

"Safely?" Her eyes misted with…wistfulness?

"In the penthouse."

She cocked her head, the mist clearing from her eyes. "Why do you never say it's your home?"

The lust and frustration churning inside him froze. The sudden memory of warm Italian sun and flowing Italian wine and a strong Italian hug threatened to melt him deep inside.

He shrugged aside her question and the memories. "I have no idea what you're talking about."

"I'm starting to figure that out all on my own." Her stare felt like it was piercing his skin, his blood. Felt like a laser slicing straight to the center of him.

No one was ever allowed into the center of him.

Never.

"Those are your paintings." His wave towards the pictures was dismissive. His words were an accusation. He knew it and couldn't control it. Striking back was what he did when attacked. Her observation had been an attack he'd felt deep inside.

She mimicked his shrug with a nonchalant one of her own. "So?"

Yet, he knew he'd penetrated her center. Knew his words and actions had sliced into her.

An ugly howl erupted in his gut. The fact that no sound came from his mouth didn't lessen the strength of the cry. Confusion swelled in his nonexistent heart. It choked his throat and tugged at the damn unnamable thing deep inside him only she seemed to be able to twist.

"I'm done." Her smile was fake, but he gave her credit for attempting to shift the conversation away from this cesspool swirling between them.

He lifted a brow in response and felt his usual control over his memories and emotions returning. "I won't pay if I don't like it."

Her pout was a classic. Plump and wet. Her lips set off the wild in him. "I warned you before I started. Therefore, you owe me the standard fee no matter what you think of it."

"Show me."

Totally unintimidated at his tone, she gave him a knowing smirk as she twirled the caricature around for his review.

Horns. Forked tongue. On what was a extremely good likeness of his face.

But no clichéd pitchfork.

Instead, there was an exaggerated drawing of his phone clutched in his hand.

∼

MARCUS LA ROCCA was completely and utterly gorgeous when he laughed. The sunlight lit his olive skin with a golden shine. His white teeth flashed bright. The sound he made was deep, masculine, joyful. The man should laugh constantly. He would end world strife, create peace and harmony between all.

And bring every woman to heel.

Including her.

Darcy sighed and leaned on the warm leather seat of his limo. Today had been as wonderful a day as the SoHo day. She'd tried to fight it, tried not to get sucked into the fantasy.

Yet, he'd got to her. Precisely like before.

The laugh at her caricature of him had turned her insides to mush. The surprise she felt when he hadn't demanded her immediate removal to his penthouse? It had been nothing compared to her sheer disbelief when he lounged around for hours with Al and several more of her artist buddies, talking football. Her disbelief had grown as he stayed the entire day, bringing her fish and chips for lunch, chatting with her potential customers. Good grief, even persuading several of them to buy her oils.

What was a girl to do in the face of this rampant appeal?

The coup de grace happened, though, at the end of the day. He'd told his security to pack her remaining art and transport it to his penthouse, where she was to have a room of her own to paint. With one wave of a bold hand, he commanded the head of his security to attend to the details. One of the cold, lifeless bedrooms was to be turned into whatever she desired and needed.

What was a girl to do?

The leaden feeling of disillusionment and disappointment she'd felt during the last few days had slowly but surely turned back into the bright, happy feeling she felt as she strolled SoHo. It had whispered inside her as she saw him laugh at something Al said. Brightness wiggled through her heart as she noticed the lines of stress disappear around his eyes. Happiness had shouted out loud when he gave her a gift she'd never, ever had.

A place of her own. For her art. The one true love of her life.

Maybe not the only love you now have?

The thought had shot through her and brought her up short. No. No. *No.*

For the last few minutes, she'd waged a determined, frightened fight against the thought, the feelings, the happiness. Yet all of the emotions continued to bubble inside her. Peering at him, she watched as he fingered his mobile. Went through his emails, answered his texts, and frowned once more, allowing tension to overtake him once again.

Why? Why did he do this to himself? He must have more money than almost every person in the world. Why didn't he spend his time laughing, enjoying life? Loving…

Her.

The beat of her heart blasted inside her chest. *Useless*, she told her heart. It would never happen. She wasn't up to the fight to save him. She couldn't imagine ever really, really breaking through his tough hide to the man she'd only glimpsed a couple of times.

The fighting spirit inside her rebelled.

Someone had to save him from himself. Someone needed to show him his work was nothing compared to what he could have. Someone should give him the gift of living life to the fullest.

"What are you thinking?" His low voice was taut with frustration.

She glanced across the seat to meet stormy eyes. What was his problem now? Other than she'd made her escape earlier today. Something he'd alluded to, but seemed to have put behind him.

"Not much." She certainly wasn't going to pour out her dilemma to him. The cause of it all.

He muttered an Italian oath under his breath and focused on his trusty phone, frowning at a message. The lines encircling his lips turned white.

She couldn't stand it, couldn't stand to see him this way.

Slipping across the seat, she placed a hand on his cheek. Turning his mouth to hers…

She. Kissed. Him.

His big body stiffened. His lips went slack beneath hers and she felt the slip of his breath hissing deep in his throat.

Then, he changed in a split second.

His body burned with hot passion along her side. His mouth firmed and took control. His arms surrounded her in a tight, hard grasp. The taste of him filled her as his tongue lanced inside, pushing into her deeply, sliding along her own tongue and sipping her soul.

Masculine power, male need, potent virility.

"*Ti voglio*," he murmured, his lips hovering over hers.

Her arms went around his neck, her breasts plastering against his chest. With one strong tug from him, she found herself straddling his legs. The heat of him surrounded and enveloped her, and the pulse of his passion pounded through her blood. There was no fear, no instinctive need to draw away, to pull away from his touch.

Only him.

The smoky light in his eyes, the gentle curl of his hair twining through her fingers, the warmth of his body beneath hers.

"*Ti ho volute dal primo momento che ti vedi.*" He slurred each word, the richness of his accent making the phrase an ode to seduction.

"What?"

The grey of his eyes turned darker. "I've wanted you from the first moment I saw you."

"Me too," she managed before his mouth took hers once more and she fell headfirst into the lust he always inspired.

His big hands slid under her jumper, onto her hot skin. A low, hoarse sound came from him as he touched her, slipping his fingers across her belly and then higher. Higher. She gasped as he reached her sensitive breasts, her tight nipples.

"No bra," he groaned. "Do you wish to drive every man insane?"

"Only you, Marcus. Only you." She kissed the side of his cheek, her hands smoothing across his broad shoulders.

He stared at her. "Call me Marc."

This was important. She didn't know why. But she knew. "Marc."

The limo jarred to a stop.

Jerking away, she stared into his face. A wicked smile turned him into the devil incarnate. "Should I tell the driver to keep going, *Tesorina*? Or would you prefer to take this upstairs where we can be more comfortable?"

A blush of embarrassment heated her cheeks. She scrambled off his lap and onto the seat beside him.

He let her go, but the smile grew wider. "I'll take this to mean you wish to finish this in the penthouse."

"I don't know," she whispered. She'd lost her mind, her soul in his kiss. Was she ready for this? She was sure to disappoint him, wasn't she? Her piddly little experience wouldn't be a match for this man's.

"No, you don't." He lunged over and drew her into his warm arms again. "You made the first move. I won't let you back down now."

His kiss was fierce, primeval, and intense. It told her clearly she'd gone too far down the road and this powerful male was intent on convincing her to not run away.

The limo door opened and Marc let her go for only the time it took to step out into the underground parking lot. With one swift move, she was in his arms again. Marching to the elevator, he stared at her, his face stark and tight with passion. "Push the button."

His gaze was full of challenge. If she pushed the button, his look told her, she was agreeing to finish what she started.

She stared at him. Stared at the smoky passion of his eyes, the curl of his hair, mussed by her hands. The wicked mouth beckoning to her desire.

Leaning down, she pushed the elevator button.

He groaned deep in his throat, an animal call to her female core.

Lifting her arms to twine around his neck, she kissed him, sweet and tender, giving him everything.

The elevator doors slid open. He stepped in with her in his grasp, their mouths locked.

The trip to the penthouse passed in a blur of kisses, growing more and more passionate. Heat poured from his body, and a trickle of sweat ran between her breasts. A fire deep inside pulsed an electric desire through her blood. It pooled between her legs. She felt the warm, wet welcome for him.

He breathed Italian words on her skin, his mouth skimming over her brows, her eyelids, her cheeks and ears.

The door slid open and somehow, they found themselves at his penthouse door. Nerves mixed with excitement as she told herself she could make him happy. In bed. In life. She should take this chance.

He finally got the door open. But then, he stopped cold, his grip on her tightening. "Blake?"

"La Rocca." A tall, blond man stood in the middle of the penthouse living room. "I'm afraid I've got bad news."

CHAPTER 8

The hospital smelled of bleach and dread.

Darcy sat on the edge of a vinyl couch, hands clasped on her lap. A cold cup of coffee held its droopy position on the table beside her. It had long ago given up any warmth or comfort. She'd barely sipped it before setting it down and forgetting it existed.

The only thing rattling in her head was her father's heart attack. Her father at death's door.

The father she hated.

Her knuckles turned white as her hands fisted. She shouldn't think like that. The bitter thought wasn't sending out good vibes and her father needed all the luck he could get right now. It didn't matter how he treated her when she was a kid. What mattered was he needed to get through this surgery and then recover.

So she could walk away from him for good.

"Darcy." Marc's husky voice slanted across the room from the open door of the waiting room. "*Il mio piccolo uno*, you appear as if a strong wind will blow you away."

She glanced over, noticing his pristine perfection. How did

the man continue to appear as if he'd stepped off the cover of a *GQ* magazine? His hair swept back from his forehead in impeccable precision. His white shirt lay smooth on his broad chest. His black linen slacks, with not a wrinkle to be found, highlighted the long length of his legs. The leather jacket he'd slipped on before they left the penthouse gave him a cosmopolitan, continental elegance.

She, on the other hand, still wore the ratty old jeans and scraggly jumper she'd put on more than twenty-four hours ago. Her hair probably stuck out like electric needles on top of her head. And she didn't even want to think about the bags under her eyes from no sleep and constant worry.

Her, a wet rag. He, a crisp linen handkerchief.

The comparison came to her in stark clarity. Along with the memory of when she'd felt it before. A brief astonishment coursed through her. It seemed light years away, the time in the splendor of the Plaza. When she'd been afraid of his perfection, afraid of what he did to her. Another lifetime.

During the last few days, during the last twenty-four hours, he'd become something much more to her. She shied away from what exactly he'd become, still she knew it wasn't fear she felt around him any longer.

"*Piccolo.*" He paced to her side, slid down on the ancient, uncomfortable couch beside her and gathered her into his warm arms. "Don't worry. Everything will be fine."

She leaned her head on his shoulder and closed her eyes. All right. She could define one thing he'd become to her during the last day: her rock. "I hope so."

"I know so," he said with authority. "I have been assured your father has the best surgeon. He will have the best care after the operation is done. On that, you have my word."

Marc had taken immediate control as soon as they arrived at the hospital. In moments, the hospital staff was in a flurry. Her father was no longer waiting in a queue for the next available surgeon. As a substitute, a top flight doctor was flying in from Edinburgh to take charge. A private room instantly became available. Over a fussy nurse's objections, Darcy had been allowed a few private moments with her father before he was wheeled into surgery.

Tough odds, the surgeon intoned to Marc in her presence. The Great Man had given him a frosty glare. *Make it happen*, he commanded.

Glancing at the clock, she sighed and shivered. "It's been almost six hours."

"These surgeries take time." His arms tightened on her.

She peeked at him. His gaze was as clear as iced glass and filled with certain knowledge. Hope, mixed with fear, wrapped around her throat. "How do you know?"

"I had my staff do some research. I want to have all the facts before me going forward."

"Why?" The haze of disbelief and fear surrounding her for these last hours blew aside. Why would he do this? It wasn't his problem. It wasn't his father.

Dark brows lowered. "I had to know what the possible outcomes were before I made plans for when your father comes out of surgery."

The haze diminished some more. "Why, though? Why are you doing this? It isn't part of our deal. It isn't something you're obligated to do."

The body beside her stiffened. "It is nothing."

"It's going to cost thousands. Maybe more."

"*Tesorina.*" His grey gaze turned silver in warning. "Leave it."

"But—"

"I said, leave it." Tugging her closer to his side, he slipped one hand into his jacket pocket and out came his most formidable weapon at ending any conversation he despised.

Darcy hid her affectionate grin by snuggling into his shoulder. For a moment, the worry for her father lifted. In its place came the memory of what had been happening right before the bad news hit her between the eyes.

She'd been about to make love to this man.

She'd been about to become his real mistress.

She'd been about to claim him as hers.

Glancing down, she admired the long length of his legs, the hardness of his thighs beneath the linen of his slacks. She allowed herself to sink into the lovely swamp of lust and relish the thought of actually being with him. The warm burn pulsed inside her and the agony of waiting and worrying diminished. For a moment.

He scrolled through his emails apparently oblivious to her presence.

Ha! The man didn't have enough acting skills to carry it off.

Amazingly, astonishingly, she knew he was vitally aware of her beside him. The heat of his arm still wrapped around her back and side. One bold, masculine hand cupped her hip, keeping her close. She also knew, instinctively, he was hoping and praying she'd drop the conversation and sit beside him completely complacent and compliant.

Double ha! The man did not have a clue who he was dealing with.

"I'm not going to let you do it." Her cheek rubbed on the warm leather of his jacket.

"Mmm." He ignored her. Or appeared to. His thumb danced across the screen of his phone.

"Dismiss me. Ignore me."

A dimple showed on the side of his mouth. Then, he threw his head back and laughed. The rich, redolent sound swirled through her and she let herself relax in his comforting, warm presence.

The man could laugh.

Comforting. Warm.

Safe.

Something inside her stirred and shivered.

"*Tesorina*." Wry humor filled his words and his amused grey gaze swerved to her face. "There is not a second since we met that I have been able to get you out of my mind."

His words touched her heart. The warm, comforting feeling blossomed inside her, blanketing the shiver in a blissful bath of happiness.

Then, she looked at him.

His face abruptly tightened and his body went taut along her side. The amusement in his eyes faded, to be replaced with a cool chill.

The shiver sliced through the happiness, trailing a cold frost down her spine.

"Ms. Moran?"

She jerked her head around to stare at the surgeon hovering in the doorway. Jumping off the couch, she wrung her hands. "Yes?"

Marc stood more slowly at her side.

"Your father made it through surgery," the surgeon announced, slipping a hand across his bald head. "He's got a good shot at recovery."

"R-r-really?" Her voice trembled.

"The next twenty-four hours will be tricky." He pushed his glasses up his long nose and peered at her.

"Okay." Her heart dipped and dove, clunking inside her chest.

"He will get the best care." The dark growl of Marc's voice steadied her emotions.

She took a deep breath in.

"I have no doubt you'll make sure that will happen." The surgeon's wry smile lit his tired face.

"*Sì*."

"Well." The older man smoothed his hands together. "I'll be

in touch with the nursing staff and will check in tomorrow morning to see how our patient is doing."

Marc strode over to the man and ushered him out the door, their low voices uttering indistinguishable words.

Darcy slumped onto the couch.

Her pop was okay. He'd made it this far—a minor miracle. She knew that. She'd seen the look on the surgeon's face before going into surgery. She heard the whispers of the nurses as they wheeled her father from the room. She felt the deep, dark dread in the center of her stomach these past six hours.

Knowing, hoping, worrying.

Praying.

Another chill ran through her, zipping along her spine. It blended with the earlier chill, making her hands cold as ice. She shuddered.

"*Tesorina.*" Marc's tone was harsh.

She wrenched her gaze up to meet the silver flash of his own.

"You are trembling." His big hands grabbed her shoulders and yanked her into his arms. "It's not needed. Your father will be fine."

A sob choked her throat. No, she couldn't. She wouldn't allow herself to be such a wuss. A wimp in front of this man? *No.*

"If you say so." She forced the words through the growing chill with a bit of her usual spirit.

He murmured an Italian word. One of his hands moved across her head, smoothing his fingers into her hair as he pressed her face to his chest.

Another sob escaped her control, breaking her determination to be strong.

He sighed. "Cry, *Tesorina.*"

She let herself go in his arms.

∼

HE HELD her until she finally ran out of her seemingly endless supply of tears. The sprite appeared to have stored quite a lake of sorrow inside her tiny body. She quaked and quivered in his arms for what seemed like hours. Her hands clutched at his shirt as she burrowed deeper into his grasp. Somehow they'd ended up sitting once more, and she huddled by him, her slight body molding to his side.

Her touch did not arouse any thoughts of sex or lust. Only concern. Only a fierce desire to console her.

Her weeping also did not inspire in him a need to run or ridicule. The tears did not elicit his usual response to attempted manipulation: a cynical putdown or mocking rejection. His mother used tears as a weapon, as had Juliana. He'd learned the lesson well. Learned to not be moved.

Yet this was very different. This time with this woman.

The realization shook him. However, now was not the time to dissect these emotions coursing through him. Now was the time to concentrate on comforting Darcy.

Her wet cheek nestled into the crook of his shoulder. She gulped another low cry.

The thing, the thing tied to her, twisted inside him.

He was absolutely positive the *ninfa* didn't even realize she held him in the palm of her dainty hand right at this moment. That she could ask him for anything—the moon, the stars—and at this moment of time, he would move heaven and earth to get it for her. With every gulping gasp, his heart ached. With every warm tear falling on his neck, he tightened his grip on her, trying to pour reassurance into her soul.

Finally, finally, the sobs faded into small hiccups. Then, silence.

He slid his palm along the fragile bones of her spine.

"How embarrassing," she muttered, her words brushing on his skin.

A chuckle escaped him at the disgusted tone in her voice.

"Now you pour humiliation upon humiliation." Her head popped up. The red rims of her eyes only highlighted the deep blue. A defiant sparkle lit the depths. "Laughing at me."

"I am merely amused you would be embarrassed for crying. Every woman cries."

"I don't."

"After the last few moments, this is clearly untrue."

She wiped at the tears lingering on her face. "It won't happen again. I promise."

"It was not a problem. I am used to womanly emotions."

"Are you?" She cocked her head, the harsh light of the waiting room throwing blue-black highlights on the strands of her hair. "You're used to your girlfriends crying all over you?"

More like having tantrums when he told them they were through. Which he ignored. "No, my mother."

Her immediate reaction told him he'd revealed too much. The elfin creature before him sparked to attention, her gaze aflame with interest, her lithe body glowing with energy. "Tell me more."

He cursed inside himself at his slip. "No."

"I'll tell you something, if you tell me something."

"This is not a time for games."

"I'm not playing a game," she said with breathless importance. "I'm serious."

His phone buzzed. With relief, he reached into his pocket.

A tiny, pickpocketing hand beat him to it. "No, you don't."

"This is becoming a habit of yours I do not appreciate," he snarled as he saw his mobile disappear into her jeans pocket.

"Tough." Her blue gaze pierced him. "I'll go first since you seem uncomfortable with sharing."

"I don't share."

"Thus, the feeling of uncomfortable." She gave him a moue of pity.

He glared at her, willing her to let this—whatever this was—go.

"I hate my father." Her words fell like rocks before him.

The stony words tore into his memory. His own father stepped from the past, right into his present. He had purposefully put all thoughts of his papa behind him long ago. It was the past. Nothing could bring him back.

But now, in this moment, his father returned to him, if only in painful, bittersweet memory. His big, booming laugh. The happiness he exuded when he was with his friends, sitting at the corner café, enjoying the warm Italian sun. The joy on his papa's face when, as a boy, he came home from school and leapt into his welcoming hug.

Marc, his father would croon. *Marc*.

The old ache of loss echoed through him. Only his papa had ever called him Marc.

"Say something," she whispered.

"I loved my father." The words ripped out of him before he could stuff them down.

Her small hand caressed his cheek. "Tell me about him."

"He was a good man." He stood, needing space. Pacing to the doorway, he leaned on the frame, staring blankly at the long, bustling hospital hallway. Loud voices echoed through the corridor, yet it seemed to him as if a cocoon of stillness surrounded them.

"He's dead?"

"*Sì*." He made himself turn to confront her.

"I'm sorry." Her expression filled with sympathy.

Rolling back on his heels, he closed his eyes.

Sympathy. Something he'd never seen on a woman's face before. He was used to, expected to see, calculation, greed, expectations. Over the years, he found a certain amount of relief in knowing he could easily satisfy any womanly desires by doling out the required funds to make her happy. It released him from any messy emotional demands.

Once, long ago, a woman had observed him with sympathy. Or that's what he'd thought. But he soon understood it had been pity. Juliana's deep-brown gaze had welled with fake tears as he poured forth his love and begged.

The pity in her gaze had destroyed him and enraged him.

Had driven him for years.

Marc took a long breath in and opened his eyes to stare at another woman's expression. The emotion he saw was completely different. Soft, comforting, accepting. The awareness of the difference struck him deep inside, disconcerting him and making him restless. "No need to feel sorry. It happened a long time ago."

"It still hurts though." She stood, walked to his side and wrapped her arms around him before he could move away. "I can tell."

This had to stop. He wasn't going to go down this road any longer. He laid his hand on the back of her head and pressed her face against his chest. He didn't want to look into her eyes again. It might make him babble more inane memories. "Enough of this."

She snuffled. "Don't you want to know why I hate my father?"

Safe territory. It didn't matter that he'd never before allowed a lover to confess any great secrets. He hadn't cared about their secrets, only their bodies. Yet he'd much rather have Darcy rattling on about her past than digging into his. Even more astonishing, he actually wanted to know why she hated. The sprite didn't seem the type to hate.

"Tell me."

"He left me." She sighed, a tight burst of air. "After Mum died."

"Left you?"

Leaning back, she gazed into his face. Her eyes were no longer brilliant blue, but a hazy blur as if she were seeing across the years. "When I was twelve. He claimed he couldn't handle bringing up a brat by himself. So once Mum went, he turned me over to residential care."

An imaginary snapshot sprung into his head. One of a little girl: black curls, blue eyes. A little elfin child alone. *"Buon Dio."*

She pulled out of his arms as if she too needed space. "I survived."

Had she? How could a child recover from such a desertion? She still claimed hatred. Obviously, she hadn't survived the experience with no repercussions. She continued to carry it with her—the memory of being abandoned.

A dark, yawning ache blossomed inside him. One he'd ignored and pushed aside for years. The teenager standing by his papa's bed while the priest gave last rites. The kid who'd sat numb and distant as his father's friends arranged for the burial. The boy who thought his world had come to end.

Yet, his father hadn't left him willingly. Getting cancer had not been his choice. He'd also been a teenager, not a child. "If he weren't so sick, I'd strangle him myself."

"My knight in shining armor?" She threw a jaunty grin over her shoulder as she walked to the couch again. "Somehow, I don't see you in that role."

The thing curled in his gut. "Not a knight, true. But perhaps an avenger?"

"It's in the past." She waved his words away as she sat. "It's behind me."

"Yet you hate him."

She hunched her shoulders.

"You also give him money on a consistent basis, according to the report I read about you. A man you supposedly hate."

She stared at the faded linoleum floor.

"Can you explain that, *Tesorina*?" He needed to know how she ticked. Needed to know for what reason he could not articulate. Still, the need beat inside him, exactly as his heart did.

She pursed her lips.

Watching her keenly, he noticed as she folded her hands primly on her lap. The action told him she was trying to pull back from her confession. It told him she was trying to put distance between them. At any other time, with any other woman, he would have felt relief.

Now? Now, he felt a compulsion to rip aside her defenses and delve deep into her mind and her past. His desperate desire to know every inch of her body had somehow turned into a dogged need to know every inch of *her*.

The thought shocked him.

"What?" The sprite immediately sensed the change in him. She tilted her head, giving him the same keen attention he'd given her. "What's the matter?"

"Nothing."

A look of disbelief filled her face. Her hand smoothed down her jeans-clad leg in a familiar gesture.

Touching herself. Again. Disturbing him. Again.

A thought jumped into his mind, swallowing his lust whole. In its place his conscience suddenly came to life and screamed. "Why the hell did you take my deal?"

"Huh?" She frowned.

"Why would you agree to my blackmail in order to save your worthless father? A man you supposedly hate?"

"Well." Her gaze grew dark. "He's my dad. He's the only family I have."

The only family I have.

The words ricocheted inside him, hitting his gut like pieces of spiked glass. When his papa died, he'd been devastated. Felt totally alone. Within hours, though, his mother descended back into his life with her new husband and an unknown younger brother, Matteo. A brother who unwittingly filled the hole howling deep inside him.

His little brother had become his family.

During the past years, he'd forgotten. Purposefully. Forgotten the joy of being with his brother. Of celebrating life's journey with a member of his family. He'd forced himself to do what had to be done to salvage his pride and his honor.

His cell buzzed in her pocket.

She stared at him and then slowly slipped it from her pocket and held it out for him to take.

The buzz came once more.

The jangle of emotions and thoughts inside him whirled. The memories collided with the purpose that had driven him from the moment of Juliana's rejection.

Another buzz.

Her night-blue gaze burned into his soul.

He took the phone and answered it.

~

HER FATHER's eyes were blurry with medication. But for the first time in years, they were the clear sky-blue she remembered from her childhood rather than red with liquor or drugs.

Why this comforted her, she couldn't for the life of her say.

"Darcy," he rumbled. "It's good to see you."

"You too, Pop." She perched on his hospital bed. Sunlight sprinkled across the white sheets and downy blue coverlet. It had been five days since she landed in the dismal waiting room at the public hospital. Five days of constant waiting and constant hoping.

All with Marc at her side.

A funny little something fluttered in her stomach. A flutter of happiness or joy or something. A feeling of being cherished.

Or maybe it was because she was tired and had a stomachache after drinking so much bad coffee. For whatever reason, he had stuck around. He'd been there to advise her and console her. His phone blasted away all the time, still, he never ignored her if she really needed him.

She'd come first.

The flutter erupted in the depths of her once more.

There'd been other flutters and feelings, though, hadn't there? There'd been five days to sit and contemplate her past. Her pop. Her mum. It wasn't in her nature to contemplate her history. She'd much rather charge into the future. Yet somehow, the lack of anything to do but wait, and the solid male presence at her side—somehow, quite a bit had come out.

As she sat, cuddled to Marc's side, she found herself confessing about her mum's heroin overdose. About how she'd been the one who took care of her parents. She'd done the cooking and the washing and the cleaning. She'd made sure their limited funds, most of the time, paid the bills.

He'd listened. Simply listened.

Darcy sat in the sunlight and felt the warmth of his acceptance of her past. Although he left her today for an important business meeting he couldn't miss, she still felt him inside her heart.

"Pretty fancy digs." Her father interrupted her happy meanderings.

"Yep." She pulled herself away from her delirious dreams. Straightening his covers, she smiled. In only a short time after his operation, her pop had recovered enough to be transferred to a private clinic specializing in cardiac patients. The place was a miracle of the most advanced medical science combined with elegant surroundings.

Everything paid for by Marc.

"I know I told you I'd come to visit you soon." Her pop

rubbed his hand across his face. "But I got busy with other things. You know."

"Yeah." Childhood memories crowded around her. "I know."

A strained silence fell between them.

Her father finally chuckled under his breath. "You've sure landed on your feet with this one, baby."

"What?" She narrowed her gaze at his tone. The tone she'd heard her entire life. A tone of a man on the take, a charmer seeing his next big deal.

"Come on." He chuckled again. "Don't play innocent."

"I was never an innocent," she snapped. "Not with you as my father."

"Now, now." His hand smoothed across his chest. "Don't get cranky on me. I'm not at the top of my game."

She puffed out an exasperated breath, but fell silent.

Her father eyed her. There was still the sparkle of a con artist in the sky blue gaze. "All I'm saying, baby, is you've got yourself a winner this time."

Considering this was the first time she'd introduced any man to her pop, his statement was— "Don't be a nutter."

"He had a word with me before he left today."

Darcy stared at her father, trying to stifle the urge to ask. She couldn't help herself. "Okay. I'll bite. What did he say?"

His eyes twinkled. "You were always a curious child."

"What did he say?"

"Told me to behave myself with you."

"Pop." She gave him a wry smile. "We both know that's never going to happen."

"Well, he sure knows how to lay down the law. If I wasn't a tough old bird, he'd have scared me." He chortled, a cunning, caustic sound. "I saw it for what it was, though."

"What was that?"

"A declaration of his intent."

"I have no idea what you're talking about."

"You've got your hooks in him good, baby girl." His voice was rich with pleasure. "He's all protective towards you."

The flutter batted inside her. She waved his words away. "You've got it completely wrong."

"I rarely get these kinds of things wrong. I know a jackpot when I see one."

A fiery burn of temper erupted. "Marc is not a jackpot."

"Whatever you say." Her pop winked.

"He isn't." Frustration mixed with fear flooded through her. Had her dear old dad insinuated such a thing directly to Marc? If so, what were the chances the cynical man she knew lurked behind his kindness would reemerge? "I don't care about his money."

"Sure you don't." Her pop's laugh sounded rusty, scratching down her spine in an irritating grind.

His mocking take blazed a path of fury inside her. She'd never seen Marc as a mark. Never. In fact, as she'd gotten to know him, his money had turned into an obstacle. Or rather, his damn need to make more and more money became the problem.

A sudden thought struck her. Is this how he'd become so cynical? Did everyone approach him as a potential sugar daddy? Did he see the same gleam of greed in the eye of every woman and man who approached him?

No wonder he was so cool and contained. No wonder.

"He could be poor as a church mouse and I wouldn't care."

"Hell." Her father eyed her with immediate distaste. "Don't be like your stupid mother."

"Don't talk about her." The old rage bubbled in the pit of her stomach.

"Darcy, lass." His wiry hand tapped a beat of disgust on the covers. "Your mum did some stupid things—"

"Stop—"

"But the stupidest thing she ever did was fall in love." His voice was laden with rueful resignation. "With me."

"Look where that got her."

"Exactly."

She took a deep breath. "I'm not in love with him."

"Good," her father stated. "That's good."

"I'm simply grateful for what he's done for you."

"Keep it that way." Her pop's eyes burned bright. "Don't be a fool and fall in love and give everything of yourself to him. He'll only use it and you. Before discarding you. Keep control of the situation and you'll come out on top."

"What top would that be?"

"Walk away with your dignity," he snickered. "And a big pot of money."

"Bye, Pop." She jerked herself off the bed. A slick coating of humiliation slid up her throat as she confronted what she'd come from, who she called family. "I have to go get something to eat."

As she marched down the hospital hallway, she clenched her fists and bit her lip. She was not. Not after Marc for his money.

She was not like her pop.

She was not like her mum.

She was not.

CHAPTER 9

"Put it on." Marc's accented voice made her shiver inside.

Darcy inspected the dress hanging in the walk-in closet of her temporary bedroom. It shimmered in the light from overhead. Deep blue mixed with aqua and turquoise. The tiny straps clung to the hanger and the long, flowing silk called her name.

"The color made me think of your eyes."

She turned, instant surprise rising inside. "You picked this out yourself?"

Leaning on the doorframe, he arched a brow. "*Sì.*"

"You didn't have one of your minions pick it out?"

"No." He shrugged. "Is there a problem?"

"No problem at all." Turning back to the dress, she couldn't resist sliding her hand across the cool silk. A flash of joy exploded inside her at the thought of Marc actually taking time away from his busy business schedule to shop.

A low growl came from behind her. "Touching. Always touching."

A smile whispered across her lips. It had been a long ten days since her pop's heart attack. And it had seemed even longer during the last five days when Marc had left her side to return to work. She'd hardly seen him since. She spent every minute at the recovery center, often sleeping in the chair beside her pop's bed. It had only been last night she felt secure enough in his improving condition to return to the penthouse for a good night's sleep. By the time she rolled of the bed this morning, Marc had already left for work.

She glanced over her shoulder as she slipped her palm across the silk once more. "It feels lovely."

His silver gaze glowed with hot heat. "The dress will feel even lovelier with you in it."

Her smile widened and she took pleasure in watching the muscles of his shoulders tighten in reaction. She'd missed him. The memory of where they'd been, what they were about to do before her father's crisis had stopped them, swept in.

The want for him had not dissipated.

Exactly the opposite.

The want had grown from a sexual need she was afraid of into a driving desire to make this man happy in every way. During the past days—as he stood by her side, held her in his arms, did whatever needed to be done to make her more comfortable and her pop more secure—every wall inside her fell. The lust swamp which had bubbled inside her even during the grimmest moments of waiting for news, that swamp had now turned into a warm, willing lake of need and desire.

Don't be a fool and fall in love and give everything of yourself to him.

She shoved her pop's words aside and the sea of emotions threatening to rip her apart. Time enough to take them out and analyze them half to death. Right now, she wanted to do something entirely different while she had the guts. Taking her courage into her hands, she took the few steps to reach Marc's side.

He eased off the doorframe and stared into her eyes. "What?"

Placing a hand on his hard chest, she smoothed her fingers on the sleek silk shirt covering his pectorals. "I like to touch you."

He took a deep breath in. "You pick a damnable time to do it."

"You don't like it?" Taken aback at the unexpected rejection, she started to snap her hand away.

He grabbed it and tugged her closer. "I like it too much, but now is not the time."

Relief surged through her at his words and gave her the license to play with him just a bit. A pout was one her favorite weapons to get the reaction she wanted. It was an effective weapon if his reaction had anything to say about it. His gaze immediately zeroed in on her mouth. She swore she felt his temperature rise. His chest expanded once more with a heavy breath and the heat of him blasted against her hand.

Then, he laughed, dimples flashing. With one swift tug, he turned her back to the dress and stepped out of the closet. "You are temptation personified. However, I'm afraid I must insist you put on the dress. We have somewhere we need to be tonight."

"Where?" Curiosity warred with lust. Still, she dutifully slipped the dress off the hanger.

"You'll see." His voice carried across the bedroom as he paced to the hallway door. "Be ready in a half hour."

Dress in hand, Darcy strolled into the bathroom and shut the door.

She'd been tired when she arrived at the penthouse this afternoon. Yet now a vibrant energy pulsed through her. It washed away the long hours consulting with doctors, monitoring her father's care, and most especially, the times she'd had to listen to her pop's explanations of things long past. There were no apologies, naturally. She long ago abandoned any hope of that. It would have been nice to hear at least once that something had been his fault, but dear old dad kept to his party line.

Her mum forced him to marry when she'd been pregnant.

Her mum was the one to start the fights with her constant flirting.

Her mum had been the reason he became addicted to heroin —she'd been the one who introduced it to him. It had been her mum's decision to start taking customers in order to foot the drug bill. He'd had nothing to do with it. In fact, he objected to it.

The biggest line of them all—it was her mum's fault for dying. Her death had forced him to give her to foster care. A man couldn't be expected to care for a young twelve-year-old girl, now could he?

The long days listening to her pop had definitely been a trial.

She made a face in the mirror. She'd survived, as usual. Plus, she had something to look forward to at this moment. Marc was taking her out once more, like he did in New York City. Somewhere spangly and sparkly. Somewhere with a spot of champagne and new people to meet. This is what she needed to focus on. She deserved a bit of fun after listening to endless ridiculous excuses.

Excitement bubbling inside her, she turned on the shower. A quick wash. A fluff of her hair so it spiked and curled around her head. A touch of mascara and lip gloss, and she was ready for the dress. Slipping the slinky gown over her head, she tugged it into place. The silk wrapped lovingly around her breasts, slicked down across her waist, and hugged her hips.

My, my.

Every move she made was going to get her noticed.

She glanced into the mirror. Her slight smile turned into a

wide grin. She was going to swing her hips in honor of her dear mum and also swing them to catch a certain man's attention.

Swish, swish, swish.

She sauntered into the bedroom and stopped.

"You're ready," the certain man said from the open doorway.

She met his gaze, remembering another time when she presented herself for his inspection and been shot down.

A ping of anxiety made her straighten her spine.

The fighter inside made her lift her chin.

His perusal leisurely slid from her wide eyes to her mouth, making it tingle. The scrutiny continued over the skin of her neck across her silk-covered breasts, making them tighten. The silver gaze turned molten as he continued to concentrate on her. Sliding across her waist, the curve of her hips, down the length of her legs. To her silk-covered toes, making them curl.

He gave her a grin, dimples flashing. "No shoes. Are you planning on playing the part of Cinderella tonight? Or perhaps you wish me to carry you to your ball?"

Not a putdown. But no compliments either.

Emotions tumbled inside her.

This intense desire she felt for him even through the old fears. The leftover anger she held because of his dismissive attitude towards her when they'd first met. The contrasting emotions mixed and tangled with the appreciation she felt for his patience during the last few days. Then there was the gratitude for what he was doing for her pop battling with the old resentment because he'd used her father as a weapon against her.

Yet, none of those emotions could compete. Compete with the one, overwhelming emotion shining through the morass in her head and heart.

Love.

No. *No.* Not that emotion. Not the one emotion she never wanted to feel towards a man.

The man who caused all these jarring emotions inside her swung his tuxedo jacket over his shoulder and leaned on the doorframe. A slight frown appeared, drawing his dark, satirical brows down. "What's wrong?"

"Not a thing." Jerking her attention away from the jumble of confusion roiling inside her, Darcy slid on a pair of matching high heels. It couldn't possibly have happened, she told herself. She couldn't possibly be such a stupid git.

She gritted her teeth in a smile and threw it his way.

His frown deepened. "Tell me what you're thinking."

"I'm thinking I'm ready to go." She pushed her smile even wider.

"Tell me what you're feeling."

"Feeling great." She gestured to her feet. His earlier teasing questions came back to her and she grasped onto them as a way to turn the conversation. "See? Got my dancing shoes on. I'm definitely not the kind of girl to play Cinderella, you'll be happy to know. I'm sure you're even more relieved to find there's no need for you to carry me. Anywhere."

A clipped silence fell.

"*Sì*," he finally replied, his scrutiny no longer warm. "I'm delighted to be reminded of your independence."

She forced herself to keep meeting his gaze, even knowing she'd thrown cold water on the evening. But she didn't know how to put every one of her emotions in perfect order so she wouldn't blurt out stupid sentences designed to tick him off.

He slipped his jacket on, taking his time as he adjusted the sleeves and buttoned the coat. When he glanced over, his eyes were as opaque as glass. "Shall we?"

The silence in the limo was deafening. Darcy clutched her small tote with tight fingers and frantically tried to think of something to say. Something that would smooth over whatever this was that had come between them. This pulsing wall of distance, one she erected with her words. The realization clunked inside her. Suddenly, she wanted so much to return to the moments in the closet, when he'd been smiling, warm, wanting.

"We're here." His tone frosted her soul.

Rather than focusing on him, she stared at her feet as she climbed from the limo. Wherever *here* was, she didn't want to be. There would be no fun or frolic for her tonight. Not with the Great Man back in all his cold, arrogant glory.

She glanced up only when he began to open the door.

To an art gallery.

A gasp escaped as her gaze fell on a very familiar painting highlighted in one of two front windows. "T-t-that's, that's…" her words stumbled to a stop.

"Yours." He continued to hold the door open as several people swept into the noise and laughter of a gallery opening. He looked down his nose at her. "Are you going to come in?"

With a gulp, she stepped into her dream world, given to her by this man. A flurry of feelings fluttered in her belly. Feelings entirely opposite of what she'd been experiencing only seconds before. "H-h-how…how—"

"Quite easily." He slipped her coat off and gave it to an attendant. "I'm in the business of making things happen."

His arrogance should have fired her temper. Instead, the fire lit something deep inside, melting her fears. "I had no idea."

"That is the general description of a surprise." He adjusted his necktie, not meeting her inquiring gaze.

Her heart drummed in her chest, hope and anguish and fear and dreams colliding inside her. "Why?"

He finally glanced her way, yet his eyes gave away

nothing. They were like two pieces of impenetrable metal. "You have talent. It should be displayed and acknowledged."

As if he would do this for any starving artist in London. But he wouldn't have, would he? He'd done it for her. However, it seemed whatever impulse prodded him to do this for her had been swept away by her odd attitude earlier this evening.

A lump of guilt stuck in her throat.

After all this man had done for her father, and now this. She'd been flippant, dismissive. She'd shut an emotional door in his face and he knew it and didn't like it. Had she hurt him? Could it possibly be that Marc was feeling some of the same emotions she was?

She peered at him.

His face was blank as he looked back at her. Still, something in the way he stood, tense and ready for another blow, gave her courage. She'd let fear—fear of rejection, of what she was feeling for this man—rule her.

Which wasn't worthy of her or him.

She stepped close to him once more and slipped her hand around his neck.

His big body stilled and then stiffened as she tried to pull his head down to hers. "No."

"Yes," she insisted, willing to fight through his rejection instead of letting it put her off.

His eyes were no longer frosty. Rather a burning light had appeared. "*Tesorina*. Why do you choose the most inopportune times to touch me?"

"I don't know." She tried to tug his head down again. "Call me perverse."

"I have other names for you." He stared at her. Hard. "What happened earlier? What were you thinking?"

She didn't want to go there. How could she explain the jumble of emotions inside her? And she couldn't confess love when she hadn't given herself time to grapple with the consequences. The only thing she wanted at this moment was his closeness. She wanted to relish this moment.

Waving his questions away, she didn't look at his face. "I don't know what you mean."

"Not true." One male finger slid under her chin, lifting her gaze to his. "I want to know."

"Why? What does it matter?"

"It matters." His silver eyes never left hers.

"I...I..."

A flash of light cut off her attempt at an impossible explanation. Both of them jerked their heads around. Cameras flashed once more.

The ancient fear blasted every thought from her head except one.

He would find her.

The paparazzi were few, and relegated to a small patch of space inside the front door. Marc straightened and tugged her to his side, turning her to face the cameras.

And the consequences.

"Smile," he ordered.

Following his order was impossible. Her lips felt like icicles.

Lights flashed once more.

Horror screamed in her brain. She might have escaped his notice when the New York photos were released, but she doubted she'd be so lucky if and when her picture hit the London tabs. She'd watched him as a kid, poring over the tabloids, laughing at celebrity antics. If he was still alive, he'd see her. If he saw her, she knew, *knew*, he'd come after her.

"Enough." Marc's arm was the only warmth penetrating the chill coursing through her.

She trembled, a cold mist of sweat breaking out on her skin.

Within seconds, he ushered her away from the cameras and

into the center of the gallery. A glass of champagne got thrust into her hand. The liquid slopped over the edges because her hand shook. Yet as he led her deeper into the crowds, away from the cameras, the panic began to subside. His arm continued to stay around her waist, a hot brand of ownership and, somehow, consolation. Dimly, she recognized he was greeting people, his voice rumbling at her side, giving her another source of comfort.

All at once, they were around a corner, into a private alcove.

"What the hell is going on?" he snarled.

The fear was so old, so deep she'd never been able to articulate it to anyone. Not after her first attempt was met with contempt and ridicule. The instinct to stuff it down was too ingrained to give her any possibility of answering his question. Plus, she didn't want to think about this, didn't want to ruin this amazing surprise he'd planned for her.

She needed to focus on the positive. As usual.

Forget the danger lurking in wait. For now.

She took a sip of champagne, not meeting his glare, trying to put the pieces of herself back in place before he saw anything to latch on to.

"Answer me."

Closing her eyes for a minute, she pulled the last bits together, pasted a smile on and made sure the ugly memories were blanked. Lifting her head, she met his steely stare. "Nothing's going on."

An Italian curse ripped from his mouth. His eyes were sharp blades attempting to rip through her mind.

The courage and fight she'd learned as a kid came to her rescue. "S-s-seriously. I'm fine."

She was. Almost. The trembling had stopped and the fear was fading for now. If only she could stop her stuttering, she'd present a perfectly composed picture to the world and to him. Eventually, she would have to confront the demon from her past. She knew it in her gut. But not now. Now was about convincing this man all was well and trying to enjoy the night he'd planned.

Leaning over, his hands splayed on the wall behind her and his head dipped to hers. "Tell me what you are afraid of."

"I'm afraid you're going to keep me in this alcove all night instead of letting me out to have some fun."

His jaw clenched. "Tell me why you were shaking in front of the cameras."

Suddenly, she wanted to tell him. Tell him everything. For the first time in years, she wanted to believe someone would listen and would believe. How wonderful it would be to lay this ugliness at his feet and let him fix it, exactly as he'd fixed her pop. The yearning swept through her, a wash of pure need. "Marc—"

"Most women would love the attention." His mouth tightened as if he were trying to figure out a particularly irritating puzzle. "Most women love the cameras."

Most women.

He saw her as just another woman. Her throat hardened around her confession. The yearning turned to instant chalk dust on her tongue.

"Tell me what you're thinking." His harsh breath fluttered her bangs.

"Excitement?" She batted her lashes, reverting to her usual illusions was the only thing she could do at the moment. She couldn't think. She couldn't feel. "Surprise?"

Another curse came from him.

Diverting his attention using some of her mum's old tricks, didn't seem to be doing the…trick. Still, she was game at keeping going. It was the only thing she could do. Wrapping her hand around his warm neck again, she tugged his mouth to hers.

He went completely rigid.

His lips were cool to her touch. A determined rejection. Darcy was more than determined, though. She was desperate. Desperate to stop this intrusive conversation. Desperate to forget what lurked in wait. Desperate to lose herself in the heat and comfort this man provided rather than confront the realization he apparently saw her as *just another woman*.

Her tongue slipped across his lips, slid across his grim mouth. Her teeth nipped at him, begging for a reaction.

Finally, she felt his control slacken, the heat from his body surging. He held onto his rejection, but she knew she was close to cracking through the wall he'd built against her. How she wished for more experience at this kissing thing. She'd seen her mum kiss often. Yet, it wasn't the same thing as doing it herself.

Well, duh, her mind dimly sassed.

So in place of experience, she offered him her passion and need. She slipped her tongue into his mouth, tasting the essence of him mixed with champagne. Her tongue danced across his teeth, delved deeper into him, asking, pleading for him to join her in this dance of desire.

Abruptly, his hands came down in a violent movement of need to grip her shoulders. Lifting her, he plastered her to his chest, taking over the kiss with a ravaged groan. His lips firmed on hers and took control. Swept her into a passion she'd never dreamed existed. In the last tiny piece of her mind that was coherent, she realized she'd never understood anything about this. Anything about sex or desire or need or love.

Love.

Yanking her mouth from his, she gasped. "Bloody hell."

The word, the emotion she'd tried to ignore earlier this evening, vibrated in the deepest pit of her soul.

Denial came flooding after it just as before. Except now it her hard in the middle of her soul where she always thought she was protected.

No. No. No.

It was impossible.

She wouldn't be like her mum. She couldn't be like her mum. Love would destroy her.

Precisely like her mum.

She pushed him away, old fears making her stronger than she looked.

It was enough to get his attention, yet he didn't let her go. Rather, he scowled down at her with frustrated male hostility. "Are you crazy?"

Quite possibly. But she wasn't going to admit it. "Let m-me go."

"This seems to be a reoccurring pattern with us." Icy distaste dripped from each word. "One that is not to my liking."

"Too bloody bad." She pushed once more.

He dropped her against the wall like a sack of flour and then turned to stare at the crowd swirling beyond the alcove.

The air between them chilled to freezing. She began to tremble once more. Wrapping her arms around herself, she leaned on the wall and tried to put the pieces of herself back together once again in a matter of seconds. An impossible task.

A low curse came from the man before her.

She took a deep shuddering breath. "I'm s-sorry."

A harsh laugh was his only response.

"I really am," she whispered. The old fear wrapped around the new fear, turning her melted heart into cold concrete.

"Hot and cold." He turned, his face like granite. "It is not a game I like playing."

"I understand. It's j-just that—"

"And I won't play it anymore." Every one of his words bit into her. "The next time you make a move, Darcy."

She stared down at the parquet floor.

"Look at me."

He wouldn't even allow her that protection. Yet, she owed

him something for her confusing behavior. Stiffening her spine, trying to find her fighting spirit again, she peered, met his gaze and notched her chin out.

"Sì," he murmured. "There's my girl."

"I'm not your girl." She stated every word as if she meant it. But the sure knowledge of what lay within her, what she would find if she even took one peek into her deep emotions, ate into her like acid. The realization edged each of her words with a brutal, hard tone.

One male hand slammed down on the wall behind her. The finger sliding across her jaw was as light and supple as a feather, though. It slipped to her curls, gently combing through her hair. His words, however, were ruthless and harsh. "I will not fight any more battles with you. They have all been won by me. Except for this last one."

She turned her head away from him, observing the laughing crowd swirling in the outer room, mere meters from where they stood. Yet it felt as if the two of them were alone, on an island of desire and anger. An isolated place filled with conflicts, contradictions, and confusion.

Leaning close to her, his lips touched her ear as his words came. "I will win this last one too. The next time you make a move, and we both know you'll make one, there will be no going back."

With a gasp, she turned her head and stared right into his blazing eyes. "What do you mean, n-n-no going back?"

His lips barely moved, but her skin felt every word. "We will finally have sex," he promised, his tone sibilant. "I'll give you exactly what you've wanted from me since the first moment we met."

Fearful excitement rippled over her body. She wanted, and also dreaded. She tried to find some cheeky words to throw him off and gain a measure of control. Nothing tripped across her tongue or stirred in her mind.

"Nothing to say?" He stepped away, never taking his gaze off her face. "Then let us return to my original plan for this evening. Attending your first gallery opening."

His big hand reached out and took her elbow in a tight grip.

And pulled her into her future.

*

CHAPTER 10

*H*is seductive sprite was at the top of her game. Which was remarkable. Only hours before she'd been a big-eyed waif, shaking with fear, slumped on the wall of the alcove where he'd tried to penetrate her secrets.

Without success.

Irritation welled in him. He sipped his champagne, and nodded in response to some comment from the circle of admirers surrounding her as she held court.

She threw her head back and laughed. Her eyes sparkled. She glowed.

Frantic. Desperate. Sick with fear. It had been written all over her. Panic screamed from her even as she denied it. Tried to pretend it wasn't real. Attempted to make him believe it was nothing.

Endeavored to trick him into believing her with kisses.

Marc signaled for another glass of champagne as he noted the sprite accepting a compliment on her paintings with aplomb. A reluctant admiration for her courage, her pluck came over him. His *Tesorina* had more than spirit. She had guts.

You don't like women very much do you?

I like them just fine. In certain areas of my life. I'll rephrase that. You don't respect them.

He stood in the swirl of the crowd and realized those words he'd exchanged with her mere weeks ago were no longer true.

He respected Darcy Moran.

Respected her decision to care for her father. A man who didn't deserve what she'd done for him. Respected her artistic talent shining on every wall of the gallery. More than anything, he respected her fighting spirit—her determination to stand tall. To take the world on all on her own.

It was something he could identify with. The driving need to prove yourself. The absolute resolve to make your way in the world without anyone's help. He'd done it himself, years ago. Been justly proud of what he'd accomplished.

So why did it eat away at him when she would not lean on him? Would not trust him with her secrets and let him take care of her?

She'd allowed him in a bit with her father's situation. She'd leaned for a time on his shoulder in the hospital. She'd grumbled a bit about him paying the bills, however, he hadn't heard much about that issue since he put his foot down.

This was different, though. Instinctively, he knew it. This secret she held inside her was much more personal. This went deeper and it cut him that she wouldn't share it.

The champagne was cool on his hot throat. But it curdled in his stomach as he realized he was in a bit deeper than he wanted to be with this woman. Faint nausea welled at the thought of being ensnared in another woman's web.

Juliana.

The memory made his throat clutch.

The sound of Darcy's laughter tugged him away from his thoughts. The chandelier light gilded blue highlights into her curls. Her skin gleamed like pale milk. Her graceful hands lifted in the air and danced as if every word she uttered prompted them to play.

Every one of her paintings had a *sold* tag on them. The gallery owner was ecstatic in his praise, effusive in his desire to acquire anything she painted in the future. The crowd around her grew as she spun her stories, chuckled at every joke, charmed the living daylights out of everyone who entered her sphere.

Including him. The knowledge lodged like a stone in his gut.

"She's priceless, Marcus." One of his mother's gaggle of crows swished to his side, the heavily-lined eyebrows like dark arrows pointing to her extravagantly curled hair. "Where did you find her?"

The churning inside him needed release. Why not stir his mother's pot for once? "Actually, my momma was kind enough to bring Darcy to my attention."

Aged eyes snapped with interest. "Really?"

"As a connoisseur of art, I was happy to make the artist's acquaintance."

"And launch her."

He shrugged. "It was the least I could do."

"Ah, so you've done even more for Ms. Moran."

He noticed it wasn't a question. As a consequence, he didn't answer.

She arched one dramatic brow and gave him a grimace of dissatisfaction. "You are always rather closemouthed, Marcus."

"*Sì.*" He'd learned the lesson well. Talking got a man in trouble. In business and especially with women. As long as he kept his thoughts to himself, he'd be fine.

Remember this when you are with Darcy.

"Oh, you." The older woman batted his arm. "I won't let you get away with it. Tell me what's between you and this lovely girl."

He gave her a grim smile. "A gentleman doesn't kiss and tell."

"Aaaah." Her heavily lined eyes twinkled with glee. "I can't wait to talk to your mother."

Why was he not surprised? He wondered if his mother would take even a moment from her busy shopping and gossiping schedule to worry about him for a change. Worry he may be getting too deeply involved with an inappropriate woman.

He doubted it.

Darcy's light laugh caught his attention once more.

"You can't take your eyes off her." The woman at his side cooed.

Her words weren't an accusation, yet he felt the sting of it nevertheless. It was a truth he didn't want to acknowledge or accept. It ate into him, the knowledge that somehow this little bit of a woman had penetrated the wall he'd erected to keep everyone out.

Clearly, he would need to do some rebuilding.

Bed her. Then, you will be free of her.

This was the plan he needed to focus on. All he needed was one more kiss from her, and he would take control. Make it happen. After, this breach of the wall around his emotions would once again be sealed.

He noted Darcy's warm smile, but also the shadow of exhaustion under her eyes. He'd had enough of this event, and obviously she had, too. "If you will excuse me."

Within moments, he skillfully extracted her from her admirers, signaled for the limo, and had her safely tucked inside it as they sped back to his penthouse. Leaning on the side of the door, he watched her as she smoothed the edges of her coat down.

Touching, he noted with sardonic humor, always touching.

The need for her to willingly touch him once more swept through him with a raging passion.

"Thank you." Her gaze was glued to her hands.

"*Prego*," he replied, trying in vain to curb his mounting desire.

Finally, she looked at him. Her eyes were wide and brimming with tears.

"No." All thoughts of sex crashed inside him. "No crying."

"I'm sorry." She forced a grin as she swiped at the tears. "I'm not usually a watering pot."

"Really?" He handed over his white handkerchief. "That surprises me."

Her muffled chuckle was her response.

A long moment later, she dropped her hands to her lap. Her cheeks were wet, still it appeared the bout of emotion had subsided, much to his relief.

"Better?"

"Yes. Fine." When she looked at him once more, her gaze was a clear, deep blue. "It's...it's been a very emotional evening for me."

"*Sì*."

His short, clipped word brought a shadow across her face, yet she straightened her spine. "I meant the showing of my art. It's always been a dream of mine."

"Which makes me curious," he responded. "I remember footing the bill on a rather large gallery showing for my brother and his friends a few years ago. A graduation present."

Her gaze shot down to her lap.

"It's surprising he did not include his lover's work in the showing." The reminder of her past love life with his brother made him want to howl. "Don't try and lie to me. I would have remembered your work if it had been there. It is distinctive."

Another dismissive wave of her hand.

The action notched his irritation higher by several degrees. "Well?"

She took a shaky breath and pinned him with a look that

choked his breath in his throat. Her eyes swam with pain. "Marc."

"*Sì?*" His whole body stiffened in anticipation of her next words.

"I can't take this anymore," she murmured. For a moment, her white skin shone in the flash of a streetlight. "N-n-not tonight."

She would not let him in. He shouldn't care, but he did. He turned away from her and surveyed the passing city lights.

"Please," she murmured again. "Please simply let me thank you. Leave it at that."

Anger pulsed in him. Anger because she wouldn't confide. Anger at himself for even wanting such a thing. He never wanted a woman to confide in him. The fact he wanted this woman's every secret appalled and stunned him.

"Marc, please accept my thanks."

"You can thank me with a kiss." He turned back to her and glared. All he wanted from this woman was sex, his brain yelled the reminder to his heart.

She gave a tiny gasp. Her eyes widened at his tone, at the fierce scowl on his face.

"Remember," he ground out. "Remember what I told you the last time you kissed me."

One of her delicate hands lifted to her mouth.

"Remember what will come next."

This was wrong. He knew it. Another demand. Another attempt at forcing her to do something she clearly didn't want to do. Rage billowed inside him like a scarlet rain. It burned the core of him with distaste at his action. She would rightfully slam him for this. His feisty girl would blast him and he deserved it.

He stared at her.

She stared back.

Why didn't she scream at him? Hit him? He opened his mouth, ready to tell her it was wrong, to forget his evil words—

When she stunned him.

Sliding across the seat, her small hand cupped his jaw and kissed him.

∽

SHE WAS HIS ENCHANTING *NINFA*. His seductive sprite.

His woman.

Her skin was pale as moonlight in the shadows of his bedroom. Her lithe body lay on his bed like a sacrifice. Her eyes were deep and dark as she gazed at him as he undressed. Let him survey her without trying to conceal or cover any part of herself.

This filled him with a fierce joy.

His hands shook as he unbuttoned his shirt and unzipped his pants. The need for her, the agony of need he'd felt for her since the moment he laid eyes on her, throbbed through every vein, every artery. Washed away any coherent thought, leaving only a primeval hunger to take.

A tiny gasp came from her as he dropped the last of his clothes to the floor.

He was big, he knew. Yet surely a woman with experience would rejoice at this.

He stared into her wide eyes. Was this an act of hers? Did she think this virginal reaction to his nakedness would turn him on? If so, she didn't need any act. He was more turned on than he'd ever been in his entire life.

The thought stopped him for a moment.

Every thought was swept away, though, when she wrapped her arms around her body. Trying to hide from him once more.

He would not let this happen. Sliding down on the bed, he took her in his grasp. "*Abbracciami*," he demanded. "Hold me."

She looked straight at him as her graceful arms slowly lifted and draped around his neck. The joy at her acquiescence, her acceptance rushed through him. Finally, after what seemed like forever, his sprite was coming to him. Wanting him. Giving herself to him. If this killed him, he would savor and prolong. After all these weeks of waiting, he wanted her to make the first moves. He wanted her to show him she wanted him as desperately as he'd wanted her since they met.

His pride demanded it.

His body wanted it.

His male heart needed it.

This had nothing to do with how they met or what he'd forced her to do. With every moment she gave to him, all that was swept away, cleansing him of any remaining guilt.

He would let her take the lead.

He would let her claim him.

Then, he would know they were together because she wanted him. Only him.

Her skin was cool in contrast to the heat of his own. With pleasurable intensity, he felt the brush of her breasts on his chest, the slip of her legs as they entwined with his. Lust pulsed in him like a living thing, barely contained.

"*Baciami.*" His voice was hoarse, husky. "Kiss me. Again."

Her gaze never left his as she leaned forward. Her eyes didn't close as her lips gently touched his. The night-blue gaze pulled him in, washing over him in a clear stream of need and want. Desire burned in her stare. Yet something more, something he couldn't quite define lurked on the edges.

His heart stirred and trembled with a sudden panic.

Then, the emotion he couldn't name was gone from her eyes as she slowly closed them. Her mouth moved on his and he lost every thought as her soft, supple skin melded with his hard, hot need. Unable to wait, he thrust his tongue into her, tasting the sweet zing he remembered with aching longing. She played with him, slipping her tongue around his, answering his demands with a giving sweetness that only drove him further into mindlessness.

Wrenching his mouth from hers, he stared at her. "*Toccarmi.*"

A slight frown furrowed her brow and she glanced at him with inquiry. "Tell me what it means."

"Touch me," he groaned. He thought of the times he'd watched as she smoothed her hands along silk and leather and herself. Now it was his body she would explore and stir and feel. The anticipation turned something wild inside him, something untamed and feral. Sweat dampened his forehead and his back.

At his words, her frown turned to a winsome, womanly smile. A smile as old as humankind. One that twisted every cell in his body into blinding lust.

One dainty hand cupped his jaw, smoothed across his hot neck.

He tensed with exquisite enjoyment.

The hand slid down to his collarbone and went slower as it trailed across his chest. Her fingers tangled in the hair lying in a patch between his nipples before wandering over to lightly circle one of them.

She plucked.

He gasped.

"Cor," she said, wonder in her voice. "You like that."

"*Sì,*" he managed to say. "*Certamente.* And you will too when I do the same for you."

Was she truly blushing? It shocked him, confused him. What was with the shy attitude? It didn't fit what he knew of her. A scraper who'd seen everything. A girl who'd grown up hard and tough. Surely sex was something she was experienced at. Hell, she'd been with his brother. A cold shot of jealousy pulsed through his hot body at the thought.

A gentle hand sliding across his stomach poured heat right after it. His entire body tensed.

"You like this?" Her voice was enchanting, luring.

"*Sì.*" He held his breath as her hand slowed.

Then, stopped.

A slight frown of concentration furrowed her brow as she watched her hand move on his body.

"*Tesorina,*" he panted. "You're killing me."

She peeked into his eyes. Hers were filled with…not fear…nerves. She was nervous. Once more, it hit him. The virgin. An act. Surely an act. She was torturing him.

"*Toccarmi,*" he demanded, his patience long gone.

Her focus went back to his body. She bit her lip as if she were about to jump off a cliff. But his girl wasn't a quitter. She had courage.

Grazie Dio.

She slipped her silky fingers around him. Slid them up, then down.

His blood roared. He stiffened and arched into her touch. A low, animal moan of pure want poured from him.

"Blimey." Surprise and pleasure echoed in her voice.

His brother was clearly the worst lover on earth. The thought dimly penetrated the passion pumping through his body. Had the idiot merely stuck himself into her and done his business? The thought of his brother in her blistered his brain. Another blast of jealousy, hot and fierce, scrambled with the overwhelming need to take, to imprint himself into her.

His hand roughly grabbed hers and pulled hers away.

She glanced at him, startled. Her eyes widened at what she saw on his face.

"Did I do it wrong?" Nerves jittered in her tone and her body grew stiff.

Taking a deep breath, he bent his head, slid his mouth along the side of her neck, hid himself from her. Hid the jealousy he never allowed himself to feel with any other woman since Juliana.

"No," he murmured on her skin. "It was too much."

"Too much?" Again, there was the questioning, the timidity, that confused him.

Her skin tasted like salted candy. Sweet and ripe. The soft hair at the base of her neck touched his cheek and nose, warm whispers of her tickling him. "I was close to coming." Why did he have to explain this to an experienced woman? "I was about to lose myself in your hand."

There was a short pause as his sprite seemed to take it in. He felt it as she sucked in a deep breath. Next, her body turned from stiff rigidity to warm, womanly welcome. Her hands came back on his body, slipping down his shoulders, moving over his sides.

"I love your body," she said it with a tentative tone as if testing out the words.

Lifting his head, knowing he'd succeeded in pushing his emotions back, confident he'd soothed her fears, he latched onto her mouth, tasting and taking. He couldn't endure any more of this shy exploration. He needed her. Had to have her now. There was no more finesse and patience in him.

It was time he took the lead.

A rain of kisses moved from her lips to her neck, down to her pointed, tight nipples. He laved and lashed them with his tongue, bent on creating the same frenzy of lust in her that she'd given him.

"Aaaah." She writhed in his arms.

"*Sognavo di te*," he murmured, brushing his lips on her sweet skin.

He was mindless, driven, primitive.

His mouth drank her in, moved across her taut belly, darting a tongue into her navel. Sliding down, farther, down.

"I d-don't know—" Her words ended in a shriek of surprise? Delight?

He couldn't tell as he pushed her legs apart and sucked the essence of her into his mouth. He couldn't decide which emotion she was feeling because his mind had gone completely blank as the primal animal in him took over.

"God," she moaned.

She tasted as sweet and spicy as he'd dreamed. His tongue tormented her folds, his lips nibbled at her. He lifted his gaze and saw his woman arch away from the bed, her breasts wet from his attention, her skin a pale, gleaming gloss on the sheets.

A broken cry came from her as her entire body tensed and bowed into his touch. He felt her bliss roll into her, shuddering through her chest, her belly, her thighs. For a long moment, he continued to pleasure her as she shuddered once more before collapsing.

He finally moved. Leaning over her, pressing her warm body to the bed, he reached for protection. With shaking hands, he ripped open the silver packet and slid the condom on him. Turning to her lax body, he took her in his arms. "Talk to me. Are you all right?"

Her eyes slowly opened. They were dazed with the passion and pleasure he'd given her. Her hand lifted and tenderly grazed his cheek. "That was amazing." Awe rang in her voice.

Fierce pride pumped inside him. He'd won her. He'd conquered her. It was time to take her and make her his.

"*Ho bisogno di te*," he groaned as he positioned himself.

The blue of her gaze turned to midnight as he thrust into her warm, wet channel. Her mouth opened in a gasp as she arched her head back. For a moment she tightened, stiffened, seemed to pull away.

"*Tesorina*." The one word whispered from his lips, whispered in his heart. Had he hurt her?

"Keep going." Her soft voice soothed his concern.

Words escaped him at that point. He had only his body to communicate. Involuntarily, he thrust once more, wanting and needing her to let him in.

Her hands flickered on his shoulders, like gentle butterflies. Her head tilted back and her eyes met his. Secrets swirled in the mist of her gaze. Along with something else, something clutching at his heart.

But it was swept away when she softened, when her core let him all the way in.

He gasped as he surged to his hilt.

Her hands smoothed across his chest, sending streaks of lightning need across his torso. With feral intensity he lifted, thrusting into her once more. She felt as tight as a virgin. As plush as velvet, as wet and warm as he'd ever dreamed.

One of his hands slid down her leg. "Put them around me."

Her eyes shone with surprise, yet she instantly wrapped her lithe legs around his waist, causing him to sink even deeper into her body.

"*Dio.*" What was going on with her? Why was she feigning this passivity, pretending not to know what to do? Except his body didn't care. It plunged and thrust and lusted. The feeling was exquisite, infinite. Fire burned in his groin, shooting out to the tips of his toes and fingers. He shook and shuddered with need.

His woman sighed and grew still.

She was not participating. She was not moving, lusting, wanting, as he was. She wasn't with him in this dance of desire.

He stopped and stared at her. "Move with me. Be with me."

Worry lanced across her face. "I'm not doing it right, am I?"

"There's no right way." Astonished amazement flashed through him at her question. Doing it right? Was she playing her games? Sudden frustration pulsed behind his words. "Lose yourself in me."

His hands grasped her hips, pulled her and pushed her into his pace. Determination surged in him along with his overriding lust. She would fall first into this desire. He would lead her into the frenzy before he allowed himself to fall into it with her.

Her hips caught his rhythm. Her face flushed and her chest rose with a deep breath.

"*Madonna in cielo,*" he groaned as her tight passage clamped around him.

They finally moved as one, their bodies slick with sweat. He felt every inch of her skin, saw every emotion and feeling as it crossed her face. He reveled in her every sigh, her every gasp.

The pace quickened. The dance became frantic.

His body teetered on the edge. Sucking in his breath, and his lust, he drove into her once more. "Come for me," he moaned. "Now."

Her eyes widened as she did as he commanded. Her fingernails bit into his skin and she arched in a bow underneath him. Her inner core squeezed his cock. Elation swept through him as he watched her come once more. Watched the pleasure he'd given her seize her and throw her into the need and want he felt as well.

His time. He let go of the final thread of control. His body stiffened, shuddered. Sweat poured off him, slicing down his hot skin. His hips pounded out a drum of fervent taking. He tightened his hands on her slick skin, pinning her to the bed with his body. He felt her breath on him, felt the beat of her blood. Felt himself bind and blend with the center of her. Trembling and shaking, he thrust one last time. Pushing himself over his own edge.

Into the oblivion of utter fulfillment.

Into an ache he thought never to feel again.

Into a fear rushing through his pleasure, fracturing his heart.

As he poured the last of his pain, and his fear, and himself into her, he realized he was in too deep with a woman once more.

Not only physically.

Emotionally.

CHAPTER 11

She woke alone and cold.

The silk of the sheet slid cool on her skin. She knew instinctively he was gone, gone from more than simply the bed. The shadows of the room were lighter now. She could tell by the way the sunbeams splintered through the shades it was day, but early. Very early.

Apparently late enough, however, for the La Rocca work ethic to kick in.

Her mouth twitched into a grimace. Clearly her sexual appeal hadn't lasted longer than one night since her lover had bounded out of bed to get to his all-important business.

She rolled over and surveyed his side of the bed.

Empty.

The pillow held the imprint of his head. She pulled it to her and curled into it. It was cool. He'd been gone for a while. Yet, she still could smell him on the silk. Masculine virility mixed with the sweet sweat of sex.

Closing her eyes, she pictured him as she saw him last. His dark lashes long on his cheeks as he slept at her side. The beginning of a five-o'clock shadow on his jaw. His olive skin glistening from the heat of their coupling.

The pure beauty of the man.

The pure joy she felt with him at her side.

She rubbed her cheek on his pillow. A tear dripped down, darkening the silk.

Except, she couldn't be angry at him. Not yet. Not now. What he'd given her. The gift ran through her like a clear stream of healing. The night had been a revelation. A reawakening. She still found it almost impossible to take in. Sex had always been a transaction to her. A way for a woman to pay her bills, keep her man. Her mum had showed her the moves by her example. And Darcy had taken it all in. Sex was something she never wanted to have.

Sex was something dirty.

Sex was something that ultimately killed her mum.

Plus, there was also her fear of sex. That had come later. But the experience at seventeen put an iron seal on the lessons she learned as a kid.

Last night, though, he'd changed everything.

It hadn't been sex she'd experienced last night. It had been love.

Another teardrop splattered on the fine woven silk.

She was in love with Marcus La Rocca. She'd given her body in love. She'd found more pleasure, more intimacy in this one single act than she ever found in any other interaction with another human being.

But this morning, when she desperately wanted him, wanted to sink into his warm arms, taste his lips, feel him move inside her…when she wanted to once more find this amazing bond between them…this morning, he'd left her.

She popped her head up and listened. Listened to complete silence. He wasn't in the flat. She knew it with a bone-deep certainty. Looking around, she saw no loving note to tell her where he'd gone. She didn't need one. He wasn't out buying her a breakfast pastry. He hadn't raced from the flat to buy her flowers or chocolate.

As sure as she knew herself, she knew him.

Marcus La Rocca had gone to work.

Exactly as if it were another day.

What did it mean? Was he disappointed in her? Had she showed how naive and untrained she was at the act? Last night he seemed satisfied. But she'd been so overwhelmed with all the emotions and feelings running through her head and heart and body, she'd barely been able to focus on any of his reactions.

Her scrambled thoughts ran through her head driving her crazy. Why was she sitting here torturing herself? It wasn't in her nature. She wasn't going to spend her time mooning over a man while lying here stupidly waiting for him to come back.

Which probably wasn't going to happen if she'd disappointed him last night.

The memory of him arching above her, his face grimacing, the low groan that tore from his mouth as she moved with him—

No. She was sure she'd given him pleasure too. Enough that he'd want to do it again.

The thought of doing it again with him brought a flush of anticipation to her face and body. She really, really couldn't wait.

Still, right now, lallygagging around in bed wasn't what she wanted to do.

A burst of energy rushed through her.

She got herself out of the bed and into the bathroom in record time. As the hot water poured on her in the shower, she took an inventory of the aches she'd never felt before. She had a slight bruise on one breast. A love bruise. How batty was it that she liked it? She liked the thought of his brand on her skin.

Okay. She was as bad as all those women she used to scorn.

She was seriously gaga over her guy. If she didn't get herself together before she saw him, she was likely to drool, say brainless things, and generally make a fool of herself.

"No way," she promised herself as she wrapped a towel around her body.

Instinctively, she knew, he wouldn't want that. She'd have to be careful with him. Not show the joy and love pounding inside. At least, not yet. Staring into the steam-covered mirror, she took stock of her situation. Tried to bring some reality to her sex-fogged brain and love-soaked heart.

Marcus had only ever claimed he wanted sex with her.

In a little more than a week, her time with him would be done.

She swished her hand across the mist and encountered two worried blue eyes.

"You can change it," she whispered.

What she wanted more than anything in the world was to stay with him, be with him.

Forever.

A man who held women in contempt.

A man who'd blackmailed her.

A man who'd never indicated by his words he felt anything for her other than lust.

Her throat tightened. "Stop it."

She would focus on the bright side of this. And there was lots of bright.

He'd helped dear old dad for her sake. Spent a fortune on private medical care. He'd given her a room to paint in his penthouse. Spent a fortune putting it together. He'd arranged her first gallery opening. Been there at her side the entire time. Launched her art career into the stratosphere.

There was a lot to build on, a lot to hope for if a girl simply examined the guy's actions.

Actions spoke louder than words, right?

"What you need," she announced to her mirrored image. "Is a strategy."

Marching out of the bathroom and across the hall to her bedroom, she threw on a pair of jeans and a sweatshirt. What was the best way to win a man once and for all? She'd never had to think about it. This was completely unfamiliar territory—but she was determined to master it. Some way or another, she was going to win Marcus La Rocca's love.

And teach him how to live.

The man had serious issues about his lifestyle. Working day and night was not how a person should live. She was going to lure him away from work if it was the last thing she did. She was going to teach him how to laugh and love and give and take. She was going to show him a woman could be trusted, respected.

She was going to love him so hard he'd have to learn how to love in return.

Darcy strode down the hall and into the kitchen. The pristine, precise, polished, and utterly soulless kitchen. From the beginning the room had intimidated her with its bare counters and every cooking utensil known to gourmet chefs gleaming as if daring her to mess with them.

Well. She was going to mess with them for real now instead of using only one pan to warm some soup a time or two.

She propped her hands on her hips and glared at the congregation of *don't-touch-me* appliances, tools, and gadgets. Cooking was something she'd learned as a survival skill as a kid. When your mum was too busy entertaining men to earn money and your pop was too busy spending said money on drugs, what else was a kid supposed to do if she wanted to eat?

Over time, cooking had become not only survival, but therapy. Then it had been a way of showing love to her friends. She couldn't do it by hugging or touching. So she did it by serving great food to an appreciative crowd.

Especially Matt.

A pang of distress twisted in her stomach. She hadn't done right by her buddy. She hadn't even thought of him during the last few days. Disappointment at herself mixed with the distress.

Still, she had time. Granted, not much. But if she could win Marc's heart using her charm, her love, her body—a girl could hope.

There was also her famous stew. The one Matt always raved about. *Peposo*, he called it. Peppers and tomatoes and beef and all sorts of spices. She wondered if one brother would be as susceptible to her best dish as the other.

"I bet he is," she stated to the barren kitchen. "I just bet he is."

A first step towards her goal. If she did say so herself, a very good first step.

∽

HE WAS AN IDIOT.

Sognavo di te.

I've dreamed of you.

He glared down at the stream of traffic rolling past his office. Watched as the people hurried across the street, winter wind whipping in their faces. Noticed the beginning slices of sleet on the window pane.

Ti desideravo nelle mia braccia dal primo memento che ti vedi.

I've wanted you in my arms since the moment I met you.

He rolled back on his heels. Closed his eyes. Fisted his hands.

Ho bisogno di te.

I need you.

The last memory of what he'd whispered to her tore into him with a savage rip.

His breath whooshed out in a gust of rejection. "No."

Pacing to his desk, he sat down, flipped through his

messages, tried to push all the memories, all the emotions, all of *her* back into the box he'd labeled ignorable.

He found it impossible. Staring blankly at the data streaming on his computer, Marc saw only her. His charming Darcy. The small sprite who had enthralled him against his will. The lithe elfin who'd lured him into deep waters before he even knew he was in danger.

Dio. At least he could be thankful he'd only confessed those words in his native tongue. He shuddered at the thought of how a woman could use those words against a man.

Ho bisogno di te.

No longer. He'd known it the moment he'd pulsed inside her. Known he had to put a stop to it even if he was in the thrall of the best orgasm he'd ever experienced.

Apparently the virgin act turned him on. This surprised him. His usual woman was inevitably experienced both in the bed and in the parting. It was what he wanted. Yet somehow, Ms. Darcy Moran had figured out his jaded appetite yearned for something fresh and new.

She'd played the act very well.

Played it so well in fact, it had sucked him into caring for her, feeling for her. Believing for a moment he was the only one she wanted or ever had wanted.

Last night hadn't been only about the sex, had it?

There was the problem and one he was determined to fix.

His phone buzzed.

Glancing down, his mouth twisted in a wry smile. Momma. What excellent timing she had. Right on time to remind him of why this fixation with the *ninfa* was a mistake.

"*Sì.*"

"So surly," his mother chided. "But of course, you must put up with that woman for a few more days, so I suppose it is understandable."

"What do you want, Momma?" Her disparagement of his

sprite drove a wedge of pure fury into his stomach. This was unreasonable of him, though. What did it matter what his mother thought of Darcy?

"I wanted to let you know about your brother."

Sighing, he leaned back in his chair. "What has he done now?"

"Don't use that tone about my Matteo."

Always it had been this way. Her second husband and second son had always been her pride and joy. He and his father were second-hand goods. Her constant flattery and coddling had nearly destroyed his younger brother. Only after he'd taken charge, took him away from her influence, had Matteo started to turn into a man. Yet, now his brother had spent almost a month in her orbit again. A recipe for disaster. Which he should have thought about when he sent him to Italy.

But he'd had a sprite on his mind instead.

"Marcus?" his mother snapped. "Are you there?"

"*Sì.*"

"Your brother is doing fine, I'll have you know."

"I am all amazement."

His mother huffed. "He's doing an excellent job in charming Viola and her family. The wedding should go off without a hitch."

Eight days. Eight more days with Darcy. Then, he would be free to return to what he did best. Do business and make money.

An ache burned in his gut.

Eight days.

"I do believe my son is really in love this time," his mother intruded, cutting off his confusion.

"Really?" His tone was riddled with sarcastic disbelief. Why his brother had only recently been in love with another woman. Mere weeks ago. A woman who declared her love for Matteo with passionate fervor. Where had that love gone?

The burn deepened, dug into his soul. The memory of Darcy's fierce defense of his brother, her clear love for him shining in her eyes; he'd buried the memory. Buried it under the driving desire to make her his.

Which he'd done last night, hadn't he?

Why didn't he feel the elation of winning rather than this ugly anger at his brother's apparent desertion of the sprite? Apparently his brother had moved on to the better option. Exactly as he'd been told to do.

Why wasn't he congratulating himself on the success of his plan?

"*Sì*," his mother interrupted his thoughts and emotions. "I see it every time he's with his fiancée."

"I don't care what he is feeling," he snarled. "I only care that he keeps his word."

"You are such a cynic," she sighed.

"For good reason, right, Momma?"

A long silence fell between them. He chastised himself. What the hell was he doing introducing long-dead issues into this conversation? It served no purpose and he had enough to deal with without revisiting old wounds.

"Marcus." His mother's voice was tentative.

"Is there anything else?" He had no time for this. "I'm busy."

His mother ignored his ploy. "Your father was a good man."

"But not good enough was he?" The old hurt pushed his words out, cold and hard.

"We've never talked about this. Maybe it is time."

"No." He wanted no more of this conversation. It layered on top of his confusing emotions about Darcy, making it impossible to handle. He struggled to shut down the feelings.

"I needed more than he could give," she explained, yet her tone held a hint of whining, a hint of the pity card she'd used so well for so long.

"More money." He hadn't bought her excuses since the

moment she left him and his papa. At a young age, he'd learned not to believe anything she claimed.

The whine escalated. "More everything. You have to understand I needed to be happy."

At the expense of his father's heart. At the expense of her first son's trust.

The image of his father as he lay dying pierced his memory. The resignation in his dead eyes. Eyes that had died the moment his wife had walked out on him. It had taken three years for the cancer to finally get him, but in reality, his papa had been already gone. Memories tore through his emotions like a dozen nails trying to drive through a wall. What his momma started, Juliana finished. No amount of pixie dust or fairy magic could lift him out of his safe and secure emotional coffin.

"Momma." He focused on the data on the screen. "This conversation is over."

The deadly tone he used had its effect. It silenced her.

He clicked off the phone.

He leaned back in his leather chair and closed his eyes. This is how he needed to be until Darcy Moran was out of his life. Until his brother was safely married to the Casartelli woman. Until the electronics deal was signed and sealed.

This blessed lack of feeling. This blank slate. A silent heart.

He would keep himself away from her temptation until he left for Italy. Surely he could control himself for six lousy days. He'd work—there was always work to keep his attention. He'd stay far from her bed. And all of her, her draw, her appeal, her trap, would be behind him.

He focused on the frozen, dead wasteland inside.

Felt the ice form over his heart.

Over his soul.

CHAPTER 12

*H*e was finally home.

Darcy stared at the bubbling stew, surprised at the word that had popped into her head.

Home.

Something she hadn't had—well, really ever. A word she'd held deep inside, hiding the hopes and dreams attached to the simple string of vowels and consonants. Sometimes even from herself. But always yearning for the safety, the comfort, the acceptance.

Home. With Marc.

The front door thudded closed and his footsteps crossed the hall into the living room.

Pushing her thoughts aside, she grabbed a dishcloth, wiped her hands, and peeked at the clock on the stove. Nearly eight p.m. The man was a maniac, working from dusk to dawn. She had her hands full if she was going to accomplish her goal of teaching the guy how to really live.

There was silence from the living room. Was he wondering where she was?

"I'm in the kitchen," she piped up, her voice purposefully cheerful and light.

He appeared suddenly at the entryway, a glass of liquor in his hand. Immediately, she knew there were issues beyond his work habits. How quickly she'd learned to read this man's body language. Her reading told her the lover of last night had disappeared into distant memory.

The realization shook her.

She'd expected something else. She thought maybe he'd come to her straightaway. Kiss her. Touch her. Or maybe he'd throw her over his shoulder and take her right to bed. All day, nerves and hope mixed inside her. One moment she'd been giddy at the thought of seeing him again. The next moment she wondered how they'd make love the next time and if she could improve her skills rapidly enough to satisfy him.

The guy standing before her now, though, had never entered her imagination or speculation. She hadn't expected her lover to disappear completely and be supplanted with this.

His shoulders were tense; his mouth held a sullen tinge to it. Grim lines of strain had replaced any hint of dimples. His gaze was wary.

"Has something happened?"

"No." He sipped his liquor, slouching on the doorframe. "Everything is fine."

Frustration mixed with a budding irritation. Why was he being like this?

"I don't think so," she stated. "Clearly something's wrong."

His mouth turned down. His eyes went cold. "Nothing is wrong."

What was wrong with him? Last night had been amazing. Hadn't it? Anxiety twisted viciously in her belly. She'd done the best she could. She only needed some more practice. However, it appeared from his attitude she wasn't going to get the chance.

Which fired her temper. "I hate it when men say that when obviously something has happened."

Rather than responding, he merely sipped his liquor once more, watching her with those guarded eyes.

Swiveling to the stove, she tried to rein in her disappointment and nervousness. Yet, both continued to simmer and grow as she stirred her stew. Why didn't he sweep her into his arms and into bed? Had she been so bad last night she'd turned him off completely?

The spoon slapped the ridge of the pot. So what if she wasn't the perfect lover right out of the box? The man could at least cut her some slack and give her another try. Instead, he was staring at her is if he wanted her to leave the premises.

Slap. Slap. Slap.

The stew bubbled over the edge of the pot. Her emotions zipped into pure anger. It wasn't as if she'd asked to be here. He'd been the one to insist. To blackmail. If he didn't like it, too bad. All thoughts of creating a nice dinner for him, teaching him how to enjoy life, loving him—every one of those thoughts disappeared.

Replaced by another.

She'd like to punch him in the nose.

"Cooking?"

"Yes. Good thing I didn't decide to make something requiring specific timing. If I had, your dinner would be ruined."

"I had work."

"Naturally," she scoffed. "What else is new?"

"Did you think one night in bed with you would change the way I operate?"

His words shot across the kitchen like pointed arrows aiming straight for her trembling heart. While she didn't think her lovemaking would alter him completely, she'd hoped it might at least lighten his mood or give him a bit of joy. How foolish to think mere sex with her would inspire him to... Change.

"I'm not that stupid." Her hand tightened around the spoon as if it were a weapon.

"Did you think becoming my lover gave you license to turn into a happy homemaker?" His voice soured to sarcastic disdain.

Her heart stopped as his words hit with deadly accuracy. But she rallied, her pride demanding a rebuttal to his scorn. Spinning to glare, she met his icy eyes. "I l-like to cook. I've liked it since I was a kid. Sue me."

A flash of surprise whipped through the grey, quickly followed by—was that fury? At who? "Your careless parents didn't have time for cooking, I take it."

"Don't talk about my parents." She turned back to glare at her stew and slammed the spoon back into the bubbling food. "They're none of your business."

A tense silence fell.

"That is not entirely true, is it?" he finally replied. "After all, I am footing quite an expensive bill for one of them."

"Go ahead. Throw it in my face."

He met her fiery words and angry attitude with cool silence.

How had this gone so wrong so fast? How had she gone from wanting him to come home with desperate anticipation to wanting to choke him? Rather than soothing him, loving him, seducing him; she was yelling at him.

Exactly like her parents.

The painful realization pinned her to the floor.

She was doing exactly what her mum had done with her pop. Loving him too much. Willing to do anything for him. Then, inevitably, when hurt, when rejected, striking back. Yelling and screaming at him, trying to get him to express a love he didn't feel. And finally dying for him. Dying at a customer's drunken hands while her pop had been out buying another fix.

Fighting and loving. Fighting and loving.

Dying. Dying because of that twisted love.

"Bloody hell," she whispered.

"What?" Marc's voice went sharp. "What is it?"

"N-nothing." She took in a swift, deep breath.

"Darcy."

She slammed the top on the pot and flipped off the stove. Turning, she stared at him. "Never mind. I was being dumb."

His eyes were alert and focused. "Tell me what you are thinking."

"I'm thinking I was close to being a fool. But you'll be happy to know I figured it out before it was too late."

"What the hell are you talking about?" Irritation sizzled around each word.

Tugging down the tight, red jumper she put on a few hours ago, thinking he'd like the way it hugged her body, she walked towards him, past him. "It doesn't matter anymore. Especially to you."

A firm male hand stopped her before she could escape.

They stood together in the kitchen entryway.

A hush fell.

She concentrated on the tiled floor, trying to get the energy to pull away. Yet, the warmth of his body, the scent of his skin, took away her will. How she wanted to lean into him and touch him. How she wanted him to take her in his arms and love her.

What a silly little fool she'd become.

His hand tightened on her arm. "I'm hungry."

She forced herself to meet his gaze. His eyes were simmering with desire. His mouth was no longer tense, rather, a slight smile edged his lips.

A ripple of shock ran through her at his about-face. What had happened? Had her temper washed away his? Confusion made her frown at him. "The food's ready," she retorted, her words clipped. "Help yourself."

He chuckled and his dimples flashed.

Her heart flipped over. Even as she despised herself, she still reacted to his magnetic pull.

"There are different kinds of hunger," he murmured, the smile continuing to edge his mouth. "But I will be satisfied with feeding a particular one for now. Eat with me, *Tesorina*."

"It's late." The fear inside forced her to rebel. "I'm not hungry."

"No? Why is it I don't believe you?"

A tremble of need quivered through her. She yanked herself from his hands before she succumbed and did something idiotic like throw herself at him. Nerves and temper and desire billowed inside. She tried to move past him, but he stepped in her path. Forced her to press against the wall to keep from touching him.

"Darcy." One long finger slid along her jaw and pushed at her chin.

His gaze was deep, a swirling grey. Misty and smoky and keen. "Tell me what is going on in that head of yours."

Nothing was going on in her head.

Everything was going on in her heart.

The memories of her mum clashed with her driving need to be with Marc. To lean into his solid presence and trust.

Trust him.

Yet, how could she trust this man who so clearly didn't trust her?

She couldn't do it. She was too full of fear and pain.

"*Tesorina*," His voice rasped the nickname, rich with promise.

"No." Darcy jerked herself away and marched into the living room. She tried to pull back from the painful memories and hurting fears stemming from them. Tried to stuff them back into the box she'd labeled *the past and not worth thinking about anymore*. Pacing to the windows, she stared at the lights of

London. The snowflakes flitted down, white tapestry on a black sky.

His brooding presence behind her lifted the hair on the back of her neck.

"I had a chat with my mother today." His tone had turned cold once more. Icy and cutting.

A strange sort of relief slithered inside. She'd angered him and he'd drawn back. There were different kinds of safe, she realized.

"Did you hear me?" he snapped.

"Sure." She forced herself to turn and meet his chilly scowl. "What's it to me?"

His antagonism suddenly filled the room. It poured from him. The rigid stand he took. The biting hardness of his gaze. The beginning of a sneer on his mouth. "You will be interested, I think, in the news that your past lover is now supposedly in love with another woman."

"Matt?" She was so aware of the man before her, what he made her feel and want and dread, it was hard to process the sudden subject of her buddy. But then his words caught up to her and the guilt she'd been fighting for days rushed in. She was so overwhelmed by one brother, she'd lost focus on the other.

"*Sì.*" The sneer covered his face. "I am sorry to inform you that you've lost one admirer."

Apparently, she'd lost this one, too. His cynical words and tone ripped into her. She wanted to weep. Or feel profound relief. Instead, she let her temper go. "I don't believe you," she spat. "He doesn't love Viola."

"Really?" He sauntered over to the liquor cabinet and poured himself another shot. He might be trying for insouciance, except his tense shoulders told her a different story. "Still, the wedding is going to happen in eight short days. With Matteo's full participation."

"Because you're forcing him to do it," she cried.

Turning to face her, he gave her a ruthless smile. "I know it must hurt to lose a lover."

"Why won't you believe me? Matt and I were never lovers."

"Tell me another tale."

"Why can't you believe what I say is true?" And why, why was she such a fool that she continued to batter herself against the walls of his disbelief?

Gimlet eyes met hers. "My experience with women in general and you in particular."

His mistrust crushed her like an ant being rolled over by a boulder. But how could she blame him when mere moments ago her mistrust had been blatant as well? Had she hurt him just as he'd hurt her? She studied him, trying to read behind the fury in his gaze.

There was a flash of something. A wary need, a cautious want.

Someone needed to be brave. Someone had to fight.

"I'm t-t-telling you the truth." She met his glare, no longer hiding her emotions. "I love Matt like a brother. Not a lover."

He must have caught something in her expression because he froze.

For a second, she thought she'd broken through and made him believe. Believe her. Believe in what they could have together.

Then, he laughed. His ugly laugh. "Right."

Clutching her hands to her chest she felt the tears, the useless, welling tears in her eyes.

"Who did this to you?" she asked him once more, the cry coming straight from her soul, even though she knew it was useless.

Sipping his liquor, he didn't meet her gaze.

A long, dead silence fell.

"I learned at an early age not to trust a woman." His sudden harsh words startled her.

They pulled her away from contemplating her knotted hands. Yanked her away from her depressing thoughts of giving up on him, on them. Staring at him, she watched as he contemplated the golden liquid in his glass.

"What happened?" she whispered, afraid to spook him.

"My dear momma wanted more," he replied. "More than what my papa and I could give her."

Holding her breath, she waited.

He sipped the liquor. Gave her a swift glance before looking away. Yet, this one glance told her more about the man than he'd ever shown her previously. Even when they'd made love.

The glance held a wealth of pain and deep rage.

Showing he held a wound that had never healed.

"So she left." His words were stiff as if he could barely push them out. "Left for the richer man, the better deal."

She searched for a profusion of compassionate sayings and found only simplicity. "I'm sorry."

"It is my father you should feel sorry for, not me. It killed him."

"What?" She reached for him, even though he stood a meter away.

His hand thrust out, a clear rejection. "Not directly. But he lost his will to live. I watched him die in front of me a few years later."

"You stayed with him."

"*Certamente.*" His eyes widened. "He needed me."

"Your mother didn't."

"Needed?" His chuckle was raspy and rough. "Hardly. She didn't want me. She made that clear."

"I'm very sorry." She wanted to move to him and touch him. Yet, something about his stance told her she would meet only further rejection.

"As I said, there is no need." He rolled back on his heels. "The experience taught me an invaluable lesson. All I have to do is remember my father's face as my mother left him to remind myself that no woman can be trusted."

"Every woman? Really?" The words burst out in an instant mixture of disbelief and frustration. "It isn't that simple or easy." He stared at her, his look cool and clear and opaque.

He said nothing.

The silence lengthened as their wills fought a pivotal battle. Searching for some way to keep him talking, she latched onto the only thought crossing her mind. "How old were you?"

"Twelve." He shrugged his shoulders as if trying to appear indifferent. Except she saw the underlying tension.

The small boy inside him who'd been hurt, terribly hurt.

"The same age as I was when pop gave me up."

His eyes met hers. They were no longer blank. They were dark, almost black, with awful recollections. They both stood, staring at each other for a long moment. The connection hummed between them, not only sexual anymore.

Emotional. She was sure of it.

"It is of no consequence." He glanced back down at his liquor. "It happened a long time ago."

"That's not true." Her brain buzzed inside her head, trying to find the right words. Her heart bumped in her chest, hoping and praying she could reach him and convince him. Heal him. "You continue to carry around the baggage this left you. This only hurts you, Marc. It doesn't help you."

He barked a cold laugh. "My conclusions about women did not come merely from what my momma did to my papa."

"And you."

He ignored her addition, an intense look of revulsion crossing his face. "I have had other salient experiences to teach me all I need to know about women."

"What other experiences?" She didn't want to know or think of him with other women. But this had to be brought out so she could understand him.

He threw his head back and swallowed the last of his liquor. Then, he eyed her. Cold steel with not an ounce of give. "It isn't pertinent."

Her heart sunk when she met his gaze and heard his words. "It is."

He set down the glass on the cabinet with cool precision. Leaned on it as if he were unperturbed by anything around him. Folded his arms across his broad chest with admirable composure.

"It is," she said once more, trying to batter a wedge in the formidable wall he was building around him.

"You want me to confess about my lovers? My experiences with them?" His lip curled with dismissal. "So you can dissect me? Understand me?"

"N-no, I only want—"

"Know what I feel and think," he continued.

"I only want to—"

"Understand how to manipulate me?"

Manipulate? The word sliced her like a steel blade.

Her throat tightened. Her dreams for them dwindled. "I just want to help you."

"I do not need help." His voice clipped each word with icy pride. "I do not need you."

The clutch in her throat moved up, into her eyes. "You n-n-needed me last night."

"Did you think it was special?"

"Yes." She was sticking her neck out, confronting her fear of trusting him. But she had to. The memory of her mum, of what she'd become for a man, was no match for the surging, spreading love she felt for this wounded man standing before her. Her love for him compelled her to say the one word that would give him a weapon if he so desired. "Last night was very special."

He desired.

Not her. The weapon.

"You are wrong."

She stared at him, no more words inside.

"It was nothing more than sex." His face was tight, his gaze fierce. "Nothing more than taking my brother's leavings for a night. A brother who apparently is the worst lover on earth. Your lack of skills showed that clearly enough."

A short cut of anguish burst from her mouth.

"It was not what I'd expected. Was it an act, I wonder? Or did you merely let your other lovers take you without your participation?"

The breath hurt her lungs as she gasped.

However, it didn't stop him from slicing her one more time.

"Never mind," he continued. "I don't need to know since it won't happen again."

The last, tiny piece of her heart bled to death. There really wasn't anything more to say, was there?

She lifted her chin to meet his stony eyes with her tear-filled ones.

And then, she walked out of the room.

CHAPTER 13

*H*e'd told her far too much.

Marcus paced down the long terrace that wound around the entire penthouse. The cold wind whipped the snow and sleet on his face, wet droplets sliding across his cheeks like icy tears. Yet, the burn of their fight heated his skin.

He'd given her too much. He'd given her something of himself.

A part of his past.

A part of his soul.

The realization roared its horror inside. Never, not for years and years, had he revealed anything like he'd revealed to her. Sweat broke out over the entire length of his body. The sweat of fear.

"*Dio*," he muttered. "*Io sono un pazzo.*"

Sì, he was a fool of all fools. To babble on about his childhood. To give her even a slice of his past. To try and explain or express anything about his emotions.

To show her a piece of a wounded heart he'd long ago thought dead.

Marcus clutched the icy railing and leaned over to stare at

the snow-laden street below. Taking in a deep breath of freezing air, he felt the temperature of his body cool.

But not his long-denied emotions and heart.

He still wanted her with desperation. This filled him with disgust. Still, the knowledge beat in his loins. In his awakened heart. He'd walked into the damn kitchen and had succeeded in hanging onto his determination to stay away from her for… what? Ten seconds? If she hadn't said no, they would be in bed right now. Of that he was sure.

He glared at the city lights. "Stick to what you decided to do, *pazzo*."

Stay away from her. Keep things cool and distant. Pay attention to what was important. The wedding. The business deal.

"Cooking for me," he scoffed. *"Madonna in cielo."*

What should have struck him with revulsion instead clanged a chord deep in his dead heart. The sight of her standing by his stove, with her bright-red jumper and jeans hugging her petite figure, had brought forth a welling emotion.

Not one he cared to define.

Pushing away from the railing, he paced down the terrace once more.

Crazy. He was crazy to want to know what she was thinking. Why the hell had he suddenly developed this mad need to see inside her brain? See what made her tick? Why of all women was it this little sprite who promoted this insane desire to know everything about her?

It scared him. This driving call to know her. Know not only her body, but her soul.

Cursing under his breath, he stopped.

The wind whipped around him in a cold embrace.

Her little temper tantrum in the kitchen had only whetted his appetite to take her body, soothe her worries. Without realizing the danger, he succumbed to her lure once more. Hard and hot and ready. When she'd stepped toward him, every inch of his skin flared into flames. His blood had blazed in him. His lust had seared his control to a crisp.

Then, she'd rejected him.

The burn had immediately flashed to fury. A fury as virulent as his lust.

The fury kept roiling around inside him. Mixed with the driving, pounding need to take her. Imprint himself into her. Drive everything from her heart and head except him.

He was in deep trouble.

Clasping his hands before him, he rocked on his heels.

The words he'd spilled in front of her were all because of this spontaneous combustion in him. The safe, closed coffin he'd come to rely on had blasted open and out poured his words, his pain, his memories.

All for her inspection and her consumption.

Her use.

The fear had quickly followed, hadn't it? The fear he'd learned as a kid, as a stupid young lover, rolled through him like a wave of remembered pain and hate. It had twisted inside him like a demonic force. And then, he'd…

He'd hurt her.

A lance of pure agony cut into him. A whoosh of breath escaped.

Hurt had been in her eyes. The blue went dark with midnight torment. Despite this, his words kept coming. He'd kept lashing her, kept whipping her with his contempt and fury. It had rolled from him without any thought other than to hurt her for getting too close.

Her eyes welled with tears the last moment they'd been together, with no light left in them. Only tears and stark anguish.

The howl rose in his throat. Breathing through his nostrils, he choked it back.

The light in her eyes when they'd lain together was gone. For good, surely. He'd very effectively snuffed it out purposefully.

This was for the best. For both of them.

She needed to recognize the reality of the situation. There was nothing between them. Nothing but a deal. It would all be over in a few short days. She'd be free to walk out his door and his life. Forever.

The howl escalated inside him. It became a shriek. Then, a scream he barely controlled.

~

Splashing paint on a canvas while tears splashed on her cheeks was a new experience. Maybe it would add to her art, this level of heartbreak. Maybe the torment would somehow come out of her and into the painting and she'd be left free to feel—

Nothing.

It wasn't working so far, still a girl had to persevere. The conversation with him that ended minutes ago would be used to fuel her art, not her pain.

She was a fighter and she'd fight, wrestle, cudgel her useless love into submission.

The black slash of paint contrasted nicely with the bold red she'd splattered on before. The colors matched her mood—stark and severe. However, it didn't match the original idea she'd imagined for this piece. Of a woman being held by a man in love.

Which was all to the good, she told herself as she wiped away tears. *That* painting was a farce. A total farce.

Another slash of black whipped across the canvas, destroying the original.

She was a fool, but she'd survive. She'd fallen in love with a man who was so wounded by his past he'd lost his soul. So what? It wasn't as if other women hadn't done the same and moved past the terrible mistake. She wasn't going to be like her mum and lose herself in drugs and other men's arms because the man she loved didn't love her. Nope. Never.

Free of him forever. Soon she would be and she should be glad. She *would* be glad.

Everything would be good. She'd take herself off, find another place, keep painting. Eight more days and she'd be out of this cold prison, out from Marcus La Rocca's control, out from his protection.

Her hand stuttered to a stop. The black paint dribbled down, soaking into her jumper.

The whisper of fear curled in her stomach.

Staring at the desolate painting before her, Darcy tightened her jaw. If the demon from her past appeared—and it was highly likely he would—she'd handle it somehow. She didn't need La Rocca's help or protection. She didn't need him for anything.

The door slammed open.

She jerked around, her blood racing.

Marc stood in the entryway, his clothes wet and sticking to every muscle along his shoulders and chest. Rivulets of water streaked his cheeks. His eyes blazed.

She took a step back.

"No." His voice filled the room with fierce emotion.

"I don't know what you want—"

"I want you."

Before she could think or feel or move, he was upon her. Tugging her into his wet, hot arms. Plastering her along his damp clothes, his heated body. She lifted her head to complain or yell or cry, but before she could utter a sound his mouth slammed onto hers.

He spoke to her without words.

His lips took hers in a passionate call, a masculine supplication to her female powers. His tongue lanced into her like a sword of male need.

"Stop." She pushed the word out between the kisses, trying to remember all the hateful things he'd spoken only minutes ago.

"I can't." His tense body shuddered against hers. "I can't."

The anguish in his voice made her lift her hands to his face. She tugged his searching mouth away so she could look into his eyes.

Sooty mist swirled around pure agony. "Please," he choked. "Please, Darcy."

All her determination to hold onto her pain and hold him apart from her vanished. How could she keep her love under wraps when this man needed it so much? How could she tell him stop, tell him to go? How could she not throw herself into his arms and pray that in some way they could make this work?

She couldn't.

Her hands wrapped around his neck, caressing him with her unwanted love. She leaned in, letting her tongue dance with his, accepting his need and answering it with her own.

A low groan came from the depths of him.

Lifting her into his arms, he paced out of the room and down the hall. All the while his mouth devoured hers with driving lust. Within seconds, their clothes were on the floor of his bedroom and they were on his bed.

Heat poured from his body as he lifted himself over her. With one thrust, he took her and claimed her. He filled her with himself and filled her with joy. He wanted her. Even after he'd said no, told her he wasn't going to take her to bed anymore.

He couldn't help himself. Just as she couldn't help loving him.

This time she was determined to be the lover he needed and deserved rather than lying beneath him stunned and overcome. This time she was going to be a full participant and leave him wanting more and more of her. Only her.

He'd given her a second chance.

She wasn't going to waste this opportunity.

"*Tesorina*," he rasped as he thrust once more. His gaze was filled with a silver desire and something else. Wasn't there something else? Or were her dreams getting in the way of reality?

"*Toccarmi*." His accent rolled around the word, making it sexy and seductive.

She remembered the word. Knew what he wanted. Her hands slid down his sides, stroking his heated skin. His muscles bunched at her touch. His hands pushed him up, arching over her, displaying the width of his shoulders, the delineation of the muscles of his stomach.

He was all male magnificence and he was hers.

His virile splendor built her desire to take him, pull him into a need so great he would never reject her again. Her fingers danced across his chest and slid down to his abdomen.

"*Dio*." His big body shuddered. He threw his head back as he thrust into her warm, willing core.

Remembering, she slipped her legs around his hips, lifting herself into him. Her hands whispered across his back and down over his surging buttocks.

A string of Italian words poured from him. The music of his native tongue husked a magic that spoke to her heart. She didn't need to understand with her mind. She knew in her soul.

This was a joining for both of them. A coming together that wasn't about lust—it was about spirit.

He looked down and met her eyes.

And told her everything she needed to know without words.

∼

THE SUN SHONE bright and warm, yet the air was crisp and cold. Darcy didn't mind. She was bundled into a nice new coat Marc had brought her the night before. Insisting she needed more clothes. She didn't. Still, she appreciated the gift because of how he'd gazed at her as she opened the package.

With love. Surely it was love in those grey eyes.

She held on tight to her hope. The hope she'd secretly nurtured these last five days. His passionate loving every night fed the hope. The gifts of flowers and chocolate and clothes he continued to give her every evening sprinkled more hope in her heart. The way he watched her when he came home nourished the hope even more.

Home.

The word trembled inside. She'd begun to dream. She dreamed as she cooked him another dinner. Dreamed of the changes she wanted to make to his penthouse. Dreamed of a life with Marc filled with laughter and love.

She stepped onto the sidewalk of Bayswater Road and browsed an assortment of watercolors as she chatted with the artist. The wind picked up, whisking the last of the autumn leaves around her boots.

A shiver ran down her spine.

They hadn't talked about his past or her fears. No final confrontation about Matt or blackmail or what they felt for each other. They'd both avoided the issues bubbling between them and instead settled into a fragile peace. But every minute they spent together, the fragile peace was building a bridge between them.

A bridge of trust.

At least, that's what she hoped and dreamed was happening.

Time was running out, though. In three short days, her buddy was going to get married. She hadn't had the balls to bring it up to Marc. Which was wrong of her. Tonight, she promised herself, tonight she was going to take the chance and say something. And hope this bridge of trust would be strong enough to hold the weight of her words.

Her heart lurched. Because what if he said no? What if he

went even further and told her she was out of his life in three short days? What would she do then?

This wouldn't happen. It couldn't.

One memory of the way he gazed at her when they made love was enough to bolster her confidence.

Her new mobile phone jingled in her pocket.

Another one of his gifts he'd insisted she carry around all the time. She'd objected, the old one she owned was fine. She didn't need new doodads. Plus, the last thing she wanted to do was become as obsessed as he was with his phone. In spite of this, when he insisted, she capitulated. How could a girl turn down a masculine god when he was whispering sweet nothings in her ear?

Darcy slid it open and smiled when she saw who was calling. "I'm here."

"Where is here?" The words might have been demanding, yet his tone told her all she needed to know. He was simply interested in what she was doing.

"Bayswater Road."

"*Tesorina*," he replied. "You no longer have to waste your talent on drawing pictures of tourists. As I told you last night, I have contacted several gallery owners."

"I know and as I said last night, thank you."

"You weren't thankful at first," he said. "I had to convince you."

"True. But you're pretty good at convincing."

This was another reason to hold onto her hope. No man who planned on ditching his lover would take on the task of setting up her career, would he?

A masculine chuckle rolled through the phone. "Which is why I'm telling you that hanging out on a street is not something you need to do as an artist anymore."

She passed by the fish-and-chips vendor and waved at him,

enjoying the salty smells emanating from his stall. "I just like it down here on Bayswater. It's fun."

"It's cold more likely. Are you wearing your new coat?"

"Yes." She cuddled into the sturdy wool. "Thank you. Again."

"Security?"

She glanced over her shoulder, spotting the man in the familiar black suit trailing behind her by half a block. They were always present when she left the penthouse, though never overbearing. She supposed it was to keep her under surveillance and in control. Still, it gave her a great sense of relief, to be honest. As long as she had Marc, she was safe. Another one of his many gifts to her.

"Yes," she replied with a note of gratitude in her voice. "Right behind me."

There was a pause on the line. He finally said, "It is interesting to me, Darcy, that you don't object to the security. Never have."

For the first time in five days, one of them was brave enough to step onto the fragile bridge they were building between them. She stopped in the middle of the walkway, taken by surprise.

"Which is unusual for you." His voice turned wry. "In my experience, you initially object to everything I try to do for you."

"Not always."

"*Sì*. Always," he returned. "So it's interesting you do not object regarding the security. Why?"

His blunt one-word question echoed in her head. He was willing to confront one of the many shadows lying like a heavy weight on their budding relationship. Was it a good sign he was willing to take this first step? Was she willing to meet him halfway?

"It makes me feel safe." A tiny admission, but at least she'd tried.

Another pause. "You don't feel safe without it?"

Could she take another tiny step onto the bridge? "No," she whispered to him. Gave to him.

"Mmm." The low sound was drawn out as if he were mulling over her response. And jumping to conclusions. Perhaps the right conclusions.

"It's really stupid, I know." She rushed in, trying to put the dreaded topic behind them. She didn't want her past ruining their future. She didn't want this old baggage she'd carried around for years to make him think she was weak or needy. Instinctively, she wanted to show him she was his equal and not simply another piece of business he had to take care of.

He didn't answer.

The silence was deafening.

"I d-d-don't know why I d-don't feel safe sometimes." She kept babbling. "Maybe it's my childhood or something."

"Or something."

"Anyway." The babble continued. "I have to go. I see a friend I need to talk to."

"There is nothing to be afraid of."

"Right. You're right." Her heart bloomed at his words, at his assurance. "I'm perfectly safe."

"How long are you going to be there?"

"Probably another hour or so." She started walking again. Past the coffee shop doing brisk business. Past the old woman who always had her hats and bags displayed outdoors. "Until I get cold. Then, I'm going home."

Home.

She realized she'd said the word the moment it slipped from her mouth. But it was too late. She'd already confessed another of her secrets to him.

"I have to go." A faint sound of another person's voice came from behind his words. "Something needs to be addressed."

"Okay. I understand." Her voice wobbled with relief. He'd been distracted when she responded. Or maybe the word *home* didn't mean as much to him as it did to her. Maybe he found no significance in her admission of seeing his place as her home.

"Darcy," he sighed. There was a shuffling in the background, some muffled words. Then, his voice came back on the line. "It might be best you return to the penthouse. I don't like the edge of fear in your voice."

He'd misinterpreted thankfully.

"I'm good." She made sure her voice was strong. "No need to worry."

More chatter in the background. His voice became impatient. "Here we go again."

With her? Or whoever was with him? She couldn't tell.

"You arguing with me," he continued. "Right now, however, I don't have time. I will talk to you shortly."

The click of his phone told her she'd escaped from any further lectures for now.

Clicking off her own phone, she slipped it into her pocket. Apparently, Marc had arrived at a point where he was no longer willing to put off the issues between them. Anxiety churned inside her. But she resolutely pushed away any worrying thoughts about their conversation. Time enough to confront his gimlet gaze and be nailed by further questions. For now, she was going to delight in her outing.

For the next half hour, she thoroughly enjoyed herself. Friends greeted her with smiles. New art exhibits enchanted her. She stopped and bought a hot cocoa which warmed the pit of her stomach. She was about to call it a day when a tall, gangly guy stepped right in front of her.

A very familiar tall, gangly guy.

"Finally, I've found you." The relief in his voice clashed with the frustration in his eyes. "What the hell is going on?"

"Matt?" She stared at his dear face for a moment before screeching the name again. "Matt!"

For once, she was the one who initiated a hug between them.

Wrapping her arms around his body, she drank in his warmth as he reciprocated and tugged her into his lanky grasp.

"Quite a welcome," he said in bemusement. "Especially from you."

"I know." She pulled away and smiled at him. "It's just really good to see you."

"What's going on?" He frowned and instantly he reminded her of his older brother. "What's going on with you and the Great Man?"

"What do you mean?" she stalled. The question threw her, in spite of the fact she should have expected it. So much had happened since they'd seen each other, it was hard to know where to begin. How to explain. Or geez, even know if she should explain.

"I saw the tabloids only yesterday." His frown grew deeper. "I couldn't believe it when my momma showed them to me. You? And my brother? When the hell did that happen?"

"Um—"

"I couldn't believe it." His brown gaze was no longer soulful. Instead, it pierced. "There had to be some mistake. I caught the next plane to England to see what was going on. But then I couldn't find you. You're not staying at my place anymore."

"Ummm," she mumbled. "No."

His eyes widened as he put the pieces together. "What? You moved in with the Great Man? Tell me you're kidding."

"I'm not kidding. That's all I'm going to say."

"You gotta give me more than that, kiddo."

"Well." She searched in her head for some way to distract him. "What about you? What's going on with the marriage and Viola? Did you put your foot down and say no?"

"Good try. I'm not answering anything, though, until you give me the goods."

Glancing down at the pavement, she shifted on her feet. "He...I..."

"Right. You and my brother in New York. You and him at your grand gallery opening. An opening I could have given you a year ago when I had mine. You refused me, but not my brother. Why?"

"He surprised me. I had no idea what was going on."

"Or you would have refused it from him also?"

Yes, she would have. The fear almost destroyed the whole opening and only by a meager strand of willpower had she managed to pull herself together. She would have put a stop to it if she'd known. For sure.

But she felt safe with Marc. His security team helped, yet it was more than that. It was the man himself. So indomitable. So commanding. So protective.

Maybe she wouldn't have stopped it after all. Maybe she would have let him give her the dream—

"No answer," her buddy grumbled. "You can't possibly be with him. Not my brother."

"Why not? I'm not good enough for your brother?"

He gave her a look of pure astonishment. "Hell, no. He's not good enough for you."

"Don't talk about him like that."

"Oh, no." He stared at her in horror. "Don't tell me the Great Man has fooled you into—"

"I'm not a fool." *I'm not. I'm not.*

"Darcy." His hands grabbed her shoulders in a tight, desperate grip, almost lifting her off her feet. "The guy is going to eat you up and spit you out. You don't know who you're dealing with."

"How can you talk about your brother like that?" She looked at his grim face with bewilderment. "I thought, deep down, you loved him."

"I did." A muscle in his jaw clenched. "I do. But not for you."

"Why not?"

"*Dio.*" He peered at her, his eyes narrowing at what he saw on her face. "You've slept with him, haven't you?"

"I…I…"

Dropping her back down on her numb feet, he groaned. "I can't believe it."

Why did she feel ashamed of something that meant everything to her? She tried to find an answer, some way of telling Matt of the changes inside, but she was stymied by his visible anger and frustration. She honestly thought maybe, possibly, he'd be happy when he found out about Marc and her together.

"Of all the guys." His serious gaze latched on to hers once more. "You had to go and pick him?"

"He's w-wonderful. At first it was tough. Except now—"

"Darcy." He looked at her with pity. "He goes through women like tissue paper. To him, women are to be used and discarded."

"I know. Still—"

"I think he hates women." He swung his arm in a tense slash. "He has only one use for them. That's all."

"Not now." She held on to her dream with a tight grip. "Not with me."

"*Dio santo.* I'm going to have to kill him."

"Don't be barmy."

"How in the hell did you two hook up?"

She certainly wasn't going to respond to this question. Then, his desire to kill his older brother would become even more pronounced.

Matt glared at her, gaze grim. "I'm starting to get a clue here. Suddenly, I get told to take myself off to Italy."

She stared back at him, watching as the wheels in his brain ground towards the truth.

He continued. "And less than three weeks later, I find out my best bud has developed an unexpected attachment to my ruthless brother."

"I went to see him." She wouldn't let Matt think the worst of his brother. Marc needed his brother, and his brother's love, even if he didn't know it yet. "I was the one who initiated the contact. Not him."

"I see. And what? It was love and kisses from the moment you met?"

"Something like that."

"Uh-huh." Rank disbelief colored his disgusted dismissal of her claim.

"I wanted him to stop your marriage." Her hands flickered in the air as she tried to make him understand. "I still want him to stop forcing you into this marriage."

"Let me guess. My big brother said what he always says when it doesn't suit his plan. No."

"So far. I kind of got distracted."

His laugh was harsh. "Yeah. I bet. He's good at distracting women."

"But I'm still planning on talking to him for you."

"Never mind about that." All at once, the edge of his mouth lifted in a crooked grin. "I don't want you to stop the marriage."

"What?"

"I want to get married to Viola." He peeked at her, his eyes filled with a surprising emotion.

"You've fallen in love with her?"

"Yep."

"Matt." She leapt into his arms once more, smiling into his face. "I'm so happy for you."

"I wish I could say the same for you," he sighed. But a grin slowly crossed his face. "Ah, Darcy. You can't believe how happy I am."

"Stay away from her." The growl rolled between them. Before she could turn and find out what was going on, she got yanked from Matt's arms and pushed behind a man whose whole body screamed masculine outrage.

"What the hell?" Matt's face filled with stunned disbelief as he looked at his older brother. "Are you crazy?"

Darcy sensed the force of Marc's fury and reached out, touching his back, trying to soothe him. Before she could find any words to reassure him, though, he'd lifted his younger brother by the lapels of his coat and slammed him against the fence encircling the park.

"You heard what I told you." He shook Matt once more. "Stay away from her."

Dropping him, he turned and for the first time, she saw his face. It was white with anger, taut with tension. His eyes were stormy, almost black with his rage. He grabbed her arm.

"Marc," she gasped. "You—"

"*Stai zitto.*" He pulled her toward a waiting limo.

She didn't need a translator to understand his meaning. *Be quiet. Shut up.* But Darcy wasn't a *be quiet-shut up* kind of girl. He should know that by now. "You don't understand—"

"I understand completely," he snarled, as he thrust her into the car.

The cold from outside entered her body and went straight to the depths of her soul. She knew at this instant the fragile peace between them was blown apart forever. She knew exactly what was in his head. He had never believed her about Matt, and she unwisely put the whole misunderstanding aside these last five days when she might have had a chance to crack through his cynicism.

Because she didn't want to stop building the bridge. Ruin the peace. Destroy her dreams.

"Make sure he's back in Italy by the end of the day," Marc stated to his security. "Watch him. I don't want this to happen again."

"Of course, sir."

An astonished Matt was hustled into another car and driven off.

Marc slid into the seat beside her and the door slammed shut. Their limo pulled smoothly into the stream of traffic going in the opposite direction of his brother's. She heard the sound of his breath, harsh and low. She sensed the heat of his anger pulsing from his body. She felt the cold glare coming from him, boring into the side of her head.

"It's not what you think." The words were a pitiful defense, not worthy of her fighting spirit, still she knew in her heart it was already a lost cause.

His silence spoke volumes. Volumes about his cynicism, his disrespect, and his lack of belief.

"I met Matt by accident." She forced herself to meet his gaze.

His eyes were steel daggers piercing her love.

"You have to believe me."

"We had a deal." His words were cold and dead. "You broke it."

"Not purposefully."

"Yet why am I surprised?" he murmured, almost contemplative. "You are a woman."

"Marc."

He turned away from her, dropping his gaze to his jacket. The mobile phone came out.

The memory of how she'd grabbed it away from him, teased him with it—briefly, she wondered if she should try it once more. But the aura around him was like a black, icy wall of stone.

Of hatred towards her.

She was afraid. Afraid of what he'd do and it shook her. She'd never ever felt threatened physically by him. Yet now, she was and it mixed inevitably with the old fear.

"Blake." His words were crisp. "Inform the hospital I will no longer be covering Mr. Moran's bills."

Grief clutched in her throat. A tight, short cry came from her lips.

His grey eyes stared right into hers as he delivered the next blow. "I'm having the driver drop me off at the office. Ms. Moran will be driven back to the penthouse where she will stay alone until after my brother's wedding."

She dimly heard the rumble of the head of security's voice answering him.

His stare never left hers.

"Make sure she is under strict supervision from now on," he commanded. "You can release her after the wedding is over."

Click. The phone disappeared back into his suit pocket. She stared into his eyes, trying to find something of the lover she'd been with for the past five days. There was nothing except pure hate.

He broke her heart all over again. "You can't do this."

"I already have."

"My father—"

"He's not my problem anymore."

The callous disregard finally broke through her heartbreak and freed her temper. "You can't keep me at the penthouse."

"I can and I will."

"I'll call the police," she threatened, her temper continuing to grow.

"My security will make sure you don't have access to a phone."

"I'll report you after I get released."

He was totally unfazed. "The police will not be impressed with your claims. You have been seen with me as my lover in public. You have willingly lived with me for a month—"

"Not willingly," she thrust the words at him.

"The point is the police won't believe you."

The limo slid to a stop in front of his office. Darcy glanced beyond his grim gaze to the silver sign.

ROCCA ENTERPRISES

Once she'd stared at this sign, impressed and intimidated, but determined.

Her heart and soul intact.

The door opened. He took one more look at her, eyes opaque now. Clear and cold and distant. "Goodbye, Ms. Moran."

The door slammed closed. She heard the locks snap shut.

Now she stared at the sign of his power, his prestige, his pride once more.

Her heart broken. Her soul gone.

He walked away, never looking back.

CHAPTER 14

He'd done it once more.
Fallen in love.
With a woman who wanted another man.

The irony was profound and worth a good laugh. Except he was quite sure, he was never going to laugh again. There would be no sprite around to provoke him. No teasing, no bright smiles, no night-blue eyes filled with amusement.

No, he had made sure of the non-existence of laughter in his life. Very sure.

Marcus glanced at the half-filled glass of champagne he held in his hands and mechanically took a sip.

The crowd surrounding him was loud and happy. Why shouldn't they be happy? The amount of food and champagne he was footing the bill for would make any crowd merry. Why not be happy when the engaged couple appeared as if they were in love with each other? The family of the bride seemed pleased, the mother of the groom ecstatic. Why not enjoy this last party before the big, splashy wedding tomorrow?

He sipped the champagne once more. The drink tasted like metal in his mouth.

His younger brother smiled at his bride. Marcus had to give him credit. When had Matteo learned to be such a good actor? In any event, he was playing his part, doing his duty. Tomorrow, not only the marriage license would be signed, but the papers for the business deal which ensured Rocca Enterprises' immediate future. Exactly as he'd planned months ago when he set this wheel in motion.

With slow precision, he set the glass on the antique side table beside him. He wished with a desperate intensity he could leave, fly far away to a solitary beach where the lapping waves would drown out the angry words he'd uttered to her. The ones that still echoed inside his brain.

"I'm pleased." Dante Casartelli, the bride's oldest brother, walked over to him. The man was tall and big and dominant. More importantly, though, he was smart and tough. Marcus liked to do deals with men who couldn't be fooled and who knew the score.

Dante Casartelli was one of those men.

In any other circumstance, he would be ecstatic to sign a deal with this man.

Taking a sip of his champagne, the man eyed his sister with his black gaze. "Viola is happy."

"Good." He had to force the one word out because this was all at the expense of the sprite. At the expense of a little girl who'd turned into a brave, fighting spirit. At the expense of an elfin creature who'd never enjoyed the loving home Viola had been coddled in since birth. Instead, she fought for everything she'd ever had.

"I have a high regard for your brother." Casartelli swung his sharp gaze back to him. "He's got a good head on his shoulders."

Would wonders never cease? Matteo had pulled out all the stops, it appeared, if he fooled this man. "Like me."

And what that meant was—Matteo knew how to fool with

women and walk away unharmed. Just like his older brother had for many years.

The man standing beside him cocked his head, a puzzled look crossing his hard face. "I'm surprised he isn't working with you in the business."

"He's an artist." A con-artist. His hands fisted at his side, the rage at his brother seeping through his control. "He wants to go his own way."

"Ah." A twinkle lit the man's dark eyes. "I have a younger brother too. Tomas has given me a few grey hairs also."

He glanced at the thick black hair on the man's head. "Not that I can see."

Casartelli chuckled. "Nevertheless, Matteo will be good for Viola. And that's what counts in my book."

Would he? Matteo didn't love her. Of that, Marcus was sure.

The memory of the two of them together rose in him. The look of pure joy as they gazed at each other, in each other's arms.

Darcy. You can't believe how happy I am.

A tight twist in his chest made him breathe out in a sharp burst.

"Marcus?" Casartelli frowned with sudden concern. "Are you all right?"

No, he wanted to say. *I'm dying inside.*

"I am fine," he stated. "Perfectly fine."

A hard hand slapped his back. "Glad to hear it. I would not want the best man to come down with anything right before the wedding."

"Not to worry on that score." He succeeded in giving the man a tight smile. "I'll be there."

"And once my sister is happily married and our two families are joined, we will finally sign the deal you've been pestering me about for months." The man's mouth, usually firm and tight, edged in a wry quirk.

"*Sì.*" The deal he'd wanted to seal for what seemed like forever. The deal that would cement his hold on a large segment of the Eastern European bond market. The deal that would send him into the stratosphere of money and power.

The deal that would steal the man Darcy Moran loved away from her.

Thankfully, Casartelli walked away to greet some guests. If he hadn't, Marcus was very sure he would have not been able to utter another sentence. Not past the painful coil in his gut or the talons of guilt clutching his throat.

He glanced over, straight into his brother's eyes. Dark, questioning eyes.

Marcus looked away. He'd arrived in Italy three days ago, yet had successfully avoided his brother's attempts at cornering him. Spending long days at his Rome headquarters helped. The endless parties surrounding the wedding had done the rest. There'd also been the one furious glare he shot at Matteo the moment he'd seen him hugging Viola. His look had brought a blank shock to his fickle brother's face. Maybe this was enough, in and of itself, to keep him from approaching.

In any event, he'd been left alone to stew in his own pain.

He had nothing to say to Matteo. Nothing to say about his duplicity regarding the two women in his life. It was wise of his younger brother to stay away from him. He had nothing to *say*. But if the idiot kid got near him, he very likely would *do* something.

Like plant a fist in the bastard's face.

Marcus gave himself a bleak smile. What would his dear momma say if her darling arrived at his wedding with a black eye? Grim amusement ran through him for a moment. However, it quickly dissipated, replaced by the churn of regret and confusion he'd suffered with for the past three days ever since he walked away from Darcy.

He'd gone to get her because of the fear in her voice.

How ironic that what he found had reinforced the fear he'd held inside for most of his life.

Abandoned. Once more. Abandoned.

The memory of her in the limo slipped into his head. The blue gaze stark with distress. The tiny hands clutched in her lap. The whiteness of her skin.

It had taken him all of an hour to rescind his command regarding her father. Lashing out at her parent because she loved another man was beneath him. The rushing fury he felt at the sight of his brother and her together had fallen away within minutes of entering his office. In its place, a dull ache at the core of him burned. An ache of loss which stunned him. Before he lost the last of his pride, he'd hightailed it to the airport. Putting distance between he and the sprite was the only way he knew to stop himself from going to her.

Begging her.

Like he had with Juliana.

He turned sharply and walked away from the party. Pacing down the hallway, he entered his library and closed the door. Leaned back and sighed.

Shadows and silence and memories.

He put the past behind him long ago. Succeeded in convincing himself he'd been merely young and foolish. The yearning to love, to luxuriate in another's acceptance, to create a circle of connection and intimacy—all of these were only a youth's dream. Not an instinctive desire he'd inherited from his father. At twenty-one, when he was rejected by Juliana for the richer man, he'd made sure, through painful months, to pull every desire for love out of his soul.

Or so he thought.

Walking to the fireplace, he placed his hands on the cold marble and stared at the ashes from last night's fire.

The memories of his boyhood passed by him. His father's laughter as he lifted his son onto his shoulders. His father's joy at his accomplishments. The love on his father's face as he gazed at his wife. The pure happiness of his father as he enjoyed life.

His hands tightened on the mantel until his fingers turned white.

All these years, he'd rejected. Run from. Buried himself.

Yet, the startling truth burned deep inside.

He was his father's son.

Ruthlessly, he pushed away the need to love, to be close. He'd kept himself apart. Kept aloof. He thought of it as necessary and a smart way to live. Still, the entire time it had been a sham. A fake face to the world.

It had taken an elfin creature of beauty and wit to rip the façade away.

Exposing his heart.

Yanking himself from the fireplace, he strode to the window and pulled the velvet drapery apart. He stared into the dark night. The moon was full and bright in the black sky. He no longer held any anger towards Darcy or his brother. Both of them had been merely his pawns. His tools to get what he wanted. What he thought he wanted. Somewhere along the way, however, the coffin which seemed to serve him so well over the years had yawned open.

Letting her in.

Yet, this wasn't her fault. Or his brother's.

He rocked back on his heels.

With everything in him, he wished to go back in time. If he'd treated her with the love he felt, spoke the words inside him, if he'd given himself to her, perhaps he'd have a chance. Perhaps he'd be able to woo her from his brother.

But he hadn't. Instead, he'd blackmailed her and ridiculed her. The small gestures he'd made on her behalf were nothing compared to the pain he caused her with his stinging words and cutting put-downs.

He deserved this.

After years of being the ruthless, cunning bastard he fashioned out of anger and betrayal, this was to be his penance. The love he'd felt for Juliana was nothing compared to the all-encompassing passion he felt for Darcy. But he'd ruined it before the love had a chance to blossom.

Marcus closed his eyes and leaned his face on the cold windowpane.

He could do one thing in honor of this love, though. He could repay her in one way.

By giving her what she wanted.

The man she loved.

∽

MATT'S WEDDING DAY.

Darcy stared out the penthouse windows and watched as the storm clouds rolled in. Another cold, rainy London day. She wondered if Italy was having the same kind of weather. Probably not. The sky wouldn't dare rain on a La Rocca celebration, now would it? With pots of money at hand, Matt's marriage would likely go down as the wedding of the year. But it wouldn't have mattered to her if it was only a small ceremony at the local register's office. She would have simply been happy to be there.

At least, Matt was marrying for love. At least, she could be happy about that.

Turning away from the window, she looked at the small pile of her belongings on the couch. Today was the day. Freedom. A new and exciting chapter in her life. A moment to be brave and fearless and…

A lone tear slid down her cheek.

Darcy brushed it away with fierce determination.

She'd done enough crying during the last three days to fill the Thames. But now, it was time to get on with it. Get over

Marcus La Rocca. He'd proved for all time he didn't have the capability of trusting, much less loving.

The doorbell buzzed. Security coming to tell her to go, she'd bet.

The men on the security team had been kind throughout the last few days. They'd ignored her red eyes when they checked on her. They brought her chocolate along with the delivery of groceries. One of them, the blond one, had even patted her on the shoulder once with a look of compassion in his gaze.

But all the kind gestures didn't make up for the fact they'd been ruthless about keeping her under wraps.

Her new and old mobile phones were taken away.

No computers allowed in the penthouse.

There was always a man standing by the front door.

How could she blame them? She wasn't signing their paychecks. No, there was only one man to blame. And since she'd never lay eyes on him again, the likelihood of getting the chance to give him a piece of her mind or a punch in the nose was slim. Anyway, she hadn't put up much of a fight about the security. She'd been too dispirited to do anything more than lie on her bed and mope about what might have been.

The doorbell buzzed once more.

Darcy brushed the past out of her head. It was done. Time to move forward with her new life. She walked to the door and opened it.

"Ms. Moran." The tall, blond man glanced down at her with pity.

Her spine stiffened. She didn't need any pity. She was *glad* she was out of here. She forced a bright smile. "I'm ready."

Walking to her small pile of stuff, she lifted her backpack over her shoulder and yanked on the handle of the rolling suitcase. She was ready to go.

"This is all you're taking?" His voice filled with incredulity.

She glanced at him. "It's what I own."

"Your artwork—"

"I don't want any of it." Too many memories were tied to each brush stroke. Too many dreams lay nestled in every painting.

"Well, I—"

"You can destroy them." A tight welter of pain pinched in her nose. She bit her tongue, forcing the tears back. What did it matter? There wouldn't be any more gallery openings for her now, so it was a waste of her time and talent.

No more gallery openings.

The realization shot through her, bringing back the demon lurking outside these doors. But she could only deal with so much pain in one moment. She'd get herself away from the La Rocca storm first. Then, she'd deal with what she'd dealt with for years now.

"But..." The blond man frowned. "I'm sure Marcus would want you to take the clothes and other items he's given you. It's expected."

"I don't do the expected." If she left with nothing else, she'd leave with her pride and the knowledge she'd taken nothing from Marc. "I don't want any of his stuff."

The man's puzzled frown deepened. "He's not going to be pleased."

"That's the thing." She smiled, with a sudden grim amusement at the effect the Great Man had on people. This guy was worried about being called on the carpet because of *her* surprising actions? Shouldn't he be checking her bags to make sure she hadn't stowed the silver along with every other wealthy item not tied down? Instead, it appeared he was worried she was going to piss La Rocca off because she wasn't walking away beholden to him. Too bad. "I don't have to please him anymore, do I?"

He stood for a moment, staring at her. "I guess not."

Darcy rolled the suitcase behind her as she walked to the

open door. Taking one last glance at the pristine, chilly penthouse, she assured herself this was for the best. How had she ever believed she could turn a cold bastard into a warm man? She'd tackled some big mountains before, yet she'd never been fool enough to think she could shoot for the stars.

He moved aside as she passed. "Wait," he mumbled. "I have your phones."

She stopped and eyed the two items he held in his hand. Plucking the older version from his palm, she turned and walked down the hall without looking back. Not even once.

Into the elevator.

Down to the lobby.

Out into the street.

The security door slammed behind her, the doorman giving her a cheery wave before walking back into the foyer. Traffic was light so early in the morning, with only a service van parked by the sidewalk. Not even one person strolled past.

She was alone. Completely alone.

Darcy took in a deep breath of chilly air. It must be the cold causing her eyes to tear. She blinked. Blinked again. The blinking didn't help. Still, she resolutely turned and started to march up the street into her future.

"Finally." A man suddenly stood in her path. A familiar face from her nightmares leered.

Shock dried the tears from her eyes. Her heart thunked in a frantic beat while panic clawed in her throat. She hadn't been allowed even a second to recover before she'd slid right into another disaster.

The demon of her past. Now in her present.

"No." She wanted to run, to hide. But every one of her muscles froze.

His hand reached out and grabbed her arm. "I've been waiting for one whole week to get you alone. Damn security always around."

"*No.*" Her spine went rigid at his touch. She would have screamed, but her throat was now thick with fear. She shuddered and tried to wrench away.

He was strong, though, and she was in shock.

The struggle was over in seconds. There was no one there to help. No one to intervene and keep her safe.

The van reeked of him. Cigarettes and rum and sweat.

Darcy clutched her backpack, shivering on the steel floor in the back, listening to his rants, his threats from the front seat.

She prayed.

CHAPTER 15

The organ music thundered as did his heart.

Marcus stood by his younger brother at the altar. The bridal party would start down the long aisle in a moment. The wedding guests chattered and gossiped under their breath, creating a low buzz of anticipation beneath the boom of the music. The cathedral was packed as expected. The joining of the aristocratic Casartelli family with the upstart, but so-so-wealthy, La Rocca clan was important. Everyone who was anyone had wanted an invitation. Once received, they would never have missed being included in the most exciting social event of the year in Rome.

His jaw tightened.

Time was running out. A decision had to be made.

Uncharacteristically, he'd avoided, put off, dodged. However, he no longer had time to indulge. It was now or never. Stop this fakery of a marriage and lose a deal he'd been working on for months. Or keep his prestige and power and pride.

Agony burst in his heart.

Yet it wasn't for the loss of his stupid pride.

It was for the loss of his *Tesorina*.

For if he did this thing, if he stopped what he'd put in motion, then the loss of pride would be nothing compared to what would happen next. What would surely happen.

Darcy and Matteo. Together.

For the rest of his life, he would have to watch them loving each other. Watch them marry and have children. Watch them as they lived life.

While he lay in his cold, safe coffin slowly dying inside.

A trickle of sweat slid down his neck.

"What the hell is wrong with you?" Matteo whispered at his side. "I'm the one getting married, not you."

These were the first words spoken between them since the moments in front of Darcy, when Marcus was filled with a territorial rage he hadn't been able to contain.

Now all he felt was overwhelming misery and defeat. "I'm fine."

"Yeah, right." His brother snorted.

Their mother, in the front pew, frowned at them. Marcus could almost see the words in her head.

Behave. Both of you. Don't make a fool of me.

Always about her. Typical.

"I'm worried about you, Great Man." Matteo's voice was quiet, yet deadly serious.

He glanced over to meet two brown eyes filled with concern and love.

His brother's gaze sliced him to the core. Ripped open the memories he held of this brother. This *piccolo fratello,* whom he met for the first time at twelve, when his mother was forced to take him in after his papa's death. Two-year-old Matteo had been the only source of love and acceptance he found in that chilly, unwelcoming home. His *fratello aveva* latched onto him with hero worship. Begged him to come with him to his football practices. Cajoled him out of his dark, dingy bedroom in the basement to play and laugh in the Italian sunshine.

A memory pierced him.

Matteo's small hand slipping confidently into his as they walked towards the park.

"What?" His brother's forehead creased in worry. "What's wrong?"

Marcus jerked his gaze away and closed his eyes.

He was wrong. About everything.

His entire life was wrong.

But there was one thing he could do to make amends to the two people he loved in the world.

He could give them each other.

The decision was made.

"Come with me." His hand shot out and latched onto Matteo's arm.

"What are you doing?" His brother yanked back. Yet, the pain and love and anguish running through his veins was more than a match for his younger brother's astonished reaction.

He didn't let go as he tugged a struggling groom off the altar.

The crowd's buzz burst into a frenzy and he heard his mother's sharp cry right before the solid wooden door of the presbytery closed behind them.

"Are you crazy?" Matteo's face was filled with a mixture of shock and antagonism.

The confession stuck in his throat, still, he forced it out. He owed them. "I'm sorry."

"I didn't hear that." His brother stared at him. "Those words are not in your vocabulary."

He grimaced at the sarcasm. "I mean it. I am sorry for not being the brother I should have been."

"Okay." Matteo shrugged, trying for nonchalance. But his body was held tight. Tight with old disappointment. "This isn't the time, though, to say your mea culpas. Plus, it's too late. Too late by years."

"It is not too late." He jerked around and started to pace the room, a frantic need to make it right pounding in him. "It is never too late."

"We could have this conversation another time."

"No." He glanced at his brother, then away. The disillusionment he saw in the brown eyes hurt. Hurt like a punch in the gut. "We have to have it now."

"Now is not the time for my cold-as-ice brother to have a meltdown." The words held a certain fascination in them. "You losing your cool is something I've wanted to see for a long time. Still, you've chosen the worst possible moment."

His pride roared, but he shut it down. "I am not losing it. Actually, you could say I've come to my senses. Finally."

His *fratello* leaned on the door and folded his arms in front of him. "If you haven't noticed, I'm about to get married."

Marcus wrapped a shaking hand around his sweaty neck. He looked at his brother, allowing him to see the turmoil, the emotions. "No, you are not. I'm calling off the wedding."

His brother straightened and his mouth grew grim. "The hell you are."

"I am."

"You say you've come to your senses. That you're sorry." Matteo's harsh laugh echoed in the cool, dark room. "Yet, some things never change do they?"

"Matteo—"

"Get this, Great Man. You can't stop it. I won't let you. Viola loves me and I love her. There's nothing you can do to change that."

Rage flashed like sparks of explosives in his blood. His brother's rejection of the sprite tore into his soul. Without thinking, he strode over and grabbed Matteo's tux, slamming him against the door.

"Liar," he roared.

His *fratello* glared right back at him. "Here we are again. This seems to be your new modus operandi. Instead of cold commands, you've turned into a raving lunatic."

Marc's breath rasped in his chest, catching and cutting across the emotions emptying into his head and heart. The feelings swelled, overwhelming his tongue.

"Nothing to say?" His younger brother stared at him, his dark gaze direct and discerning. Whatever he saw, it stilled him. "No demands? No directions?"

"No." He couldn't hold the gaze. He was too raw inside. Too new at giving.

He felt his brother's instant withdrawal.

But he couldn't force himself to answer it. Show all of himself. He let go.

"What have you done to my brother?" Matteo's voice turned mocking. "Has your body been taken over by an alien?"

"No." He stepped away and forced himself to glance over. His throat closed when he saw the expression on Matteo's face —one of contempt and scorn.

He deserved it. For years, he'd pushed his brother away. Ever since Juliana, he'd focused solely on his mission. To make more money than any other man. To amass more power. He'd avoided contact, it would have distracted him. He thought throwing money at the kid would be enough. Yet it hadn't been, had it? Money was nothing compared to time and love.

He dropped his head and closed his eyes. "I know I don't deserve a second chance with you. I understand."

"Good. Like I told you, it's too late."

"Right." He looked at his *fratello*. "But I can do one thing for you. One thing that will start to atone for my actions."

Matteo stood silent before him.

"I can give you Darcy."

A scowl crossed his younger brother's face. "See. There's another sin you have to answer for. What the hell do you think you're doing messing with my—"

One hard rap at the door cut him off. They both stiffened.

"La Rocca." Dante Casartelli's deep voice shot through the closed door like a pointed missile. "What is the meaning of this?"

"Go away." Marc shot back with brutal inflection. "This isn't your fight."

"However, this is my sister." The man's words were edged with menace. "I will not allow you to hurt her."

"*Merda.* I don't have time for this." Matteo turned to open the door, but Marc's hand slammed down, stopping him.

"Marcus." If it were possible, Casartelli's voice had grown deeper and darker. "Come out right now or the deal is off."

"To hell with you," he yelled. "And the wedding."

"So be it." The deadly words were followed by the slap of the man's shoes on the stone floor as he paced off.

His brother whipped around, pure hatred contorting his face. "You can't stop this wedding and neither can Dante Casartelli," he snarled. "No matter what, I'm marrying Viola."

"You don't have to. I'm not asking you to do it anymore."

Matteo sneered. "What about the deal? What about your all-important deal with the Casartellis?"

"I am calling it off."

The words clearly stunned his brother. He slumped on the door, his face blank. "What?"

"You heard me." He stepped back, after noting Matteo was no longer making an attempt to leave.

"I heard. I don't believe though."

"Believe it." He didn't flinch from Matteo's astonished gaze. "Believe it."

A hushed silence surrounded them. The buzzing of the

crowd penetrated, yet it didn't cut through the breathless connection between them.

"You'd give it all up?" Matteo finally said. "Everything you've worked on for months?"

"Sì."

Shock ran across his *fratello's* face. "But you told me it was ultra-important. That it would ensure the survival of Rocca for years."

"It doesn't matter anymore." He waved the objection away. Weariness abruptly settled inside him. The only thing he wanted to do was get this done with and find a place to hide. "The business doesn't matter anymore."

"The business doesn't matter anymore," Matteo stated the words as if he were speaking a foreign language.

Marc walked to the lone window. Faint light splintered through the stained glass. It slashed red and black across his hands as he leaned on the wall and placed his sweaty forehead on the cold marble. He felt as if he'd been whipped, tortured. His body was drained to the bone. His heart dead. His spirit crushed.

"The. Business. Doesn't. Matter. Anymore," his brother stated again.

"Right." The word came out tired and soft.

The click of the door lock wasn't enough to penetrate his lethargy. Why Matteo was locking them in rather than leaving him, he didn't have a clue. He heard the footsteps approaching, yet he couldn't seem to move. Couldn't face his brother any longer.

A hand touched his shoulder and then, gripped.

"Okay." Matteo's voice was husky with forgiveness. "Let's talk."

His throat tightened and he had to fight back unexpected and unwanted tears. "It's pretty simple. I'm an idiot."

"True." His younger brother's tone turned wry.

"But I figured it out in time." The emotions ate at his soul, gnawed at his wasted dreams. "In time for you."

"In time to save me from sacrificing myself for the family business."

"*Sì*." He couldn't bear the touch of another human right now. He lurched around, turning his back on his brother and taking two steps away. "Don't worry. I'll take care of everything."

"As usual." The wry tone was edged with unexpected affection.

Wiping his hand across his sweaty brow, he forced a smile as he faced Matteo once more. "You don't have to worry about Viola or the Casartellis anymore. You only have to worry about Darcy."

"Darcy." His brother leaned on the stone wall.

"Correct." The final words that would nail him into his coffin needed to be given. "Find her and make her happy for the rest of your lives."

Matteo's gaze was contemplative. "My impression was that you and she—"

"No." The word came out harsh and tortured. Still, he managed to meet his brother's eyes. "Not anymore. It never meant anything. She's in love with you."

"Is she?" A dark brow, much like his own, rose. "She told you this?"

"*Sì*," Marc muttered, the pain of losing her cutting, cutting into his heart. "Many times."

"You slept with her, though." His brother said the words as if it mattered little to him.

He fisted his hands as the knot of regret twisted inside. Regret mixed with a growing frustration that Matteo wasn't running with the opportunity he'd given him. "It meant nothing."

"She slept with you."

"I'm telling you it's you she's always wanted."

"So you forced her?"

"No," he snapped. "Of course not."

Then, the realization hit him. The contrast in their voices. His brother's voice was calm and distant. His was loaded with pain—even though he'd tried to keep it under lock and key.

He observed his brother, who was slouched on the marble wall as if he didn't have a care in the world. Matteo's eyes held… not joy at his release. No, they held a slight amusement. A growing knowing. Of something.

He cursed under his breath. "What the hell is wrong with you?"

"Nothing," his brother murmured. "In fact, I'm rather enjoying this."

He should be insulted, yet he was too tired to object. "Fine. Have your fun. Just make sure to treasure her."

He strode to the door, intent on leaving and taking care of what was left of this fiasco. But before he could turn the lock, a male hand, much like his own, slammed on the door. "Now it's my turn to say you're not leaving until we've had this out."

"There is nothing left to say."

His brother chuckled. "There's plenty left to say."

"I have nothing left." Which was the truest statement he'd made in eons. Nothing left inside him. No more words to utter. Nothing except yawning darkness and a numb feeling of death overtaking him.

He leaned his head on the door and tried to breathe.

"Well, I have plenty to say," his brother said cheerfully. "You can just turn around and listen."

A short pause enveloped them. Marc concentrated on breathing past the numbness. Then, his brother's hands grasped him, turned him. It wasn't worth the effort to fight. It wasn't worth the effort to do anything except stand here like a dumb animal ready to die.

Matteo's eyes were bright with laughter. "I always knew

Darcy was special. But not even I could have predicted she was *this* special."

A dart of pure jealous rage pierced his apathy. However, it quickly subsided, consumed by the wretched numbness making his bones ache.

"Who would have thought," his brother continued, "she'd bring you, the Great Man, to his knees."

"Enough." The torture was more than he could stand. Hadn't he paid for his sins sufficiently? He'd never thought Matteo malicious, yet clearly he was. "No more."

"Admit it. You love her."

The howl burned in his throat. The emotion welled, overtaking him, sweeping him away into a wasteland of regret. "It doesn't matter."

"*Dio*," his *fratello* gasped. "You do."

He closed his eyes and leaned his head on the wooden door.

A sharp hush descended.

"She loves you, too."

The words fell like drops of hope on his parched soul. He rejected them, though. Pushed them far from him. "No."

"*Sì*," his brother rebuked. "*Sì*."

The confidence in his voice caused Marc to open his eyes and glare. "Don't be stupid. She loves you. She told me so."

"Yet, she never slept with me. But she did sleep with you."

Shock coursed through his body. He stiffened and swore. "She wasn't a virgin. Don't take me for a fool."

"Yeah." Matteo's gaze was clear and direct and honest. "She told me about the one time. Claimed she had something to prove to herself. Which she never really explained."

"What?" The word was hoarse with disbelief.

"Told me the guy was harmless. The one she picked to do the deed."

"*Merda*."

His brother's eyes never left his. Still clear. Still honest.

"Darcy told me she didn't like it and she wouldn't be doing it again. Ever."

"It can't be."

Matteo grimaced. "Something happened to her before I met her. Something that put her off of touching."

That wasn't true. Darcy touched all the time.

"I think she channels her need for contact into her artwork," his brother mused. "She touches all sorts of stuff, paints and canvas. That kind of thing. But never people."

She'd touched him those last few days together. She'd initiated contact. Slipping her hands across his jaw. Whispering her lips on his skin. Taking him deep inside of her until they were one. Until he'd found the place he was meant to be.

"Darcy doesn't do hugs, much less sex." His brother observed him with a keen gaze. "Until you, apparently."

The memory of her, naked under him. Her surprise, her naïve moves, her widened eyes.

It hadn't been an act.

It had been real.

He'd lost control. He'd taken her roughly and quickly instead of with finesse.

The sins mounted, overtaking him.

"*Jesu.*" Horror leached into his gut. "I took her like a—"

"She gave herself to you. There's no way you'll make me believe you raped her."

"No, but I—"

Matteo punched him lightly on his shoulder. "Did Darcy come to you willingly?"

The memory of her graceful arms coming around him, her eyes hazy with desire for him. "*Sì.* She did. But I kept—"

"Then that's all I need to know." His *fratello* paced away and then turned. "She loves you."

Marc swept a hand over his face, wild hope and fear pumping inside him. "You and Darcy?"

"Only ever friends, Great Man. Not anything else."

His breath was harsh in the quiet room. *Cazzo*. She'd been telling him the truth all along. She'd been open and trusting and willing to give him a chance. But he'd been a fool of fools and thrown her away.

She had to hate him now after what he'd done.

It was too late. For him. With her.

"I want you by my side when I marry, Marcus."

He glanced over, tried to push away his own dilemma and for once in a long time, truly think of his brother first. "Only if you really want to, *suo fratello*. I want you to be happy."

"*Dio*." Brown eyes suddenly gleamed with a sheen of tears. "You haven't called me that in years."

"I will be calling you far more often in the coming years." The promise was rock solid, planted deep in his soul.

His brother walked to him and pulled him into his arms. The hug healed something hard inside of Marc. Something he'd slammed down between them when he was a rejected lover at twenty-one and Matt had been a mere boy.

"Now, we better get out there before your big, bad partner calls the whole thing off," his *fratello* said, stepping back. "It's time I got married."

"*Certamente*." Marc tried to pull himself together. Straightening, he tugged his bow tie tight. He tamped down on the emotions he felt about his brother and his past. His *Tesorina*. Tried to focus on what needed to be done right now.

"After the wedding, though, Marcus." Matteo pinned him with a determined squint. "I want you to leave for London immediately. Find Darcy. Make it work for yourself."

Fear mixed with lingering pride made him clench his jaw. "We'll see."

His brother grasped his shoulders. "She somehow made you human again. Don't throw this away because you're afraid."

His pride yelled, yet he knew in his heart what was

important. Now he knew what he needed to value. It was only a matter of gathering his courage and throwing himself at her feet. Opening himself to rejection once more. Risking his heart in a way he'd never risked it with Juliana. Or any other soul on earth.

"She loves you." His brother's gaze was dark with belief. "And she's worth fighting for."

"*Sì*," Marc finally admitted out loud. "She is worth it."

CHAPTER 16

Two weeks.

Marc glowered at the sleet and ice dripping down his office window. The weather was typical for December in London and at any other time he wouldn't have given it a thought. But now somewhere, out there, was a fragile little sprite. Outside in the cold. Who couldn't be found and couldn't be protected.

His gut twisted. If he didn't find her soon, he was in serious jeopardy of developing an ulcer. Or a broken heart.

Turning, he paced to his desk and scanned his emails once more. Nothing.

He glared at his mobile lying on the glass top. Nothing.

He cursed under his breath. The best damn security a man could buy. A boatload of private investigators hired and paid handsomely. Connections and contacts made with the police and Scotland Yard. All to find one tiny woman—a person with little money and no home.

And what did he have to show for it?

Exactly nothing.

Dannazione, he'd even walked the streets of his brother's old neighborhood in desperation. Prowled the Bayswater Road market for an entire day. Questioned every single damn artist on the long street. Not a one had any information. They'd had plenty of stories to tell about Darcy Moran, though.

How she made them laugh.

How she would give a person the coat off her back.

How she was a scrapper and a fighter.

All things he knew. Yet, hearing the words created a tight congestion somewhere in the vicinity of his heart. It competed with the acid burning in his stomach as he fought the growing fear. If these people had no idea where she was, how the hell was he ever going to find her?

He'd arrived from Italy with a plan, a good plan.

Soothe her with his loving. Placate her with more gifts.

Manage to tie her to him without having to confess his imperfections. Confess his ugly past, his horrible sins, his aching love. The scene with his brother had torn a strip off his pride and he had no desire to experience the same gut-wrenching interaction with Darcy. All he'd wanted was to slip into her welcoming arms and forget his past.

However now, after two weeks of agony, he was willing to say or do anything to find her and keep her. If Darcy stood in front of him right now, he'd willingly get down on his knees and beg.

His phone buzzed and with a desperate hope, Marc grabbed it and looked at the number.

Buon Dio.

His brother returned from his honeymoon. The last person he wanted to talk to right now.

He forced himself to answer the call. "*Sì.*"

"Hey, Great Man." Matteo's voice was bright and filled with laughter. "Just got back from two glorious weeks in Tahiti. Viola and I both thank you for the trip. It was wonderful."

"Wonderful." He paced to the window and scowled at the storm clouds.

"Fantastic diving. Excellent food. Completely isolated, yet with every comfort you could possibly need."

"Fantastic." He strode to his desk.

"Hmm." His brother's voice turned curious. "The one regret I had was I couldn't find out what happened with you and Darcy. No phones. No internet."

"Nothing happened."

A cutting silence fell.

Then, his brother erupted. "What the hell is wrong with you?"

Everything. Everything was wrong with him. He'd stupidly pushed away the love of his life. Forced her to leave and disappear. Forever?

Matteo's curses continued to flow.

He stood at his desk and stared at the blank computer screen. Waiting with fading hope for any news.

"Marcus."

The harsh sound of his name broke through the fog of fear hanging over him. "What?"

"I thought I got through to you. At the wedding."

You did. But I screwed things up so badly, Darcy was gone when I returned.

"Marcus. Are you listening?"

"*Sì.*"

"Well? What happened? I can't believe she rejected you. Not the way she feels about you."

A short bark of laughter was his only response. The way she felt about him was clear. She never wanted to see him again. He'd left his name and number and a message with all her artist friends. No calls. No contact. She wanted nothing to do with him.

"She rejected you?"

"You could say that."

A stunned silence echoed across the line. "I can't believe it," his *fratello* finally said.

"Believe it." He prowled to the window. "She was gone when I got back to London."

"Wait. You mean you haven't even talked with her?"

"No."

"You've been searching for her, haven't you?"

"*Sì*."

"Okay." His brother's voice became marginally warmer. "You're not a complete idiot."

He leaned on the cold pane of the window and grimaced. "I wouldn't be so sure."

"Darcy's good at hiding in the shadows. She's been doing it her entire life."

"Why?" The question shot out with a desperate need to understand.

"I don't know. She'd never say. But I do know something in her past scared her. Scares her even today." His *fratello's* voice grew grim. "She never wanted anything in her name. Bank accounts, leases. She never wanted any of her art exhibited, although she's incredibly talented."

Marc tightened his hand around the phone with a sudden sick dread in his stomach.

The gallery opening he'd arranged for her without her knowledge. The press and the photographs. The fearful, trembling waif who'd barely succeeded in holding herself up against the wall. The tears in the limo. The plea for him to stop asking questions she didn't want to answer.

The picture forming in his imagination was one that struck terror in his brain.

"*Dio*," he whispered. "I thought she was only hiding from me."

"Maybe. But she's hiding from other things too. I'd bet on it."

"We found her suitcase." His heart beat an alarming tattoo in his chest. "Outside my penthouse."

"*What?*"

"She didn't take anything I'd given her." He still felt the astonishment. When he'd opened her closet and seen every one of his gifts neatly stacked and rejected, it had hit him right in his gut. She hadn't wanted his money. Hadn't wanted the only things he ever offered women. "Just her own stuff. For some reason, though, she left it on the sidewalk."

"That doesn't make any sense."

"I thought it was some grand gesture. Some last way of telling me she wasn't what I accused her of."

Matteo made a rude sound. "A gold digger."

"*Sì.*" He deserved the ridicule.

"She didn't have much, yet what she had she held on to." His *fratello's* voice was cold with sudden distress. "She wouldn't have simply left her stuff on the side of the road. Not purposefully."

The fear churning in his gut turned to a hard block of ice-cold terror.

"You need to find her, Marcus. Fast."

"*Sì*," he hissed.

"She's afraid of someone. I'm sure of it."

Marc swore a string of furious Italian words.

"I'm going to give you a list of people and places."

"Good," he gasped through his panic. Why hadn't he thought of contacting his brother before? As usual, he'd thought he could handle it, thought he could fix it without anyone's help except his security team.

He was an idiot. A complete idiot.

Still, he now was an idiot with hope.

COMING HERE WAS A MISTAKE.

Darcy glanced around at the laughing crowd surrounding her. The King's Rose was one of her favorite hangouts when she had a bit of dough. The old bar was a haunt for artists and she'd become good friends with the crusty old man who was the owner and usually the bartender. When she'd gotten enough courage to stick her nose out of her current hiding place, it had been a no-brainer this would be a safe spot to take the plunge.

But it was no use.

She kept shaking inside. Kept jumping at every shadow.

The confrontation and her abduction had been a close call, a very close call. However, the monster hadn't known she'd grown some balls since their last encounter. Didn't know she knew where to kick a man if needed.

Darcy smirked.

She'd grown some balls and kicked his to the back of his teeth.

His howls followed her down the alley and into an adjoining street. Within seconds, she'd blended into the crowd. Within minutes, she arrived at Alvin and Sandy's doorstep where she'd been taken in and given the couch. Fed and warmed and comforted.

And not asked a lot of questions.

She let them think it was all about Marc. She let them believe she was suffering from a broken heart. That this was all she was suffering from.

It was easier. It was her habit.

The old secret had once more been stuffed into her private hell.

The fear lingered for a few days, still, she'd managed to act on a few things. She'd called the hospital and been surprised, yet not stunned, when her pop answered. Marc might be a bastard, but she hadn't pegged him as vindictive.

She'd been right.

Her pop seemed oblivious that his meal ticket had thrown her out and she hadn't the energy to tell him about her new reality. Pop didn't like reality anyway, so let him get well in peace. Sandy took the small amount of cash Darcy had on hand and found some used clothing—she had the start of a new wardrobe. And Alvin started a fundraiser to get her a few art supplies so she could start making some money and get her feet back on the ground.

Still, the heartache for her lost dreams continued to build and burn inside. She pretty much understood it was there to stay. She'd live with her need and love for Marcus La Rocca for the rest of her life.

Another fiery cross to bear in her private hell.

Tonight, though, after two weeks of her huddling on their sofa, Alvin insisted. It was time to get back out there. Time to live and let live, he'd said. Time to put this behind her. She'd tried to argue, tried to divert, but without telling him of her deepest fear, what could she say? That her broken heart would never let her leave this refuge again? Her pride wouldn't let her do it.

So here she was. Not having any fun at all. Not caring about anything at all.

"Come on, lass." Al's heavy hand landed on her shoulder. "Give it a smile. Things will get better."

"Sure." She painted a smile on her lips and forced her eyes to twinkle. "I'm fine, Al."

"There it is, there's the Darcy I know." His worried frown turned to a broad grin. "The man won't be bothering you anymore. We made sure not to give him an ounce of information when he came around asking about you."

"Thank you." She was stunned when he told her Marc had been asking about her. Stunned and shocked. Did he want to confront her about not taking any of his gifts? Was he that displeased? Or maybe he wanted to rub it in her face that her buddy was married. That she no longer had a chance to work her wiles on Matt.

Darcy snorted.

For the first time, a bit of her old temper and spirit flared. Just for a moment, she wished the Great Man stood before her so she could kick him in the shins.

Or somewhere else. After all, she'd had recent practice.

She deserved better.

Her little old heart was simply going to have to get over Marcus La Rocca because he wasn't the man she deserved. The passion in his bed, the compassion he'd shown her and her father, the impassioned way he'd promoted her art—none of it could erase the essential character of the man.

A cynic and a workaholic. A man who could not trust or love.

Darcy Moran was worthy of a much better man.

She straightened her shoulders. For days now, she'd been wallowing. Glad she escaped, yet with no real will to live or plan for the future. The appearance of her demon ensured she'd have to return to her usual pattern. She'd have to forget the gallery. She'd have to jump from place to place, never having a real home. One step ahead of him. The thoughts had crowded in on her, deepening her depression until she felt as if she'd suffocate under the weight of her broken dreams.

But it wasn't in her to accept defeat.

She'd survive. Like she always did.

A friend passed her another beer, giving her a jaunty smile.

For the first time since walking away from the Great Man's sterile life, Darcy gave a true smile back.

She'd be fine. She'd live. Not love again, but living was worth something.

"Hey! Darcy!" A jolly cry from another of her artist buddies captured her attention. Turning to her left, she kept her valiant grin on her face. She'd be the life of the party. She'd show the world what she was made of. Her chin lifted, her eyes twinkled. She was ready to meet the world once more with a cheeky attitude and a fighting spirit.

What she met was the gaze of two glittering, silver eyes.

∼

MARC STARED as if she was a dream.

Dio. He'd found her. He'd finally found his sprite. The very first place Matteo told him about and here she was.

Smiling and laughing. The life of the party.

A shaft of pain lanced inside him. Clearly, she wasn't suffering from their parting like he had. In fact, it appeared she'd already forgotten him. Nausea slid up his throat. What if his brother was wrong, all wrong about her feelings? What if he were about to make himself a fool once more in front of a woman?

So be it.

He had to know. Needed to face her and find out if he had a hope of winning her back. A hope of living the life he'd been dreaming of these last couple of weeks. A life of laughter and love. A life overflowing with acceptance and warmth. A life with…

"Darcy," he breathed.

She turned and looked right at him. As if she heard her name on his lips although the crowded bar was filled with noisy chatter. Her gaze met his from across the distance between where he stood at the door and she sat at the bar.

She stiffened and her eyes widened.

Then, she turned from him with a jerk and slipped through the crowd at a rapid clip.

"No," he cried. The people around him went silent.

"No," he said once more as he pushed his way through the throng, following her fast-disappearing form. An older man, vaguely recognizable, stepped in front of him, but one fierce glare from Marc had him stumbling aside.

He'd found her, finally found her. Damned if anyone or anything was going to stand in the way of getting to her and telling her.

Telling her—he loved her.

He gained on her, saw her sneak through the back door. In two paces, he was out the door himself into a dark, dank alley behind the long row of shops and stores. Her slight figure dashed across the cobblestone lane at a breakneck pace, yet his long legs would easily close the distance in seconds. He tensed, ready to run.

Suddenly, it happened.

A man stepped in front of her, grabbing her and yanking her towards the alley entrance where a van stood waiting.

What the hell?

Darcy froze at first, then started to hit and kick. An intense pride swept through him at her pluck and her spirit.

"There's my girl," he muttered under his breath, as he ran down the street toward the struggling couple.

He was upon them in seconds.

Wrenching her away from the assailant, he pushed her behind him, facing the danger.

The guy tried to take off, but Marc grabbed him by his arm, stopping him. "What is going on here?"

The stranger said nothing. His wild eyes were wide with fright at being held by a determined, angry man. Dark, greasy hair stood in spikes on his head, while his beer belly heaved in distress.

"Darcy?" Marc turned to stare at her.

Before him stood the waif once more. The fear flooding in her gaze, the pale skin of her face, the twisting hands.

This man. This was the man who she feared. He'd bet his life on it.

"Who is he?" he snarled.

"He...h-h-he..." His sprite stopped, gathering her courage. "He's the only son of the foster family I was put with as a kid."

"*Sì?*" Marc grabbed the guy by his ragged collar and lifted him off his feet. A triumphant rush of power pulsed through him when the man gasped for breath. "What did he do to you?"

"Nothing," she whispered. "I ran away before he could..."

Her insinuation was enough. More than enough to justify what he'd wanted to do since he saw this man grab her. His fist plowed into the sweaty face before him and the man went down cold.

Marc glared at the unconscious man, rubbing his knuckles. A primal rage pumped in his blood. His woman. No one else's. His woman would never be touched by another man.

"How old were you?" he rasped.

A short, sharp pause. "It d-d-doesn't matter."

He swung around, anger pulsing inside, needing an outlet. "It sure as hell does."

Her eyes widened at the expression on his face.

"Tell me."

"I never talk about it." She slumped on the brick wall as if every bit of her energy was gone.

"You must." He paced over to her and leaned down, gazing into night-blue eyes filled with turbulent fear. "You must get it out so the memory can be put to rest."

She stared at him, searching for something. Maybe she found it because she finally spoke. "I got placed with them when I was twelve." Her lips twisted in a grimace before she continued. "He was the only kid they had. They wanted a g-girl."

"Go on." He leaned farther in, trying to wrap her in his presence, in the safety he provided.

"He wasn't happy," she murmured. "He was spoiled, didn't want to share. He hated me."

Merda. The childhood she'd suffered. While he'd been merely unhappy, yet safe and well cared for, this little girl had been scared, alone and unwanted. His hand lifted, gently cuddling the side of her face as she kept talking.

"But as I grew up, his attitude changed."

He ground his teeth, sensing what was coming.

"He started leering. Touching." A lone tear slid across her cheek. His thumb whisked it away. Another replaced it. "I...I..."

"Say it, *Tesorina*," he commanded in a low voice.

A whimper escaped her, but at the same time her shoulders stiffened as if wanting to shake her memories off one last time. "I was seventeen when it happened. I w-w-woke and he was in my bed. Touching me."

A torrent of Italian curses erupted from him. Marc turned to the man on the ground, ready to pummel him and kill him.

"No!" Her hand clutched his elbow. "I got away before he could do anything."

His breath was harsh in the stillness of the alley. The rage roared and rattled inside him.

"No. Please." Her knuckles went white as she dug into his arm, keeping him from violence. "I ran away. His parents didn't believe me. S-s-so I left. Before he could do anything else."

Her words penetrated his fury.

Marc took a deep breath and straightened. With a shaking hand, he slipped his mobile from his pocket.

"Blake," he barked at his head of security. "I need you to come around to the back of the bar. I have something I need you to deal with."

He glowered at the unconscious man, before turning to scowl at her. "He's been stalking you ever since, hasn't he? That's why you reacted as you did at your gallery opening. You didn't want your picture in the tabloids."

"Yes." She stared down at the man, her mouth tight, her skin white.

"Why the hell didn't you report him to the police?"

Her dark head shot up and a bit of fight flitted in her eyes. "I did. Naturally I did."

Naturally, his little fighter would have fought back. He reached for her, but she shied away. "Darcy—"

"What good does any restraining order do?" She took another step away, her gaze filling with a flame of anger at the system's betrayal. "What good does it do to tell a policeman who doesn't even care?"

"I care."

Fury burned inside him at the thought of his sprite spending years running and hiding from this man. Her artistic talent denied. Her life one long struggle to survive. Her fighting spirit the only thing standing in the way of her utter destruction.

The urge to kick the unconscious man lying before him was almost undeniable. "He deserves to die."

"No, that isn't—"

Four men dressed in dark suits interrupted her as they swung around the corner coming at them with a swift gait.

"Take him away." Marc waved at the man on the ground who was gaining consciousness. He exchanged a few terse words with Blake, ensuring his head of security understood the situation and knew what he wanted done. Within seconds, the stalker had his hands manacled behind his back and was being led sniffling and sobbing out of the alley.

Forever out of his woman's life.

She made a move to shuffle past him, but he turned and tugged her into his embrace. The feel of her against him sent an intense kick of rightness to his gut. This was where she was meant to be. With him, by him. Inside his soul.

His arms tightened around her.

"He will never get near you again," he muttered into her soft curls. "They are taking him to the police where he'll be charged and put away. You will have to give your testimony, but I'll be at your side through it all. He's gone for good and I'll make sure you're safe from now on."

He held her. The rage and pain and fear he'd been dealing with for weeks slipping away.

He'd found her.

In this moment, he had found his place and his heart.

CHAPTER 17

Darcy stood in his warm, strong arms, drinking in the distinct male smell of him, spicy and sexy. Relishing the feeling of protection, of being safe. For a moment, she let herself remember her dream, drift into the hope of sanctuary.

Then, his words hit her.

Safe? He would always be sure she was safe?

Yanking herself from his embrace, she stepped away.

His expression filled with astonishment and he made a move to pull her into his embrace again, where she desperately wanted to be. But this way led to nothing for her.

Her hand came in front of her, blocking his move. "No."

For some strange reason, he'd tracked her down and thankfully been in the right place and time to deal with her stalker. All the same, that shouldn't go to her head nor her heart. She knew the real man, the man who walked away from her without looking back. The man who blackmailed her. The man who cynically dismissed love. Whose accusations had cut a deep hole in her feisty spirit.

That was the man making promises to her he couldn't, wouldn't keep.

"*Tesorina?*" His hands twitched as he slowly lowered them. "What's wrong?"

Everything, she wanted to scream at him. *Everything is wrong with you and it's torn my insides apart.*

Still, she controlled her emotions, tried to put a brave front on. She had her pride. "I don't know why you're here—"

"I'm here for you."

She ignored the words, knowing her aching heart couldn't stand another disappointment. "I appreciate you were around when this happened, though."

He stared at her, silver eyes blazing like star-streaked light. "He'll never bother you anymore. Of that, I'll make sure."

A dry chuckle came from her throat. "We'll see."

"The police will charge him."

"He'll eventually get out." She gave him a nonchalant smile as if it mattered little to her. Yet inside, the old fear bubbled. She'd never really be free of her demon. She'd come to accept the fact. "He's followed me for years. I can't see him changing his ways."

The man in front of her scowled. "What if he does get out? You don't remember the security surrounding me at all times?"

"I can't see that has anything to do with me."

"Why not? You don't think I have it in my power to protect you? You don't believe I can keep you safe?"

"Safe?" She was glad her voice held steady. Glad her tone was mocking and cool. "You plan on keeping me *safe?*"

"*Sì.*" A determined slant edged his mouth. "You will always be protected with me."

"Except that's the point." She wrapped her arms around her. "I won't be with you."

"Don't say that." He took a deep breath, his face tightening with tension. "Now that I've found you, I'm never letting you go."

Lightning-quick anger zipped along her spine. "I'm not some kind of possession you can pick up any time you want."

His hand slashed down in instant rejection. "That's not—"

"Or discard when you no longer want me."

"Darcy." He dropped his head as if he couldn't face her. "I'll always want you."

His choked words reignited the useless hope, lighting her heart with a deep yearning. She tried to ignore it, push it away. She would not subject herself to the pain she'd felt over the last two weeks ever again. "That's not what you told me the last time I saw you."

"I didn't mean it." He swung around, as if he couldn't meet her gaze and ran a shaking hand through his hair. "I was wrong."

The hope tugged at her, her heart cried for her to believe. She wanted to race to him, soothe him, and take him into her arms. But what would she get? A few more nights in this man's bed? A few more presents she didn't need? Eventually, inevitably, their relationship would end in his cynical rejection of her when she stepped out of line or did something that roused his mistrust.

She deserved better.

She deserved better.

She loved this man, yet if she let him, he would destroy her. Better to face the pain now and walk away from him with her heart hurting than subject herself to more anguish than she could handle down the road.

"You were right, actually." She tried for a careless tone, holding onto her last strand of pride. "It would never have worked between us."

"No," he snarled, swinging around to glare at her. "It will work."

His arrogance might have brought a smile to her lips at any

other time. However, she was fighting for her soul here, and his bloody insistence on having his way stoked her temper.

"For how long do you want me in your bed?" she scoffed. "For another month? Until you grow tired of me?"

"That is not—"

"Matt warned me. Told me all about you." She pushed past his objection. "Except I was stupid and didn't listen. I realize that now."

His hands fisted at his side as if he were ready to battle. "My brother wants—"

"I deserve better than you, Marcus La Rocca."

Her words echoed in the alley. A hush followed as she watched his face. White brackets around his mouth. Watched his eyes. Grey and stark. Watched as his body flinched and then, grew taut.

"*Sì*," he finally admitted. "*Sì*. You deserve a better man than I am right now."

She nearly gasped at his confession.

"Nevertheless, I'm asking you to give me a chance."

"There's no point." The ache was too harsh, the yearning too strong. Before she capitulated to his plea, she swiveled on her heels to leave.

His hand stopped her in her tracks.

"Let me go," she whispered, her gaze latching onto the road, not him.

"I can't." His words were tortured, husky with pain. "Please. I'm asking for one more chance to prove to you—"

"Prove to me what?" She turned to sneer at him. "Prove to me your cynicism runs so deep I can't ever overcome it?"

"Darcy—"

"Prove to me your mistrust will always mean I'll be under the microscope?"

"I will—"

"Prove to me you don't and never will believe in love?"

The last word ricocheted between them. His gaze burned with…She couldn't tell. Didn't want to know. She simply wanted to leave, huddle somewhere alone, and lick her wounds. But his hand tightened around her, holding her in place.

"I was twenty-one."

She watched the words come from his mouth. His grim, tight mouth. Holding her breath, she waited for what came next.

"I fell in love."

A gasp did escape her at this confession. It seemed to be enough for him to realize he had her attention. His hand dropped, he paced two steps past her, leaned his shoulder on the brick wall and gazed at the street. "Juliana was the daughter of a wealthy family. I thought she was in love with me, too. Yet, when the time came, she went another way."

"What do you mean?" She stared at him, watching the flash of emotions cross his face. Damaged pride. Remembered hurt.

"She left me and married another man."

"I'm sorry." Her heart melted in spite of her determination to stay distant. "Just like your mother."

He froze. "I never thought of that."

Men. Totally clueless in so many ways. Darcy barely restrained herself from going over to him and kissing his pain away.

"The man she married," his confessions kept coming, "was also wealthy and powerful."

She stood silent, letting him give her the gift of himself.

His past. His memories.

His gaze met hers. "Because of that experience, I decided that was what I would aim for. Instead of love."

"What?"

"Wealth. Power."

"You certainly succeeded."

He ignored her wry comment. Tension pulsed from him as if he were about to jump into a firestorm and he didn't know if he'd survive. "I promised myself I'd never be hurt. I'd amass so much wealth I could snap my fingers and any woman would be at my side. I'd gather so much power I would never take second place to anyone ever again."

"Marc."

"I succeeded, as you observed." His gaze never left hers. "Until a small sprite walked into my life and blew my priorities to pieces."

His words echoed with blunt truth, but she shook her head, not willing to believe in the forlorn hope pumping inside. She hurt for him, understood now what had caused him to become a cynic. Still, her spirit couldn't take the chance on a man this damaged. He would eventually strike out at her. Eventually tire of her and reject her. And in doing so, cut her heart into tiny bits.

"That's not true. I was only a means to an end."

His grey eyes narrowed as his mouth turned down. "The end being Matteo's wedding."

"Yes." She lifted her chin, the old anger stirring even as she yearned. "Your plan succeeded, didn't it? Matt is married. I'm of no use to you anymore."

"No use." A dry chuckle came from him. "You're right about one thing. My brother is married."

She stared right back at him.

"Your *lover* is married."

There it was. The essential misunderstanding between them. One that could never be overcome. She scowled down at the road. A pause of breathless suspense or strain or pressure pulsed between them.

"Why the hell did you let me think such a thing?" His words rumbled through the silence. "Why the hell did you let me think my brother and you were together?"

Her head jerked up. "Let you? I couldn't stop you from believing what you wanted to believe."

"Now I know better."

Her hands folded in front of her. Shock bled into a resigned relief. "Matt told you."

"Sì."

"You believed him." Her words were flat. "But not me."

"Sì." He glanced away. Now it was he not meeting her accusing glare.

"That's why I don't want to be with you."

Her hard, cold statement wrenched his gaze back to hers. The turmoil in his eyes knifed into her, yet she had to be strong. She had to survive.

"You're not capable of believing in a woman."

"No—"

She waved away his hoarse cry. "I understand now why you're this way. I can accept you were hurt—"

"But—"

"But." She forced herself to finish. "I can't handle a life with a man who won't believe me."

"I—"

"Who can't love me."

His harsh breath filled the air between them.

Futile tears welled in her throat. This was it. This was the end. Her heart cried even though her brain and pride told her she'd done the right thing.

"I love you."

His words were laced with fear. She felt it. Tasted it. It poured from him in an agony of panicked alarm. He stood tense as if waiting for a blow.

"Marc." She should walk away now. Still, she was unable to leave him in so much pain.

A short, sharp silence fell between them.

Then, he turned to look at her. His eyes, his silver eyes, no longer held a stormy brew of turmoil. They were intense, two silver swords of resolve.

With one pace, he was at her side, tugging her into his arms. A torrent of Italian slipped from him as his lips slid across her forehead, her cheeks, and her mouth. His kiss was frantic. A plea and cry she could not deny. Her lips softened, opened to his thrusting tongue and hot mouth. The kiss went on and on as if he'd given up on convincing her with his words and instead, had decided to tell her with his body.

She wrenched away from his temptation. "I'm not—"

"No," he moaned into the side of her neck. "Don't say it."

Against her will, her hands smoothed across his shoulders. "This won't work."

"It will." He lifted his head and met her gaze with a hot, determined look. "I put myself in your hands, Darcy."

She cupped his face. "I want a man who loves me."

"You have it."

The tears choked her throat. She let herself believe a tiny bit. "I want a man who wants to live. Not make money."

"I will change." His hands clenched on her waist. "I promise."

"I want a home." Her deepest desire escaped her.

"You have one," he responded immediately, without hesitation. "With me."

Her heart broke free from her pride and fear, jumping and flipping and bursting. "Really?"

The silver of his eyes deepened to pewter. "Marry me, Darcy Moran. Marry me and make me whole."

She stared at him and saw everything. Everything she'd ever hoped for, dreamed of, needed. Love and hope and need all blended into a promise she could accept.

"Yes." The one word slipped from her without thought, only instinct. "I'll marry you."

"*Dio*," he groaned and captured her mouth. The kiss was no longer frantic but intense with love. He finally lifted his head, a crooked grin on his face. "Now, *Tesorina*, I must hear the words I never thought I wanted to hear again."

She cocked her head and gave him a sly peek. "What words?"

"Do not torture me." His voice was stern, yet his eyes twinkled. "You know what I need."

She slipped her finger over his tight jaw, down his hot neck. Gave him a coy smile.

"Darcy. This is not a time to tease me."

"Could the words be…I love you?"

His hands tightened around her, pulling into his hard body. "Say it without it being a question."

She laughed and hugged him. Leaning back in his arms, she gazed into his beloved face. Yes. She was willing to give this man one last chance with her heart.

"I love you, Marc La Rocca."

EPILOGUE

The stew bubbled on the stove.

Sunshine dappled across the wooden chopping block, warming her hands as she cut the peppers. A slight breeze ruffled the white cotton curtains and filled the air with the scent of spring. A bird chirped from one of their orange trees outside.

Darcy stopped cutting for a moment and closed her eyes. Was this a dream? This life she now enjoyed. This life where she felt safe and loved and protected. This life even her pop approved of when he'd given her away at the simple wedding. Her pop had even cried real tears that day. And with Marc's firm control over any finances coming his way, her pop seemed to have gone straight much to her continued relief.

Could this really be true?

A home of simple beauty. A man who loved her with everything he had. An artist career launched with her paintings being sold as soon as they were displayed in London's galleries. To add to all of this joy, another miracle soon to come. Could she be the luckiest girl in the world?

She took a deep breath and opened her eyes.

Marc stood in the kitchen doorway, his hair mussed, a slight smile on his face. An old pair of jeans hugged his lean hips, a grey T-shirt lay on his broad shoulders. Long, elegant bare feet caught her eye.

My, my. She was a total goner for this guy. She even lusted after his feet.

"I always like to see my woman smile when she sees me." He slouched on the doorframe and slid his hands in his pockets. But his gaze held wicked intent.

Darcy chuckled. Trying to shake off the haze of lust, she scooped the cut peppers into a bowl and dumped them into the stew. She felt him approach; her skin tightened in response, the tiny hairs on the back of her neck rose as if asking for his touch.

"Smells good." One long arm encircled her belly, as he dipped his head and nuzzled her. "I can't decide what smells better. You. Or the stew."

A shiver of need went down her spine. His warmth surrounded her. As well as his love. She knew it now to the bottom of her soul. She was loved and cherished.

"You have a flair for cooking." His lips formed the words on her skin.

"And other things." He wasn't the only one who could tease. She purposefully moved her hips, rubbing herself on him like a cat.

A groan rumbled low in his throat.

She smiled in feline satisfaction.

"I think you need to take a break from cooking." Both of his arms came around her and pressed her tight to him. "Your husband is suddenly in desperate straits."

"Really?" She moved her hips once more. "What's wrong with him?"

Long fingers moved across her breasts to tweak her nipples through the simple shirt she wore. "Mmm." Satisfaction radiated in his voice. "You're so responsive."

Gasping, she dropped her head back onto his chest. "That feels—"

"There's more to come." With one decisive move, he leaned across and turned off the stove. Sweeping her into his arms, he grinned at her. "I'll show you."

He paced out of the small kitchen and down the hallway to the one bedroom in their cottage. The home he'd given to her on their marriage day. High in the Tuscan hills, it had become their hideout. During the first year of their marriage, they'd spent almost six full months here.

Marc had been true to his word, shifting a good part of his workload onto others. Now, more often than not, he worked from home. While she painted in one room, she could listen to his accented voice on the phone or his muttering as he worked on his computer. Whether it was in this idyllic cottage or in the redecorated London penthouse, she had his company day and night.

He'd learned. How to put his mobile down. How to trust her words.

How to love.

So, in the year she'd been his wife, Darcy let her heart fall completely and utterly into Marc La Rocca's capable and willing hands.

Where she would be safe forever.

Her baby would be safe too.

Her gift to him. Her gift of trust.

The cast-iron bed stood prominently by the room's terrace doors. At night, after making love, she often opened the doors, letting the soft sounds and smells of the Italian countryside wash across their naked bodies as they lay together, kissing and touching. The golden yellow quilt was one she cherished, for it had been a wedding gift from Matteo and his lovely Viola.

Matt, who now worked with Marc in the family business.

Her husband smiled at her, as he slowly lowered them both

onto the silk cover. His eyes were misty with love and lust. "*Baciami.*"

She no longer needed him to translate. She knew exactly what he wanted. Drawing him down, she nibbled on his mouth, let her tongue slide across his teeth. He answered with his own taste of her essence. Within seconds, the kiss turned to hot passion mixed with infinite love.

A short laugh escaped him as he pushed himself back. "You destroy me so easily."

"And you me," she murmured, hearing the pulse of love in her words.

When he'd broached the subject of children shortly after their marriage, she'd seen the gleam of his intent in those eyes of his. He thought if he got her pregnant, she'd stay forever. They'd still been circling each other then: she fearful of his ability to heal, he scared of what he felt for her.

So she'd told him *No*.

At the expression on his face, she'd added, *Not until I know for sure.*

Sure that he'd change. Sure that he'd believe. Sure that he'd continue to love.

The rejection almost destroyed the fragile peace between them. He'd been hurt, angry, and said so. But she held firm. She would never bring a child into anything but a strong, sure, safe love.

His hands now made quick work of their clothes and before long, he stood naked by the side of the bed, gazing at her. "*Toccarmi*," he husked.

She sat up and slid her hands down his sides, already covered with a light sheen of sweat. Running her fingers along his belly, she reveled in his swift gasp of a response. She teased and taunted, her fingers barely scraping his nipples, slipping through the coarse hair on his chest and moving steadily closer to the part of his body that rose up, begging for her attention.

Her palm caressed him, finally. Her hand tightened around his hardness.

With a sudden cry, he grabbed her hand, tugging it away. "*Ho bisogno di te.*"

His body came onto her and inside her. She arched into his taking, her body rejoicing in his need. His eyes were a wild silver light as he gazed down at her.

"I need you," he moaned, with a tone of utter surrender slurring the words.

It was his need that had driven him to surrender to her demand and accept her challenge a year ago.

She hadn't been sure. Not at all.

Yet, he proved himself over and over and over. Often at first, she'd see him physically vibrate with tension as he left a problem at work to Matt. Sometimes she would see the struggle visible on his face as he turned his phone off. However, eventually, she saw him shrug off a work issue to another day or another person.

She'd stopped taking her birth control two months ago.

"*Ho bisogno di te,*" he demanded.

Her soul responded to his want and need. Her body accepted and embraced his. Her words were intense and passionate as she gazed into her husband's eyes. "You have me."

A quick smile of pure possession crossed his face. Then his face tightened, his jaw clenched, his sex took over. Instead of words now, they communicated with their bodies.

He set a quick pace, his body jerking and plunging in a driving ride, pushing her faster and faster into a climax. It broke over her, and her mind went blank as the feelings swelled and her body bonded with her lover. Her mate. His hoarse cry echoed in the small room as he followed her into the bliss they created together.

The slight breeze drifted across them, cooling their hot skin.

She lazily slid her fingers on his back, feeling the muscles relax. His mouth nibbled on her chin and neck, murmuring low Italian praise into her ears. He finally lifted himself off her and to her side. One large male hand fell on her belly.

His gaze was filled with a masculine satisfaction. And a sliver of silver relief.

She should have known he'd figure it out. The amount of attention and care he gave her would have given him some clues. Plus, he had a way of reading her which was a bit uncanny. He was quickly developing into the most sensitive man she'd ever met.

"Bloody hell," she said, giving him a mock pout. "You know."

"Sì," he responded, his eyes dancing with delight. "I am a smart man."

"And a virile one." Her hand touched his jaw, reveling in the coarse shadow of hair.

"That, too." He watched his hand as it moved across her flat belly. He glanced back at her and gave her a blinding smile. His signature dimples appeared, entrancing her as always. "You trust me, don't you, Darcy?"

"Yes." She gave him a grin filled with happiness. "I trust you. You proved to me I would be safe in your love."

"I am a man who keeps his promises." His grey gaze was clear as glass and she saw right into his soul.

All healed. All love. All hers.

"I know." Her eyes filled with tears. Happy tears this time. "That's why I trust you with my heart."

"Darcy." His eyes glowed and glimmered with happy tears of his own.

"And my love," she whispered.

The Great Man gave her another smile filled with his own love and leaned in to kiss her.

ALSO BY CARO LAFEVER

THE ITALIANS

Mistress By Blackmail
Wife By Force
Baby By Accident

THE GREEKS

A Perfect Man
A Perfect Wife
A Perfect Love

THE SCOTS

Lion of Caledonia
Lord of the Isles
Laird of the Highlands

ALSO BY CARO LAFEVER

THE LATINOS

Knight in Cowboy Boots
Knight in Black Leather
Knight in Tattooed Armor

ABOUT THE AUTHOR

Caro LaFever (me) writes sexy contemporary romance in a cabin in the woods. She's friends with a raccoon, some wild turkeys, and occasionally, a bear. Oh. And she has a few human friends as well.

www.carolafever.com
caro@carolafever.com

ACKNOWLEDGMENTS

I appreciate every bit of advice and commentary that I've received from numerous critique group buddies, workshops, classes, and beta readers. After years of honing my craft, I still find new and important nuggets of wisdom every time I put my writing out there for review. Thanks to all those that have helped shape me as the writer I am today.

Finally, thanks to my family, who taught me to love books and appreciate a story well-told.

Copyright © 2025 by Caro LaFever

All rights reserved.

No part of this book may be reproduced in any form or by any electronic or mechanical means, including information storage and retrieval systems, without written permission from the author, except for the use of brief quotations in a book review.

Book cover: Kim Killion

Interior design: Caro LaFever

ISBN: 978-1-945007-00-2

Made in the USA
Columbia, SC
07 November 2025